A Face in the Shadows

Susan Evans McCloud

BOOKCRAFT
Salt Lake City, Utah

Library of Congress Catalog Card Number: 93-72858
ISBN 0-88494-898-6

First Printing, 1993

Printed in the United States of America

To Dr. Jack Johnson

whose enthusiastic, in-depth professional counsel
has strengthened and enlivened my books
and whose loyal friendship has enriched my life

Chapter

1

I walked home past the Chateau des
Ducs, as I did every afternoon. I had left the library in Dijon directly at four and taken the bus back to Chatillon, as was my usual
habit. It was a hot August day, and I noticed that the harebells and
poppies growing along the dusty roadway looked wilted, their
heads drooping as my own did in the intense heat. And there was
a shimmer, a glaze over the far fields that stung my eyes when I
looked at it. It was much too hot and dry to move quickly. I carried
three heavy books in the crook of my arm, my purse slung over my
shoulder, and I wore a wide-brimmed straw hat to protect my fair
skin from burning. I hummed as I walked. I felt lazy and dreamy,
and content.

As I stepped inside the cool, darkened interior of my mother's
kitchen I could smell warm bread and the herbed pungency of fish
frying. I sighed as I set my books on the table and poured a glass of
cold milk. My mother was an excellent cook. She took good care
of me. I was all she had left. That is why I was surprised by the letter she handed me, surprised by the sudden color in her cheeks and
the obvious excitement in her eyes.

"From America. From my friend in Salt Lake City, Augustine. Read."

I drew the letter out slowly. I did not share my mother's enthusiasm for all things American. I felt uneasy as I unfolded the paper and saw the English words written there. "Why didn't she write you in French?" I asked.

My mother shook her head; an impatient gesture. "It has been years since she was here. French no longer comes easy for her. You know the English better than I do, Augustine. Read."

After the first line or two I sat down. Before the letter was half finished I thrust it across the table at my mother. "You are both crazy," I said, making a thin, hissing sound between my teeth. "I do not want to go."

"You want to go," my mother said very gently. "You are only afraid."

"Maman," I protested, "why do you decide what is best for me?"

"Because I am your mother."

"I am nearly a grown woman now."

"I am still your mother."

I hissed through my teeth again. "I know my own mind."

My mother smiled. Her smile could always undo me. It was the smile of a child; open and guileless, with something soft and vulnerable in it. "*Ma petite*, you know your own mind. But that is not the same thing as knowing what is best for you." Her eyes narrowed and grew serious. "This is a miracle, Augustine. This is an answer to prayer."

What could I say to her? "You would send me to school in America? You would live alone here, scrimping and saving and lonely?" She sat smiling and nodding at me. I drew a deep breath. "You would take this woman's charity?"

To my surprise, my mother laughed out loud. "This is not charity, foolish girl. This is the gospel. This is love." Her eyes were shining now.

"No, I do not understand. And I do not wish to go."

"Read on," she said, handing me the letter.

This woman who had written the letter, this Martha Pratt living in Salt Lake City, was the missionary who had found my mother and brought her the gospel of Jesus Christ seven years ago. Now her young husband had died in an accident. She was left with two children to raise and a huge sum of money, more money than she needed—enough money to make a dream come true for her dear friend in France. "God moves in his own ways," she wrote. "And even out of great sorrow some joy may come forth."

My mother had tears in her eyes. I had forgotten how badly she wanted this. It was her dream, not mine. It had always seemed impossible, unrealistic, and I had given no weight to it; I had merely humored her obsession. Now this Martha Pratt, whom I vaguely remembered as a bubbly, bouncing, bright young American, had set her hand on my life, taking upon herself the power to change everything, to alter my very existence!

"The fish will spoil," my mother said suddenly. "Come, eat the good food I have prepared. Then we will talk again."

But for me the good food had been spoiled. The good food and the warm, languid evening, and the sense of sameness and peace, going on as I wanted it, unendangered, unbroken. I knew we could argue and discuss all we wanted to, but in the end I would go. In the end my mother, "who knew what was best for me," would have her own way. She would break her own heart securing a dream for me that I wanted no part of. She would send me away from her to this Mecca called Zion, even if it proved the undoing of us both.

༻

The following day was Saturday and I did not go to my job at the library. But that morning, buying baguettes for my mother at the market, I saw my friend, Armand.

"No sweets, Augustine, it is bad for the figure. What dainties do you have tucked in there with your mother's baguettes?"

Armand was a great one for teasing. Without knowing I was going to, I said simply, "I'm going away, Armand."

He stood blinking back at me. "What do you mean? Are you planning a visit to your brother in Paris?"

I shook my head at him. "That is not going away, Armand. I am going to school in America. In less than three weeks I am to leave. It is my mother's dream for me."

He tried to look pleased, but a slight frown was beginning to crease his broad forehead. "You, yourself, do not wish to go, Augustine?"

Armand and I had an unusual relationship. He was five years

older than I; he was like the big brother I lost when I was a child—
though he used to tease and claim he was waiting for me to grow
up enough to marry. But by the time I did he decided he was too
old to take such a foolish step. He was now just twenty-five, not
past the marrying age by any means. But he was a born tease.

He led me now to the steps of the old church and, placing his
hands on my shoulders, sat me down gently. "Tell me all about it,"
he said.

I am ashamed to admit it, but I disliked talking about Mormonism to my friends. No other people in my small town were
Mormons. Our religion was not well thought of there. But I could
not explain what was happening to me without the Church coming in.

"My mother has a friend who lives in Salt Lake City, Utah.
She has been working, with my mother's knowledge, for over a
year to obtain a scholarship for me to go to school there. And she
is willing to pay the remainder of the expenses herself—the air
fare, the cost of my living quarters when I arrive." I made the high
hissing sound with my teeth that is my habit when I get upset.

"And why is this?" Armand asked quietly.

"Because they believe it is an honor for me to get to go to the
Mormon university. This woman helped convert my mother to
Mormonism. I believe she truly loves my mother. She is doing this
to be kind."

Armand held his hands out, palms up, and scrunched his
shoulders. "It is a great thing, a generous thing, Augustine. And
you deserve an education. Everyone who knows you knows that."

I wanted to smile at him for his kindness. But what he was saying disturbed me. "It is a long way away, Armand. It is a whole different life." I had to say it: "I am afraid I may never come back here."

He leaned against the gray, chipped stair leading up to the
stone church. "I can respect your fears. I can understand them. But
the opportunity, Augustine! Without it, you could not afford an
education. Without it, you would never know what you are capable of!"

"You sound like an old grandfather," I scolded. I felt angry with
him. "You are no comfort to me, Armand."

He put his hand on my head then and stroked my hair. I liked
the touch of him. He didn't seem like a grandfather now.

"No one will miss you more than I will, Augustine. No one but your mother, that is. But how can I say anything else, if I care for you?"

We talked on. The day warmed, began to hum around us. A quiet summer's day in a quiet French village: my village, my life, that was soon to be torn from me.

When we rose to go, Armand tilted his head and said cautiously, "You are very dramatic, Augustine. You feel things so deeply; too deeply, perhaps. Do not torment yourself and suffer more than you need to."

He leaned close and pressed his lips to my cheek. I wanted to cling to him. I wanted to rest my head against his broad chest and worry about none of these things. Instead I returned his smile and went on my way without him.

I knew he was right. But how does one alter one's nature? Jean-Paul said, "The experiences of the war made you this way." But Jean-Paul blamed all things on the war. As for myself, I did not remember the war much. But the *feeling* of it went with me still, seemed to be part of the life I led.

Certainly the life of my mother had been changed by the war. In the space of three months she lost brother, son, and husband. What, after that, does a woman live for? Often I wished I could ask her that question. But she would not speak of the war, even now in 1957, years after the horrors had ended. When I was a child and would cry in the night with my terrible nightmares, she would say only *chut, chut,* hush, my little one—*tout va bien:* all is well. As I grew older and asked her specific questions, her only response would be: *n'y pense pas*—don't think of it. *Va jouer*—go and play. Did she also have nightmares that left her weak and trembling? Did she ever resent my father's giving his life as an uncalled-for sacrifice, leaving her alone, to face so many tomorrows without him? I did not know. Perhaps I never would know this.

Perhaps—ah! Armand was right about me. I was my own worst enemy. I must stop tormenting myself. I must go with my mother this afternoon to Dijon and buy material for dresses. I must inform the head librarian that I soon would be quitting my job, a job I prized highly, a job that would be snatched up with pleasure by somebody else. I must sew and plan and pack and prepare myself. And, perhaps hardest of all, I must write a letter of appreciation and acceptance to Martha Pratt in Salt Lake City. All this, and then I must go.

※

In the end I did experience some excitement, especially after the catalog came. Brigham Young University—courses offered in humanities and the fine arts. Even their titles stirred me: Baroque Art, Music of the Renaissance, Post-Impressionist Painting, Eighteenth Century Architecture—my mind tingled in anticipation. I *did* love to learn. I had done well in my classes, earning excellent marks, and some honors as well. I had merited a scholarship from the great Mormon university. Now I would have to prove myself there. The prospect frightened me when I let myself think about it. So I put it out of my mind, and kept my hands busy. Three weeks is no time to speak of. Three weeks can slip through one's fingers like sand through a sieve.

Everything became precious to me, even the smallest, most common of things: the bed I slept in, with the sagging springs, the old chipped bureau where I kept my clothes, the basin I washed in, the bright blue and white dishes my mother and I ate on, the stone bowl of flowers that always sat on her table and brightened the room. I looked at things closely, I tried to savor.

The friends I knew well enough to tell of my plans all reacted with joy. Gui, the girl I worked with in the library, said, "I wish it were me. I would love to go someplace, any place. You are lucky."

I knew many of the people in Chatillon. I had lived there all my life, and my father and mother before me, and their fathers and mothers as well. The bakery, the dry goods store, the fish market where we did our shopping had all been in business for seventy-five—perhaps a hundred—years or more. Our city was the seat of an important convention held in 1814 which drew up propositions to give to Napoleon. We were Burgundians here, and proud of it. The Hospice at Beaune, twenty miles from Dijon, was built before America was discovered. The ruins of Cluny, which date to the Dark Ages, once possessed the largest Christian church in the world. So it was here. You felt history around you, in the very air you breathed, in the bricks on the buildings, in the whisperings of the river, in the slant of the hills. America was new and brazen and awkward compared to us. Yet, why did so many admire her and glance with envy upon her doings, and think of her distant shores as lined with glittering gold?

"You should be going," I told my mother one day, as we hemmed the last of my dresses. "You would savor every impression, every experience. Nothing would be wasted on you."

"I have done what I wish to do with my life," she answered. I wondered if that was true. I glanced at her face; thin, and lined with age now. Last month she had turned sixty-three; no longer an age when one thought of life as something that would improve with the future. She had been forty-two years old when I was born—ten years after the birth of my sister, Giselle. So. What had she done with her life—Idelette Derain, who was once young and pretty, who had large gentle eyes, and who always wore a brightly colored ribbon tying back the thick curls of her brown hair? She had married Étinne Mousset, borne four children, then watched war come to her country and a hated enemy occupy her beloved French soil. She had buried her husband and two of her children, for Giselle had died of pneumonia before the occupation was over.

And, since those sad days? She had lived as a pauper, taking in laundry, taking in ironing, tending other people's children—anything to earn money. And then spending what little she had to help her children. Year after year of this; it seemed a dismal existence to me. Especially since, in the end, her children went off and left her. And what had she then? Sad, lonely memories? Perhaps nightmares? I shuddered to think of it.

What did I wish to make of my life? I did not know. But watching my gentle mother, with her pale, wrinkled skin and her veiled, faded eyes, I knew I did not want what had wrung all the life from her and left her this way.

The day before I left Chatillon-sur-Seine, Armand and I had a picnic together. We walked through the streets, which were crowded with steep, bright-roofed houses, marching in long rows close together, over the arched stone bridge in the center of town that crosses the Seine. Chatillon was the only place where this river, beloved of all Frenchmen, remained wide, full, and free. The river stayed with us, lined, nearly choked, with lush vegetation. The land slowly climbed until we reached the steep stone stairs leading to the ancient church of Saint Vorles. Here we paused to look down on the city and catch our breath for a moment.

"How many times have you and I made this journey together?" Armand asked me. His eyes were twinkling with mischief.

"Don't start that again," I laughed. "Too many times. And, yes, in the early days when I was a baby and then a toddler, you carried me up on your back, and gave me sticky candy to eat, and washed my hands in the spring—I know all the stories."

Armand threw his head back and laughed at me. "*Je me souviens*—I remember so well," he said, "as though it were yesterday. Whom shall I tease with you gone?"

"If that is all you have to worry about, I shan't feel sorry for you," I mocked. "*Désolée, désolée.*"

He shook his head at me. "*Ma chérie*," he said, "have a good time in America, do many wonderful things there, but do not forget us back here."

He saw tears gather in my eyes and added quickly, "This little gift I have for you to help you remember, to help you fight the homesickness when it comes over you."

Out of the basket he carried he drew a small wrapped package and handed it to me. I sat on one of the cool stone benches and tore off the thin paper, revealing a print of a painting by Twachtman, nicely framed and matted. I drew in my breath. I had never had such a present. I held the picture up to the light.

"John Twachtman is an American painter," Armand explained, "who studied in Paris. I thought that a fitting choice." He raised a black eyebrow at me. "But the subject, you see, is the Seine—even more fitting." He sighed as he looked at it: soft gray-green tones in an even gray light. "The source of the Seine in our own forest of Chatillon." He crooned the words, like a mother's lullaby.

"You shall wrench my heart from me, Armand," I cried at him, fighting the hot tears. He put his hand on my head. I covered the cool flesh with my own trembling fingers. "Thank you, Armand," I whispered. "It is the gift of a lifetime. It is Home, and you, and myself, my family—everything I have ever loved, somehow all woven together."

He pressed his lips to my forehead. "Let's go eat, *ma petite*," he said.

I walked with him to the lush green grotto where the river rose in a fresh, gushing spring and made a wide, tree-lined pool, backed by a great gray cliff. All was green and mossy and cool here. We spread a blanket and the contents of Armand's basket, our sounds conspicuous against the backdrop of cascading water and circling insects. This was the place where, since childhood, I had come for peace and renewal. Never had I needed it more than right now.

"Yes, Augustine, memorize every line, every slant of light, every shimmering shadow." Armand smiled at me gently. "It will all be waiting, unchanged, when you come back."

I said nothing. I could not trust myself. I savored the fresh, flaky pastry and the thick, crusted cheese. I savored the sun on my cheek, baking my skin. I savored the smell of the water, I savored the thin clouds overhead, and the green drapery of a drooping willow, weeping over the dark rippling water. Armand did not spoil it with words. He sat in harmony with me; the spell that moved through me unbroken. My eyes searched the uneven cliff face to find the carved niche which harbored a stone statue of Mary, white and still against the rough dark stone. She had never been Mary to me, but France: all that was French, all that was woman, all that was life embodied in the grace of her figure and the innocence of her soft face. I looked upon her for the last time, unweeping, feeling the peace of the loved spot enter my heart like a prayer, course through my whole being with a sweet benediction, so that it would have been blasphemy to spoil the unsullied perfection with tears.

It was a strange thing when I said good-bye to my mother. Neither of us spoke a word about when we might see one another again. I had instructions, to be sure, to call her from Paris when I arrived at my brother's house. And also to write as soon as I arrived in America. But what more could we say beyond that? We were not rich people who could contemplate the luxury of traveling back and forth at our pleasure. Even returning for summers would be a pleasure I must not anticipate. So, if my schooling worked out I supposed I must stay till its finish. But other things might happen, too. Did my mother truly wish me to find a Mormon to marry, and then go wherever he took me? The prospect was horror to me. Would she be willing to sacrifice so much to see me what she would call *safe?* I dared not think about it. I kissed her again and again and smoothed her frail, work-worn cheek. I did not let myself think beyond Paris. I would see Jean-Paul and Sylvie there. I loved Paris. It was a great adventure to be allowed to go there, ride the train by myself. Nothing beyond that. Nothing to break the composure that was so vital to both of us.

And it worked. It worked until the train pulled away, leaving behind all that was dear to me. Then I put my head down and wept, unmindful of the lovely French countryside streaming past my window, unmindful of curious-eyed passengers casting me covert glances. I wept like an abandoned child. I wept for every-thing, not just for this parting. And when my hot tears had spent themselves, I felt numb and exhausted, but in no way comforted or resigned.

Chapter

2

*S*ylvie met my train. "Augustine, Augustine!" she cried, holding her arms out, as if to a child. I stood and allowed her to smother me with hugs and kisses. She too had been devastated by the war. Her father and both her brothers were killed in the war, and her mother died seven years later. Her one remaining sister lived far down in the south of France. And Sylvie *was* family. She had loved my brother, Jean-Paul, since she was a girl of fourteen, and married him at eighteen. And both of them had lived through the war. Now they had two children, but the children were at school today and my brother at work.

"We have a few hours to ourselves," she smiled. "What would you like to see most?"

"The Louvre," I replied, though I knew my answer would probably disappoint her. I have a passion for paintings, especially the French Impressionists and the High Renaissance painters of Italy; daVinci, Raphael, and Michelangelo.

She was good-natured about it and traipsed along with me, pursing her lips in dismay at those things which sent me into raptures, or left me standing in awe before them, weak and helpless, until she dragged me away. I had always envied Sylvie: her full, sensuous mouth and her high, wide cheekbones. Yet she had not aged as gracefully as she might have, and she seemed largely unconcerned with the state of her appearance. I hoped I would never develop such laxness. A woman should remain appealing as long as she possibly can, especially a French woman.

We lunched at a little café that was one of Sylvie's favorites. I sipped a cool fruit drink, startled somewhat when she ordered wine. Jean-Paul was a grown man, off making his own way, when the Mormon missionaries found us. Though my mother pleaded with him to hear their message, he resisted every effort. "I have my own ways, Maman," he would tell her over and over again, with the greatest of patience. "I have no interest in changing." He was a good man, my brother, and he and Sylvie were very happy together. Without the gospel. Would they be even happier if they had it? My mother certainly thought so. I wondered suddenly what *they* thought of my going clear off to Utah to go to school.

"So you are to study the humanities, eh?" Sylvie was asking me. "Artists and architects and composers?"

I nodded my head.

"You are going far away, Augustine. Are you frightened?"

I nodded again.

"I would be, too," she laughed. "But I think it is wonderful." She rose and swept the crumbs from her full skirt. "Raymond wishes he were going along. He envies you terribly."

I was anxious to see the children. They were there, waiting impatiently, when we pushed open the door. Elise flew at me, wrapping her thin arms around me, pulling me down to her level. Raymond, ten years old now and above such antics, stood back at a respectful distance, watching his little sister a bit disdainfully. I petted Elise for a few moments and gave her the treat she was looking for. She was a pretty, beguiling child, but she did not fascinate me the way Raymond did. After she had skipped off I motioned for him to come to me. With a solemn air he stepped forward.

"You are going to leave us, Aunt Augustine. Why?"

I frowned at his question. "Because I want an education. Because this is a great opportunity."

"Do you wish to leave us?"

"No, no, I don't," I said honestly. "And I am a little afraid. And I wish *you* could come with me to keep me company."

"Do you mean that?"

His small brow was knit and his brown eyes two round, shining orbs. He reminded me so strongly of Gerard that I hissed between my teeth, and he noticed it.

"I would take care of you, Auntie."

"I know you would, Raymond. And I can think of no better company, besides." I drew him close to me and smoothed back his waves of dark hair. "I shall miss you especially," I said.

"Because I am like Uncle Gerard, who is dead," he responded. We had all remarked about that too often, compared him to the adored one who was lost to us. Gerard had been like a god to me; as a child I had idolized him. When I had learned he was dead, I had prayed that God would let me die, too.

"Because you are you," I told the waiting child, "and that is the truth of it." He smiled, and his smile was like a sudden light in the room. Just then Jean-Paul entered and the moment was lost to us, and I was sorry.

"So pretty, Augustine!" he said, kissing me on both cheeks. "You will break the hearts of many American college boys. Is that not so, Raymond?"

Raymond nodded solemnly. I scowled back, but at the same time winked at him.

"You do not think it crazy that I am going, Jean-Paul?" I asked. "It is so far away. And what is Mother to do?"

"She was around a long time before you came into her life, *ma petite*," he said gently. "She will manage just fine."

I was not convinced. He was kind, he was trying to reassure me. But I knew our mother far better than he did. These last few years she had suffered in ways which she tried to keep hidden. She was not strong. I did not even believe she was well. But what could I say without being laughed or scoffed at?

We spent a splendid evening together, and the hours passed quickly. As I tucked Raymond into bed I whispered, "I will write. Will you answer?"

He nodded, solemn and big-eyed.

"That will help," I smiled, kissing him, fighting back weak, girlish tears. The following morning, before he was even awake, I rode through the wakening city to the airport. I had never been on an airplane. I smiled at Jean-Paul, determined to put on a brave face, determined to say good-bye without tears.

And so I did. But I was sick inside, and I could feel my heart thumping through my thin cotton blouse. I followed very carefully all directions the stewardess gave. When I felt the plane lift I nearly cried out with a sense of trapped panic. This was real. I was hurtling like a sick insect through the blue sky above Paris, traveling with demon speed away from my home and loved ones. I closed my eyes, my hands clenched tight over my seat belt. *I am twenty-one years old,* I told myself. *Why must I behave like a child? Why must I feel no older, no more sure of myself than Raymond?*

I talked myself out of my alarm. Still trembling inwardly, I opened my eyes. All the passengers around me sat quietly reading or looking through the windows down to the miniature landscape quickly receding below. An unexpected sense of inevitability settled over me. I was truly on my way now. There would be new adventures ahead. Things I would learn from and remember with pleasure for the rest of my life.

I searched through the large straw handbag I carried and found pen and paper. I would write a note to Raymond and mail it at the New York airport. I would describe the clouds to him and the wide, checkered fields, and the thin, snaking river that looked like a midget's playground. That would please him. I pulled the lid off the pen and began to write.

෴

New York was a nightmare. I nearly forgot to mail Raymond's letter. I was a stranger among strangers there. And after the nightmare of customs I was more than content to return to my narrow seat in the airplane and settle in, with my possessions safely tucked round me, for the final leg of the journey.

I was exhausted when I stumbled out of the plane at the Salt Lake airport in a strange, rather dazed state. And I did not recognize the woman who came toward me, waving her arms and grinning widely, as though we were long-lost sisters. Sister Benton, now Martha Pratt, had grown stouter and, therefore, looked even shorter. Her brown hair was cut short as well and it bobbed up and down as she skipped toward me.

"Augustine!" She leaned forward and tried to wrap her short

arms around me and the bulging bags I carried. When it didn't
work she stood back with a laugh and surveyed me—and that girlish laugh brought the first real memories back to me, memories of
her as a missionary and myself as a fourteen-year-old girl.

"You've become a beauty!" she cried, looking me over shamelessly. I noticed one or two passengers smile in amusement as they
walked past us. I squirmed from one foot to the other, but she
didn't seem to notice. "Snow White. You look like Snow White,
Augustine. My heroine when I was a little girl."

She reached over and took everything but my purse from me.
"I'll carry these," she said, starting off. "You must be worn out after
such a trip. Do your legs feel shaky? I remember mine did. I remember I felt sleepy for at least a month straight, after I returned
from my mission."

She slowed to let me catch up with her, and smiled, rather
gently. "That's why I left the kids home with a baby sitter. No need
to overwhelm you in the first ten minutes."

I had forgotten what a chatterbox she was. Even speaking
French she had managed to go on like that; oblivious, enjoying
herself. It was a help to me at the moment; I didn't feel much like
talking myself.

". . . and tomorrow we'll *make* time to at least see the temple
grounds before I have to drive you to Provo. Though there will be
weekends. I hope you'll come and stay often, as often as you can
get away, that is. And bring your friends with you, we've got plenty
of room, and if I remember my own college days . . ."

Her voice faded a little, became a buzz in my ears. I ducked
into one of the ladies' rooms, and when I came out she had col-
lected my bags from the baggage chute, and we headed out into the
night air.

"Well, here it is," Martha said, drawing a deep breath. "You're
in Zion at last."

I smiled faintly. The air smelled sweet and clean. I followed
her pointing finger and could see the temple, softly lit, standing
out in etched splendor against the rest of the city. *Mother should be
here*, I thought foggily. *This would mean something to her. She would
get tears in her eyes the way Martha thinks I should.* But I was too
weary, too overwhelmed by the reality of being there to care about
anything much right then.

❧

I slept late. Martha awakened me, and by the time I had show-ered and dressed it was nearly eleven o'clock in the morning. Then Martha insisted I sit down and eat tuna fish sandwiches, potato chips, and grapes with her.

"We'll pick Roger up from kindergarten at quarter to twelve," she explained. "Then we can go on to the temple from there."

She had two children. Roger, I knew, was the older. "Where is Ellen?" I asked.

"In her room playing." She leaned closer over the table and lowered her voice a bit. "I haven't told you much about her, Au-gustine, because I didn't know how. And I didn't want your mother worrying, for any reason she might think of." She sat up straighter and took a deep breath. "Ellen was born with Down's syndrome. She is what you would call retarded. She'll never de-velop like normal children, never reach a level of competence be-yond twelve or fourteen years, they tell me."

She had said this before. How many times had she recited it, pretending a detachment, a clinical acceptance she didn't feel?

"I'm sorry," I said. "That must be difficult for both of you. Es-pecially now, with your husband gone."

"Heber was my mainstay, all right," she replied, wiping at her full eyes with the corner of a paper napkin. "But the Lord always makes compensations, doesn't he?" Her eyes were sparkling through the tears. "These are such loving children. They bring such a spirit of peace and purity into the home." She cocked her head at me, looking like a small, thoughtful brown sparrow. "I've often thought that perhaps Heber's death would have been much more difficult for me without Ellen to take care of, without her in-credible love to sustain me."

I reached over the table and squeezed her hand. *She's not that much older than I am,* I realized suddenly. *Probably thirty. She was one of the fussy missionary sisters, I remember that—afraid all the elig-ible men had married younger women while she was gone and she'd never "catch a husband," as she put it. And here she is married and widowed and—*

"Ellen!" Martha turned, holding her arms out. A little child of three tumbled into them. She had the roundest blue eyes I had ever seen, and a flower-bud mouth. Her head appeared a little too large, almost too heavy for her, and the skin on her face was puffy. She buried her head against her mother. She had very pretty brown hair of a light fawn shade. When at last she hazarded a peek at me her entire face broke out into a bright, laughing smile. I held my hand out.

"I have a surprise for you, Ellen." I patted my big leather handbag. "Right here in my purse."

With great care and a little apprehension she disentangled herself from her mother and took a few cautious steps forward. I undid the catch on my purse and pulled out a small cloth doll with bright rag hair, a painted face, and a colorful dress and pinafore which a young child could take off and put back on again. She reached for it almost greedily, not having learned the quelling of natural enthusiasm most children are required to master. I couldn't help liking her. I felt inexplicably drawn to her.

Martha glanced up at the wall clock. "We're late," she cried. "Come on, you two."

We hurried out to the car. The air was warm and carried the faint smell of leaves and water. Martha lived on what she told me were called the Avenues, the old streets of Salt Lake that ran above the temple. The houses were mainly large and somewhat imposing, but they stood close together and gave one a sense of neighborliness that I liked. Her own house was of modest size, but I got the impression that Heber had done well while he lived, and would have provided a good life for both of them. *Désolée*, as my mother would say. It is a pity indeed to see a man snatched away in his youth. What long, lonely years Martha had ahead of her, unless, of course, she remarried! We knew all about loss and loneliness, we French people . . .

I was drawn away from my reverie as Martha pulled up by the school where three long yellow buses sat, their engines puffing and throbbing noisily, like a sustained growl beneath the sharp stacatto of children's voices chattering, laughing, shouting in careless abandon. One slight, dark-haired boy moved away from the rest and hurried toward us. Martha pushed the door of the car open and he slid, with obvious relief, inside. He settled himself as she pulled away.

"How was school?" she asked brightly.

"All right." He turned solemn eyes on me.

"This is Augustine," his mother told him. "The French girl who came last night while you were sleeping."

"That is a pretty name," Roger said. "And I think you are very pretty."

"Why, thank you," I answered, taken aback a little. He reminded me of myself as a child. Or of Raymond, dark and serious. Or of Gerard—but I mustn't think of any of that. His dark eyes were still watching me. Poor thing, he had had his own share of suffering. I wondered if Martha had told him that he was the man now and had to take the place of his father—weighty, frightening things like that.

We pulled over on one of the broad streets bordering Temple Square. Martha was obviously eager. So were the children. Once inside the square, they skipped over to the Seagull Fountain, walking with care around the concrete rim.

"Everything is different, isn't it?" Martha said. "The currency, the customs, the food—not to speak of the language." She glanced at me with obvious sympathy. "I know how you must feel. But you speak English beautifully, Augustine. I hope you won't have much trouble. Though I'm afraid you will miss French food. I missed it terribly when I came back here."

She turned to take Ellen's hand and walk for a way with her. I felt suddenly ashamed of myself. She was trying so hard to make me feel cared for and at home here. For the first time I wondered what it must have been like for a young American girl to leave her home and go live in a foreign country for a year and a half. Not only live among a people different from her own but also try to convince those people that she had something they lacked, something they wanted.

"You were my age when you came to France, weren't you?" I asked.

Martha turned her head and nodded. "Just twenty-one, and scared to death. I hope you're not half as scared as I was, or you must be thoroughly miserable." She laughed lightly to cover the seriousness of her revelation.

"Why did you do it?" I asked, unable to help myself.

She had no trouble in answering. She looked up until my eyes met hers, and let go of Ellen's hand, letting the child continue on by herself.

"I had always wanted to go on a mission. From the time I was six years old I knew the gospel was true. I listened to the stories my father and uncles told about their missions and decided, the day I was baptized, that I would show the Lord how much I loved him by giving a year and a half of my life to his service. It sounded very noble, and even romantic."

She paused and sighed, her eyes filled with a gentle remembrance. "When the time came, it was not as easy as I had expected. I didn't really want to leave school. It wasn't easy getting the money together. Most of my friends thought I was crazy. It was all right for the boys to serve missions, but the only girls who went were the ones without prospects."

"Prospects?" I didn't understand her.

"Marriage prospects," she said, coloring a little. "I never was the most attractive of girls. I was afraid what my friends taunted me with was true: all the good men would be taken by the time I got back, or looking for younger, prettier possibilities, and I'd be left out in the cold."

"How terrible!" I said. "How unkind!"

She smiled suddenly. "I know. But it was worth it. I discovered that right away. And, as soon as I did, I tried hard to put the whole matter in God's hands. If he wanted me to have a husband, then I would somehow find one when I got home."

My heart was beginning to ache. I could see the conclusion our conversation was coming to, and I wanted terribly to avoid it.

"It's all right, Augustine," Martha said gently. "I *did* find a wonderful husband and, though he's gone now, I haven't lost him, not really." Her eyes moved slowly, almost involuntarily, up to the gray temple spires that sparkled in the clear autumn sunlight. "We were sealed in the temple, and so Heber is mine still. That's more comfort than you can dream of." She wiped her eyes. "It's hard, terribly hard; it hasn't gotten easier yet. But I'll make it." The pain in her voice was terrible. "I'm just so grateful I found him—that he's mine—"

She couldn't go on then. I reached out, found her cold hand, and squeezed it. Ellen appeared and began tugging at her skirt, saying something I couldn't quite make out. I dropped her hand and went in search of Roger. After that he and I walked together through the Assembly Hall, the Tabernacle, the small Church museum. He pointed out, with great solemnity, his favorites among the decaying Indian mummies that rested in the glass cases on the bottom floor. Back out on the grounds we stood at last before the statues of Joseph Smith and his brother Hyrum, with the temple rising, slender and serene, to the left of us. At that moment a strange peace came over me, a strange, warm sense of belonging. For perhaps the first time since I had read Martha Pratt's letter something inside me relaxed. When Martha glanced at her wrist-watch and announced, "Goodness, we've got to get going if we want to get you to Provo before nightfall," my insides did not twist into terrible clumps and knots. I was able to face the prospect before me without the weakening fear that had been with me before.

Chapter

3

My dormitory was one of a whole cluster of pale brick buildings that looked alike. Martha deposited me there with the dorm mother, after fussing over me and extracting half a dozen promises that I would call her if I needed even the least thing—no matter how silly it may seem to me, and that I would come visit often. Ellen, curious and off in her own world, was oblivious through all this. Roger helped carry my bags and belongings into my apartment with such a determined manly air that I could not resist throwing my arms around him.

"Thank you for taking such good care of me," I whispered into his ear.

"Thank you for the car and the French book," he replied. "I'll get my mother to explain the words to me, and then I'll take it to school. And tell them all about you," he added.

"Good," I smiled, through sudden tears. Then suddenly, and at last, they were gone, leaving the room strangely quiet and lifeless. I followed Judy Craig, my dorm mother, into the apartment I would live in and was politely introduced to three of the five girls I would share it with.

"Clara is the oldest," Mrs. Craig explained. "She's in the nursing program."

Clara looked up and smiled faintly. She was a short, rather mousey looking girl, but she had the most beautiful, velvety-brown eyes.

"Penelope isn't here yet, but she's your age exactly, and I believe she shares your same major. Nancy is in business, and Sally—Sally is a freshman. What will you be studying, dear?"

Sally looked the typical American freshman to me: dark-blonde hair, round "American-shaped" face with a fresh, milky complexion, and wide, long-lashed eyes. She shrugged her shoulders and laughed. "I like science. I may go into archeology; I don't know yet." Then she went back to her novel and the apple she was chewing on.

"Well, I'll check in on you later," Mrs. Craig promised, and abruptly left us.

"A roommate from France," Sally cooed, looking up at me. "Wait till I write my folks."

I smiled weakly.

"Can you understand what we say to you?"

"I've had six years of English," I replied, disturbed that my voice revealed my contempt for her.

"Wow!"

She hadn't even noticed. I took my things into my room and began arranging them in the closet and dresser. It was a square, tan-colored, unimaginative room with not one thing to make it look homey. Armand's picture would help immensely; I was more grateful for it than ever. A spread over the bed and some of my trinkets set out—I began to picture it as I hoped it would be.

"Penelope will be your roommate. She's mellow and easy to live with."

I looked up to see Nancy standing in the doorway, leaning against the frame, regarding me with eyes that seemed cool and appraising. I didn't know what to say. I mumbled something and bent again to my work, but she didn't move. "Do you need any help?" She sounded like a receptionist at a medical clinic.

"No, thank you. It just takes a while to figure out where to put things."

She nodded in agreement, or approval. "Right. I'll get back to work, then."

I worked on in peace for a few more moments. Then a blonde head popped into the room.

"Want to go to the drive-in for milkshakes? With me and Clara?"

I looked up slowly. I was a last child, virtually an only child. I had lived all my life in a quiet house with a quiet mother, having things entirely my own way, with no interruptions, no irritations. To live in these close quarters with *five other girls!* I shuddered.

"They make great chocolate malts," Sally urged.

"I'll come," I said suddenly.

"Great!"

I grabbed my handbag and followed her. "Why isn't Nancy coming?" I asked, as we shut the door to our apartment.

"Such things are below her," Sally said, with a giggle.

"Nancy and I were roommates last year," Clara added. "She's very meticulous and organized, and she has a job that starts first thing tomorrow morning, so she's getting everything in order tonight."

Sally looked over and rolled her eyes at me. I smiled at both of them, suddenly hungry for chocolate and ice cream and girlish nonsense. We strolled out into the cool night and I breathed in the fresh mountain air.

"Squaw Peak," Clara said, watching where my eyes went. "It's really quite beautiful here. I think you'll like it."

I pray I do, I thought. *It will make things so much easier if I can.*

The day following my arrival was freshman orientation. Sally and I were both freshmen, though she was eighteen and I twenty-one. She went off with a group of giggling girls who smelled of hair spray and wore too much makeup. I struggled through the day alone, learning some admittedly necessary essentials, but at a tedious price. Masses of people, long lines, forms to fill out; I was exhausted at the end of the day and found myself longing for a tall glass of cool milk and one of my mother's fresh salads, almost forgetting that there would be no one to "go home to," no one waiting to take care of me now. Though my feet were aching and my right shoe was rubbing my heel uncomfortably, I walked to the grocery near our apartment and purchased salad fixings, milk, cheese,

oranges and apples, and a loaf of what these Americans were satisfied to call bread. I could see that, somehow, I was going to have to
find time, between classes and study, to do my own baking. I had
not located watercress, but I had found fresh mushrooms and decent tomatoes.

After eating my simple meal I worked out the schedule of
classes I wanted. I had already heard nightmares about what registration would be like the following morning. But it wasn't really
too bad. I spent over three hours traipsing from line to line, getting
my cards signed and in the right places, but when I was through I
had made it into every class I wanted. Some of the freshman re-
quirements were waived for me, since I had classes to my credit
which were more advanced than most American high school students had experienced. I was grateful for that. I would work hard
this first semester and earn excellent grades. Though I was expected to take Humanities 101, I was given permission to register
for a Theory of Tragedy course. I also had English, Geology, third-
year Italian, and Book of Mormon. I wondered what that would be
like.

Immediately after registering I walked over to the bookstore
and filled out a job application. Between the scholarship and
Martha Pratt's assistance all my major expenses had been taken
care of. But I had refused a personal allowance, letting my benefactress believe that Mother and I could handle at least that much.
And yet, the truth was that I had spent most of my small reserve
just in getting out here. I would need food and pin money for day-
to-day expenses. I also wished to send something back to my
mother whenever I could. So I tried my best to appear pleasant, as
vivacious as I could, despite the fact that every job on campus had
at least fifty applicants. The young assistant manager who took my
completed application gave it only a cursory glance as he explained the unfavorable odds. But something caught his eye, and
he looked more closely.

"You come from France, from Burgundy—I've been there." He
was grinning from ear to ear now. "I served my mission in Paris."
He began an enthusiastic tirade in French, passable French, and
when I responded he sighed, his eyes warm and misty. "How I've
missed the sound of that language."

I couldn't help relaxing a little myself. It *was* good to speak in
my native tongue again. I had experienced very little difficulty

with the English—only when people talked too fast, or turned their heads away from me as they spoke. As soon as people detected my accent they seemed to react in one of two ways: *Oh, you speak English. How wonderful!* And then they would go on as though that matter had been dealt with and put aside as thoroughly unimportant; or they would become flustered and begin speaking louder and more slowly, and simplifying their sentences as though they were addressing a child. Either way, it proved somewhat annoying. But here was a boy who grew starry-eyed at the chance to speak French with me.

After a few more moments he circled my name on the application form. "I'll do what I can, Augustine." There were matters which wanted his attention, yet he dismissed me with obvious reluctance. I smiled as I turned away from him, the encounter making me strangely homesick. I went back to my apartment and wrote a letter to my mother, then a short note to Raymond, with a few sentences in large print for Elise. I washed some clothes out by hand and decided what I would wear the next morning for my first day of classes. It was still very hot here, although we were into the last week of September. I missed the fragrances of home, the roadside flowers, the ripening fields. I missed the close, narrow streets; the streets were so wide, everything was so spread out here. I missed the library—I ought to apply for a job at the university library, if they even allowed freshmen to work there. But I did have experience. I would go first thing in the morning before my first class started.

That night I gave Martha a phone call and told her that I had lived through registration and everything seemed fine and in order. She was reassuring to talk to. I didn't tell her I had applied for a job. If I got a position, I would probably have to work weekends, and she would have to find out, wishing me to come to the city often to visit the way she did. Well, I would cross that bridge when I came to it. I hoped she would not object. I desired at least a measure of independence in this new life where everything was different and foreign, and decided for me in advance.

☙

Late on the second day of classes our last roommate arrived. Her name was Anja Bates. She was from a city near San Francisco,

California, and she was only eighteen. She looked about fifteen, with bleached-blonde hair, eyes more gray than blue; cat eyes, and long, tanned legs. She was as nonchalant about things as I was tense and timid.

"What will you do about your schedule?" Sally asked, her eyes wide with interest, her voice breathless.

"I already have my classes," Anja replied. "We were on vacation in Hawaii, and I'm officially excused." She blew a large pink bubble with the wad of gum she had been chewing.

"How did you *manage* that?" Sally persisted.

"She has an uncle who teaches here," Penelope offered, passing through the small living room on the way to her bedroom.

"It isn't my uncle," Anja corrected, disdain obvious in her voice. "If I *do* have any pull, it's cause my dad donates huge sums of money to the college each year."

That stopped all questions for a time. I thought: *six girls living together in such cramped quarters, and no two alike. Thank heaven I don't share my personal bedroom with this teeny-bopper Californian.*

"Teeny-bopper" was an American term I had learned. One of the few. I didn't like American slang. I didn't like American food. I didn't like American manners. I didn't like—but I mustn't do that. I mustn't.

∾

Late Friday afternoon, soon after Anja had made her grand appearance among us, the friendly boy from the bookstore called our apartment. The job was mine if I wanted it. Fifteen to twenty hours a week, if I kept my grades up. I felt light and tingly, really happy inside for the first time since I had arrived. I thanked Michael Allen, then wrote his name in my little lesson planner so I wouldn't forget it. I was to go in tomorrow at one o'clock for training and stay until five. Something to do, something all my own, a beginning.

A few minutes later we heard the loud, staccato beepings of a car horn right outside our apartment, annoying and insistent. I stuck my head out the window. A shiny red convertible had pulled up to the curb. There were three boys inside. They were calling up to some girls in the next apartment, who hung over the window ledge shamelessly, flirting back with them. Sally came up beside me and, to my amazement, she waved her hand to them.

"Do you know those boys?" I asked her.

"No, but they sure are cute," she replied. "Especially the big one with the wavy black hair. The driver. I bet it's his car."

To my horror the driver of the car looked up at us, caught Sally's expression, and waved. "Anybody free," he called, "to go to the movies? What about you, honey—" His eyes shifted. He was staring straight at me! "How about it, Snow White? Is it a date?"

I quickly ducked back inside. I felt that my face had gone hot, and I put my hands to my cheeks. Sally was giggling, calling something back to him. Anja came up behind me, almost pushing me out of the way. The look she gave me was withering.

"Tell him there are two here, Sally, and we'll be down in five, if he's serious."

"You're going to go with them?" I asked, unable to stop myself. "You don't even know who they are."

"This is a college campus, Frenchie," Anja replied, pulling lipstick out of her purse and smearing it over her lips, making her tan look even more luscious. "How else are kids supposed to meet each other?"

There must be a better way, I thought to myself. *There must be something here besides this mindless rudeness!*

I walked over and picked up my book and settled into the lumpy, uncomfortable sofa. There must be other foreign students here, there must be some decent Americans; I had to give myself time. Tomorrow I would go to the bookstore. Perhaps we would have another conversation in French. Perhaps . . . I must not look ahead! Count my chickens before they hatched, as the old saying goes.

I tried to concentrate on my book, our first novel assignment in English. But it was such a lovely night. A mild, cool breeze sifted in through the open window. I could smell water, what Sally said was the canyon air. It was reminiscent of home. I sighed. Anja and Sally had behaved disgracefully. And yet, they were out in the night air, feeling its sweetness blow through their hair. I was restless. I was homesick. I was lonely. I bent my head to the book. If I was to work four hours tomorrow, I had better get this read now. I wanted good marks—I wanted to earn excellent grades here. I wanted Maman to be proud. I blew air in a low whistle through my teeth. I wasn't here to indulge myself, to "have fun," as the Americans said. There was much more to living than that.

❧

When I arrived at the bookstore the following day I learned that Mike, as everyone seemed to call him, wasn't working today. I would be trained by the manager herself; a woman by the name of Sharon Hall. She appeared to be in her thirties, and was kindly enough, though "no nonsense" in her approach to business. So there would be no one speaking French to me, complimenting me in little ways. But I was pleased when Sharon decided to place me in the book section; my experience in the library having some influence, I knew. I would far rather be immersed in the smell and feel of books, the sense of thought and emotion that seemed to hang in the very air above them, than peddling sweaters or perfume or watches or, worse, re-stocking shelves of gum and candies, tissues and handcreams and toothpastes.

The hours of my training passed quickly enough. I walked back to my dorm as the first gentle shadows of evening were softening the sky. I walked slowly, as I used to at home, enjoying the sensations around me, and entered the confinement of my apartment with some reluctance.

"Augustine, Augustine! Look what's come for you! You have some secret admirer," Sally cried, racing toward me as soon as I pushed the door open and tugging impatiently at my hand.

I let her lead me to the small end table in the living room. There, beside the squat, unattractive lamp, sat a vase of lovely red roses—a dozen, I could tell, with sprays of baby's breath, like tiny white stars, sprinkled among them.

I put my hand to my throat. "They could not be for me," I said, "I know no one here."

"Exactly!" Sally breathed. "Wait till you read what the note says."

"It *is* rather romantic," Penelope said, coming up to join us. "You must have made quite an impression."

With trembling fingers I drew the little card out of its envelope. *To Snow White*, it read, in a firmly-drawn hand. *From one who has recognized and admires your beauty.*

I was stunned. I felt a warmth creeping into my cheeks. "This does not mean me," I maintained. "And who is *Snow White*, anyway?"

Both girls laughed.

"She's the one in the fairy tale who is treated so cruelly by her wicked stepmother, who is jealous of her beauty," Penelope explained patiently. "She tries to kill *Snow White*, but the dwarfs in the forest care for her, and eventually her prince comes and carries her away."

Sally nodded, as if in agreement, her eyes round and shining still. "They *are* for you, Augustine, from that handsome smart alec in the red convertible last night, who fancies himself a prince charming."

I put my hand to my mouth. I remembered now that, when his eyes had met mine directly and fixed there, he had said something like, *How about it, Snow White?*

"Did he ask about me when you and Anja went off with them?" I queried Sally.

She shook her head at me, so that her dark-blonde curls bounced. "Course not. He's far too cool for such a direct approach." She leaned closer and breathed in the fragrance of the dark flowers. "One thing's for sure, you'll be hearing more from this Romeo, Augustine." I could detect soft laughter in her voice.

"What was he like last night? Is he nice?" I asked.

"Yeah, he's quite a gentleman. Has a southern accent and that makes him, you know, dreamy—kinda harder to resist."

"Is that how it will be for Augustine?" Penelope asked, gently teasing. "Will she be irresistible to boys because of her accent?"

With that, chaos took over. Clara came into the apartment and wanted to know what she was missing, and every little thing had to be explained again. It was all too much for me. As soon as I could I slipped away to my room, taking the flowers with me. They looked almost elegant standing on top of my dresser, just to the side of Armand's picture. I did not have to close my eyes to see Armand's face, to hear him laughing at me, as he most likely would if he were here with me now. The Seine, in my mind, was more liquid and alive than in the painting before me.

I leaned close and buried my face in the fragrant blossoms. *Do not build something out of nothing, Augustine*, I warned myself. *Right now this is a flirtation only. Chances are you will not even like this arrogant, willful young man.*

I knew I was probably right; but I didn't want to be. I wanted some romance and happiness in my life.

૭৪

We had campus branches, I learned, and ours met in the Maeser building. So everything about the Sabbath seemed foreign to me, especially hearing the prayers and the hymns and the talks in English. I had to smile at my own arrogance in preferring French when, after all, English had been the favored language of the Restoration.

There were very few of what I would call "adults" in this ward; most were young students like myself. There had simply been too many people and too many sensations for me this week. When the meeting ended, my intention was to slip away as quickly as I could. But as I walked out of the meeting room into the hallway I saw him: the convertible boy. He was literally surrounded by a swarm of colorful, sweet-faced, fragrant females, reminding me very much of the buzzing bees in the lavender fields at home. I paused and studied him a moment. He was dreadfully handsome and had a bold, overpowering presence, being taller than most men, and broader; though not heavy in any way. His shoulders were broad, which made him look a little uncomfortable in the suit he wore. His hair was blacker than mine, and it fell in waves over his forehead. Just as I determined to turn and be on my way, his eyes moved, scanning the room, and resting on me.

I saw him begin to remove himself, politely, from his admirers. But I had already turned and was walking quickly out of the building. *This is your own fault!* I told myself angrily. *You should not have stood there gawking at him like a smitten thirteen-year-old.*

I prayed that he would lose me in the crowds, that I would outdistance him. But no such luck! I was scarcely five steps down the broad approach to the building when I felt him coming up close behind me. It took all my self-possession not to turn back and look. Then, to my amazement, I felt his hand on my elbow and a soft, almost lazy voice spoke close to my ear.

"Why do you run away from me, Snow White? What *are* you afraid of?"

He stressed the word *are* and it came out sounding like *ahhh*— a long syllable that held a hint of mockery. I turned to him then, and replied as evenly as I could, "My name is not Snow White, and I do not know you, and you do not know me. So, how then could I be running away from you?"

He threw his dark head back and laughed at me, but the sound was pleasant, almost delighted.

"Ah knew you were special, Ah knew from the beginning. Mother would simply adore you!"

I had kept walking, and he lengthened his stride to keep up with me, yet he moved with a casual, loose-jointed ease. I noticed that the jacket he wore was of linen, and was obviously costly. And he smelled of something fresh and tangy, despite the warmth of the afternoon.

"Must your mother approve of any girl you admire?" I asked a bit tartly, as he sidled close, too close on the narrow sidewalk.

"If anything serious were involved—more than you know, honey-dear, and for good reason," he answered.

A *strange reply*, I thought, and began to veer left, heading across the campus toward Heritage Halls. But he touched my arm and very deftly guided me where he wished, so that we crossed the narrow road skirting a grassy hill that led down to tree-lined paths, heavily overgrown with plants and bushes. It was quiet and peaceful there, and silence seemed to swallow us, so that I felt a pang of alarm and looked up, almost involuntarily, into his eyes.

His smile was slow in coming, but it softened every line of his features and melted his eyes into pools of tenderness. "It's very lovely here, isn't it?" he asked. "Reminds me a little of home— South Carolina," he added, seeing the question in my eyes. "There's no place on earth like the South."

I couldn't help smiling; a warm, responding glow lit his own eyes. "You're French, aren't you?"

"Yes."

"Not Paris?"

"No, a small village in Burgundy called *Chatillon-sur-Seine*."

He repeated the words, and they sounded beautiful in his mouth. "How romantic," he said.

"It *is* romantic there," I affirmed, suddenly wishing to defend it against his Southern arrogance. "Lush fields and cool forests, architecture that can rival any in the world hidden in small, modest villages—"

He was listening. I could see it in his eyes.

"And the river, always the river, warm and melodic, whispering of old memories and other times."

He nodded, his eyes contemplative and serious. "As a Southerner Ah can understand what you're saying, Ah believe. We have our own old memories and sad songs. And nothing, honey-dear, is more admirable than love of country."

"Do you call every girl 'honey-dear'?" I asked. The words made me uncomfortable.

He laughed, very low, very gently. "What is your name? Ah do not even know what your name is."

"Augustine," I replied.

He repeated it, as he had the name of my city, and I felt a pleasant chill trickle along my spine.

"A proper gentleman would introduce himself, Augustine." His eyes were sparkling. "My name is Emory Charles Tuckett the third," he said, pronouncing the words firmly.

"Is that a very Southern name?" I asked. "And is it meant to impress me?"

"Yes to both questions." He pushed a lock of black hair away from his eyes and leaned so close to me that I could feel his breath on my cheek. "Ah am going too fast for you," he said, but the words were only a murmur. He drew away, and I felt I could breathe again. But then he took my hand in his, as though it were the most common, most accepted thing to be doing.

"Will you do me the honor of allowing me to escort you home in my shiny red convertible?" He was the flippant ladies' man again.

"Since that will be obviously the quickest way to be rid of you, by all means."

"Ah like your spirit," he said, "you're not at all like other girls. Ah'm not sure what the difference is—" he seemed to be musing to himself, almost unaware of me. "Another girl could have said those same words, but the meaning would have been different, and the sound and the *feel* of them." He tightened his hold on my hand. "Is it because you are French?" It was not a question he expected an answer to. We walked along the narrow, fragrant path for a moment or two in silence.

"You have nice hands," he said all of a sudden. "Long slender fingers and the softest of skin."

I looked down at my feet. I felt very uncomfortable. I had never met anyone like him; indeed, the closest thing to a boyfriend I had ever had was Armand, and he wasn't a boyfriend at all. Oh, I had experienced occasional dates with boys from Chatillon and one or two in Dijon, but they had not amounted to much; nothing there to make my heart skip a beat. But this boy . . . this boy!

We reached the road and crossed it to where his car was parked. He held the door for me and tucked my skirt up before he closed it. As he got in the driver's side he said, "You don't approve of what Ah was doing the other night, do you?"

I wondered what he would do if I answered honestly. "No," I replied. "Something in me recoils from such common, calloused—"

I didn't get the rest of my sentence out. He laughed at me again, in the way one would laugh at an endearing, adorable child one could not resist. I watched his profile, square-jawed and confident, as he drove. I wondered if his laughter was good or bad.

Chapter

4

*D*r. Bekker will be in class this morning," Penelope said, as she put the finishing touches on her make-up. She had beautiful, almond-shaped eyes. They smiled at me now, through the bathroom mirror.

"You mean our Theory of Tragedy professor?"

"Um-hum."

"Where has he been?"

"Off in Germany, I believe." Penelope pulled a brush casually through her thick auburn hair. "You'll like him. He's such a good teacher. And, besides, he's a dream."

I hadn't expected such a statement from Penelope. Watching my reaction, her brown eyes sparkled. "Everybody thinks so. Wait and see. Oh, and did you know he's assigned as your advisor? I saw the list posted Friday. Probably because you're both a Humanities major and a foreign student."

I nodded somewhat absently. Penelope and I shared the same major, though she intended to become a teacher, and I was not certain what I intended as yet. Although we were both twenty-one, she was a junior and I was registered somewhere between second semester freshman and first semester sophomore.

Theory of Tragedy was a fairly large class and, despite my reticence, I found myself stretching and craning my neck to get a glance at the professor before taking my seat. Penelope and I were somewhere near the back but, even from this distance, it was easy to tell how handsome Hans Bekker was. He was not a large man, and was slender of build, with a lean face and blonde-gold hair. Perhaps his appeal would have ended there. But when he spoke, his voice was so rich in timbre, low and melodious, measured and controlled, yet laced with a strain of excitement that enhanced its musical quality.

For the first few moments none of the words he said registered. When I realized that the students around me were taking notes and consulting their textbooks, I struggled to make the necessary distinction between the sound of his voice and the words that he said.

He was a brilliant lecturer, sharing his love of his subject as well as his knowledge of it. *This is because he is European*, I thought to myself. *He understands and values the heritage of thought and beauty which is mankind's most important heritage.* But I caught myself up short with the realization that Dr. Bekker was German: his name, his Aryan looks. The old barrier within me creaked and threatened to close shut like a trap. *You are grown up now*, I scolded myself impatiently. *The war is over, the war was another world ago. It has nothing to do with today.* So I told myself as Dr. Bekker bent his gold head over the painting of Parnassus depicted in our book, and explained the Greek beliefs of the structure of the universe.

After class at least half the students seemed to flow down the slanted room toward the podium where Hans Bekker stood glowing beneath a golden halo of adoration. I would have gone on my way in a heartbeat, but we had no class to hurry to, and Penelope wanted to introduce me. We waited in our seats for at least ten minutes, then took our place, like dutiful disciples at the fringes of the thinning throngs. My disdain and skepticism were in part a shield; I knew that. Close up, Hans Bekker was taller than I had thought, and his jaw was broad, his chin somewhat jutting, which gave an impression of strength to his finely-etched, almost delicate features.

Suddenly he turned half round and fixed his gaze upon us. His eyes were a penetrating blue; I found myself unable to look away from them.

"Penelope! It is so good to see you again. How is your brother? Is your sister home from her mission yet?"

There was no hint of patronage in his questions, nor in his manner; he was genuinely interested. And, once he had turned his attention upon us, no one else existed; time, itself, seemed to stand still.

I heard Penelope "explaining me" to him: who I was and why I was here. Her words grew dim before a growing sense of panic I felt building within me, a strange sense of unease that took me completely by surprise. As his gaze isolated me in its intensity, I felt myself tremble.

"Augustine, I am happy to make your acquaintance." His hand reached out for mine. It was a strong slender hand, the hand of an artist, but it held mine gently enough. "I have been to your part of France; indeed, I once did research in the library where you must have worked. And the museum in Dijon—there is none finer."

With quiet, unhurried sincerity he spoke to me. I was drawn to this man. Then why did such a cold, nameless fear tremble through me?

I was only half aware of our conversation. By the time we left I was perspiring and felt cold all over.

"Are you ill?" Penelope asked, leading me out into the sunlight and guiding me to the shade of a tree where we both sat down.

"Perhaps," I said, shakily. "Something just came over me."

"Well, close your eyes and rest for a few moments," she instructed, concern in her voice.

I leaned my head back against the rough-barked tree and did as she bade. I could see his face inside my mind, as clear as a picture. His eyes were smiling, his hair tawny and gold-flecked.

". . . so I'll drive you tomorrow afternoon, if you'd like. And, do you want to sign up for the conference trip?"

I opened my eyes and lifted my head up. "What did you say?"

"Augustine, *are* you ill? I said I'll drive you to your interview with Dr. Bekker tomorrow afternoon."

"Did he tell me to come then?"

"Yes, he did."

"Why? What does he want of me?"

Penelope looked at me a little strangely. "An initial interview to review your qualifications and make sure you're getting what classes you need to take you where you want to be going. You're very lucky to have him, you know. Some advisors couldn't care less. You can bug them all semester before they'll spare you a minute or two. Even then, they aren't much good—I had one like that my first year here."

I nodded and drew in a deep breath of air. My head was clearing a little, the panic that churned my insides had disappeared.

"Did you even hear him ask if we'd like to go with a group the department is organizing to attend the Sunday sessions of conference? Then we'll take a driving tour, if we have time, to see examples of different styles of architecture in Salt Lake." She paused, still watching me. "Sounds fun, doesn't it?"

"I've never attended general Church conference before."

"Course you haven't. Won't it be wonderful?"

I had to agree. "Yes, sign us up," I said.

Penelope had a car, an old jalopy, as she called it, painted a gruesome, but luckily faded, shade of green. She insisted upon driving me home now. I let her. I still felt a bit strange.

Later that afternoon I met Emory on campus, and we studied at the library for a couple of hours with some of his friends. Afterward we went out for ice cream. His was a noisy crowd, bordering on obnoxious. There were three boys and five girls, counting Emory and myself, and all the girls flirted shamelessly with him. He favored them now and again with one of his slow, languid smiles, or a gentle tease that set them giggling. But, by and large, he only had eyes for me. And he could act the gentleman, if he wanted. I could not help enjoying his attentions; I'm only human, and he was so very charming, so male, so attractive.

When he took me home he walked with me up the long path to our apartment. The night was cool, with a breeze coming down from the canyons. He had put his sweater over my shoulders. It carried the faint reminder of the pleasant, pungent scent that always clung to him. When we reached my door I began to remove it, but he shook his head.

"Keep it," he said. "You may need it again some time. The cold days are coming." He hunched his big shoulders in an imaginary shiver. "Now, if we were at home in the South, the mockingbird would be singing us a melody right now, so sweet in our ears—as sweet as the smell of you, Augustine, and the sound of your voice . . ."

He was wooing me with his voice and his words. He leaned very close and touched my cheek with his lips. How warm they felt on my skin. I wanted to sigh, I longed to move closer. He drew slowly away.

"See you tomorrow, Snow White," he said, his voice a murmur, a caressing murmur in the indistinct darkness that both separated and united us. I put my hand on the doorknob and slipped reluctantly inside.

∾

That night, for the first time since I had left home, I had The Dream. I never had The Dream without wakening suddenly, cold and perspiring and shaking uncontrollably. Since I was a child of four this dream had tormented me—ever since that dark night when my father had been shot to death before my very own eyes.

I got up as quietly as I could and went out for a glass of cold water. Penelope seemed undisturbed. She slept on the top bunk, usually huddled close to the wall, and she usually slept the sleep of the untroubled young. None of the girls in our apartment had known what hardship and trial were; that's not true, there was Clara. Clara wasn't fat, but she was what one would call dumpy, with mousey brown hair and short, thick legs. She was shy and usually kept her eyes down, and that was her biggest mistake. She had the most beautiful, velvet-brown eyes I had ever seen. Clara's soul spoke to you through her eyes, and you forgot her less-than-attractive body and experienced the delight of communicating with a bright, compassionate, caring person.

When I sat down to the table with my glass of water her anatomy notebook was sitting there. I thumbed through it idly. Clara was studying to be a nurse, and she was a natural for it. She had a father who was a doctor and a mother who was an alcoholic. I had heard her say once or twice: "Thanks to my parents I have both the money I need to study nursing, and the compassion I need to practice it."

She could have gone the other way; she could have grown narrow and bitter, and bereft of compassion. *Look what has happened to you!* I told myself harshly. *You have become narrow and frightened and, yes, somewhat bitter—or, at least, untrusting.* But I was so young, so young to watch soldiers with guns break down the door of my house and pour into it, through it, like black, filthy floodwaters. Shouting and crying and machine guns barking, and the look on my mother's face—it was all too vivid still! Vivid with a small child's terror that I had been unable to touch, unable to diminish since I had grown old enough to start trying.

I pushed up the sleeve on my nightgown and traced the fine white line of scar tissue with the tip of my finger, that scar that rippled like a drunken stream along the inside of my arm. Not a terrible scar, as such things went, easy enough to hide, if one was careful to always wear sleeves, even in summer weather. At inconvenient times, such as when one went bathing in the ocean on a hot July day, a little caution would usually do. I could hold my arm close against my body, being careful not to expose it. Except that some times I would get caught up playing with the others and forget, and then . . .

I yanked the sleeve down and stood up. I must get back to sleep now; tomorrow would be a busy day for me. Whenever the dream awakened me, my mother would know. She would come into my room and sit on the edge of my bed and stroke my arm gently and caress my hair until I relaxed and began to feel the kindness of sleep overtake me. The dream did not come often now. But, when it did, she was always there.

N'y pense pas, n'y pense pas . . . I chanted to myself as I crawled back into my bed and pulled the rumpled covers around me. "Don't think of it now." *Ma petite, ma chérie, ma chérie, dors: sleep.* I could hear my mother's voice, but I longed for the feel of her, the solid presence of her sitting there on my bed. I closed my eyes and wept softly into the darkness, until my tears exhausted me, and I slept.

∽

Late the following afternoon I kept my appointment with Dr. Bekker. Penelope drove me there in her car and insisted upon walking me all the way to his office and getting me settled; even then she was loath to leave me. She had a late class, and then would be spending the rest of the evening with Thomas, her boyfriend of over a year.

"Stay up so you can tell me all about it," she whispered into my ear as she scooted out the door. *What should there be to tell?* I thought. She was a bit strange where this Professor Bekker was concerned.

He came into the room. As though someone had turned a light on, everything brightened, a warmth stole over me.

"Miss Mousset," he said, his eyes meeting mine. "Would you like to come into my office now?"

He was the first person I had heard pronounce my name correctly since I had come here. I told him so and he laughed, and his laughter made me feel that all things must be right with the world.

"We Europeans have a harder time than people think." He spoke the words somewhat lightly, but then added in a more thoughtful voice, "Especially those of us who have lived through the war."

I did not know what to reply. I dropped my eyes. I found myself thinking, *How dare you speak to me of the war? It was German soldiers who barged into my home, German soldiers who—*

I felt his hand on my shoulder; a warm, comforting weight there. "I am so sorry, Augustine," he said. And I felt his sorrow, like a cry of pity that wrapped itself round me, like the gentlest of lullabies . . .

"The war means something entirely different to you than it does to me. And I wish you to know, I respect that."

He was telling me clearly that he respected my hatred of Germans, my bitterness, my inability to let go. My mother had never allowed me to speak ill of the Germans. From the shopkeepers and the schoolmasters I learned to continue my hate for them. My mother would say only, *c'était un moment très dur; on avait beaucoup de difficultés:* "That was a hard time; we went through many difficult things then . . ."

So I said those words to him now, in my own language. His eyes grew sad, his voice quiet. He answered me also in French and, without my quite realizing it, we continued our conversation in that language, speaking of classes, of goals, of memories, of a possible future for me in the museum system of France.

When I stood up to leave and glanced at my wristwatch I realized that nearly two hours had passed! I apologized for the use of so much of his time. In English he thanked me for the sharing of so much of mine.

I felt vulnerable around this man. Late that night, when Penelope and I talked, I contrived to ask her about him. As far as she was concerned, there was nothing strange in that.

"No, he isn't married!" she breathed. "Everyone knows that, Augustine. He isn't yet thirty, or barely so, and the most eligible bachelor on campus!"

"For the unmarried teachers," I amended.

"For the students," she persisted. "Some of us get pretty ancient before we're through." She winked at me, knowing my own concerns at being so much older than most of the other beginners. "Sorry, Augustine, but the way the American system works, the man is fair game."

"And he knows it?"

She paused briefly. "I suppose so; he must." Then she looked at me more closely. "He's not a wolf, my dear, he's not after all the young, pretty girls, though I know some professors who are." She relaxed, almost laughing at me. "You can trust Dr. Bekker," she assured me. "Besides, he's not really interested. Rumor has it that the girl he was once in love with was killed in the war, and he's never gotten over her. Sad, isn't it?"

She was enjoying the poignant drama of the situation, as though it were no more real than something she had read in a novel or seen in a film. I began to understand what the man, himself, had said to me: Penelope could not help herself. How could she know the harsh and terrible and unromantic nature of true suffering? The war had set us apart. We were, as the poet, Byron, said, "among them, but not of them."

And yet, what was I saying? Hans Bekker was the enemy. Without the pride and greed, the awful ambition of his nation, my people would not have suffered. And I would, perhaps, be as pleasantly naive and content as my roommate, Penelope.

I shuddered to think about it. I must not!—there was my answer! Dr. Bekker was merely one of my professors who taught a class I must go through and earn a good grade in; nothing more. Our lives would touch briefly, temporarily, and then go their own ways.

The thought ought to have comforted me, but it didn't. I felt a strange fog of misery and confusion close around me: I could not explain it, I could not understand it, nor had I any power to chase it away.

Chapter

5

My days were full and demanding, they slipped too quickly away. I had no time to be bored, or even homesick. In addition to classes, studies, and my hours spent at work, there were things about the apartment to do, a schedule of chores and responsibilities. Some of the girls were great at carrying their share of the load; others, Anja and Sally in particular, seemed to be able to ignore with great equanimity anything they did not wish to concern themselves with. Sally was feather-headed and cheerful and, at heart, had good intentions. Anja seemed sullen, usually withdrawn from the rest of us with an air of mild disdain about her.

Clara, eating breakfast with her huge anatomy text propped in front of her, the pages smeared with jam from her toast, offered a short and simple explanation for Anja: "She's from California," she said. "What else can we expect?" She made the statement matter-of-factly, without any malice or air of criticism. Nancy, wearing a tight suit and heels, already looking the successful executive, nodded agreement, her black hair glistening like a raven's wing. "I prefer her ignoring us to having to deal with her any other way."

So we all worked around her and made adjustments, and things went, really, quite smoothly.

And, in addition to all this, there was Emory. He was quickly becoming a daily fact of life. I never went as long as twenty-four hours without having some contact with him. Tuesday night he called. Wednesday we went for a ride in the canyons and ate a picnic supper, a bit late and a bit cold, because I had worked at the bookstore till six. But the night was heavenly, and I loved the strong smell of the cold, brackish creek water mingled with the pungent, almost sweet, odor of the drying leaves we crushed under our feet. Emory was easy to be with. He was clever, he was attentive. If he was also a bit pompous, a bit taken with himself, that could be forgiven.

Friday night we went out to the movies, as the Americans say, with a group of his friends. I didn't like Emory's friends as well as I liked Emory. Perhaps because they did not hide or mask their affluence and snobbery as well as Emory did. I liked Leroy Blount best, Emory's buddy from the South. He was a tall, gangly boy, all legs and ears, and I had the feeling he was a bit of a tagalong, not quite belonging socially, but accepted by the others because Emory wanted it that way; much as I was. Though the girls in the group who had designs on Emory did not accept me at all. They *endured* me, and I felt the difference. I believe Penelope thought me a fool to even go out with him. Clara was too nice to make judgments, and Nancy too preoccupied to care. Anja and Sally were obviously green with envy, though Anja would never deign to admit it. I sidestepped everyone for the time being, and basked in the flattery of his attentions, not really caring to determine whether that was foolish or not.

I slipped in barely before the dorm curfew, but I could not sleep. I turned on the little light above my bed and caught up on my English reading, that being perhaps my most troublesome subject, despite the fact that my whole life took place in English now. The thought half-amused, half-disconcerted me. I was French: I thought in French, I spoke in French, I *saw* in French. Now all that was changed. I was not certain that I wished to be Anglicized; I was not certain at all.

About two o'clock I got up for a drink and some crackers. That is why I was there to hear the door open and then swish shut very quietly. Anja had her shoes off and she walked with a cat's stealth across the floor. But she jumped and nearly snarled like a cat would when she looked up and saw me watching her.

"What are *you* doing here?" she asked, her voice implying that a person as boring and commonplace as myself could be up and about for only a most mundane purpose. Of course, this time she was right.

I made no reply; only giving her a searching look as I went back to my own room and shut the door.

The following morning I took an early bus to Salt Lake City. I had arranged to spend the day with Martha and the children. I would sleep overnight there and Penelope would pick me up early Sunday morning to join the others and attend the conference sessions on Temple Square.

It was raining when Penelope dropped me off at the bus station, but by the time we crossed what they call the Point of the Mountain the sun had come out again and was glistening along the backs of the raindrops, so that the whole world looked scrubbed and new. I felt Martha was truly pleased to see me. Ellen smiled her open, disarming smile, and Roger reached for my hand and squeezed it as we walked to the car.

We did crazy things all day long, spending most of our time in Liberty Park riding the Merry-Go-Round and walking through the Aviary, eating American hot dogs and ice cream cones for lunch. We went shopping and I found a gift for Raymond, who had a birthday coming: an American truck with English words written on it, a coloring book in English, and a box of Crayola crayons. Being with a family made me more homesick than ever, but I loved every minute of it. It was such a blessed relief from the strain of living in the unnatural compression of college life.

That evening, after the children were bathed and in bed, Martha and I sat and talked. She made me tell her every little thing that had happened. And she was wise enough—or kind enough—to offer no advice. I drew a few little things from her as well. It was easy to see how lonely she was.

"I had forgotten how nice it is to have someone to talk to," she admitted. "That was what I liked most about being married—having someone to share your thoughts with, share every little thing with."

There were tears in her voice as well as in her eyes, and my heart went out to her. Despite the blessing that she was, Ellen was also a burden; a worry, at least. Martha was raising two small children alone, with no one there, ever, to shift any of the load to. I thought of my own mother, and my heart grew even more tender.

"Have you ever thought of going back where your family is?" I asked her.

"Idaho?" She raised an eyebrow in such an enigmatic expression that it made us both laugh.

"I'd be lonely there. My mother has been dead for five years, and my brother has the farm that adjoins my father, so Dad has someone to care for him. There are better schools here in the city for Roger and special schools for Ellen."

I nodded agreement. She hesitated just a moment, then added, "Besides, all I have left of Heber is here—all the places we went together, this home that we lived in."

I put my hand out and covered her cold, trembling fingers. I could not say, "I understand." But I did know suffering, I did understand loneliness and confusion and fear. I could only pray that my spirit would communicate that tenderness to my grieving friend.

❧

The hour was very early, the morning soft and whispery when Penelope knocked gently at the door, and I slipped out to join her.

"I didn't want to awaken your friend," she said.

"Her room's in the back," I answered, "and we were up pretty late talking, so she ought to be sound asleep still."

"What about yourself?" Penelope grinned as she started the engine and backed her old rattly car down the narrow drive.

"I just hope this is worth it," I responded, and I meant it. I am not one to feel good around crowds, and to stand in line for hours and then sit, packed in like sardines, just to say I had attended conference, did not make my heart skip a beat. I suppose, to be honest, the Church did not mean a great deal to me. I had been converted with my mother, or I thought I had; I wanted to be, wanted to please her, wanted to be part with her in something that seemed, to her, so important. I had even begun to read the Book of Mormon back then when I was fourteen. But the novelty faded, going to meetings was a difficulty, especially in bad weather, especially if one is young and one's friends are doing something else and want you to come, too.

My mother tried to nag me at first, then she grew strangely silent and resigned on the subject. She was faithful herself, and she read in the scriptures daily. I had suspected from the beginning that one of her motives in sending me to Utah was to re-convert me to Mormonism. I still wondered at her logic. Did she really wish all this to reach its natural conclusion, which was for her only daughter to marry an American Mormon and live half a world away from her?

Temple Square *was* crowded, and there were lines or, rather, clumps of milling people, waiting for the Tabernacle doors to open. The crisp air tickled my nose with half a dozen odors, all tantaliz-ing. I felt alive; as keen and fresh as the morning air.

There were two teachers and about twelve students in our group. When the pressing crowd shifted and began to jostle into movement, we did our best to stay close together, like a herd of timid, obedient sheep. But, once inside, we saw the impossibility of finding a block of fourteen seats. In unspoken agreement we slid into any empty spaces that presented themselves close at hand. One could spy a likely open spot two rows ahead, but never reach it before someone else crowded into it. I am not very aggressive in such circumstances, and I do not move quickly. Three or four times I found myself heading toward a seat, only to stand there blinking as someone else claimed it. In my confusion I felt a hand on my arm, firmly propelling me forward, actually pushing me onto a bench, with a resolution I appreciated. Once seated, I looked to see who had saved me. The surprise I felt must have shown in my eyes. To cover my confusion I blurted out, "Where is Penelope?"— as though I were a child and needed her near for assurance! Dr. Bekker laid his hand briefly, lightly on my shoulder. "I haven't the slightest idea." His voice sounded amused.

"Well, thank you for securing a seat for me. I don't believe I could have done it myself."

He laughed gently, kindly. We were sitting so close together. I was very aware of him: the touch of his leg against mine, the scent of his hair and skin. His blue eyes were too piercing for such close quarters. I felt myself shrinking back, then turning my gaze, my at-tention, to anything else but this man beside me. And I found there was much to distract me. So many people to watch; so many faces, so many expressions, so much beauty and enthusiasm. Suddenly I sensed a shift in the crowd, a settling, the beginnings of a hush, and then a sense of expectancy. The organ, deep and solemn, began the strains of a song that even I was able to recognize: "We thank thee, O God, for a prophet to guide us in these latter days." As one person, the whole congregation rose to its feet, and the very air held its breath. Then I could see, coming up the aisle, a tall, white-haired man; a magnificent man with a strong, gentle face, and eyes that held the peace of eternity in them. I felt a pure sensation of love and joy surge through me, and was not surprised to look around and see that many people were crying openly or stood with tears brimming their eyes.

The prophet of God! I had never in my life seen a prophet, but I knew I was seeing one now. I felt the power of his presence sweep through me like a benediction, and I uttered my mother's name as I would utter a prayer.

That meeting was perhaps the first truly spiritual experience of my life. I leaned forward in my seat. No matter who the speaker was, his words seemed to be meant just for me. The music, the atmosphere of love and acceptance, the sense of peace that surrounded me, blotted everything else out of my consciousness. I was not aware of the hardness of the benches and the ache I felt in the small of my back. I was not aware of the noises, the coughing, the occasional giggling or whispering of young children. Once or twice they broke through, then faded away again. Once or twice the man who was sitting beside me would meet my eyes, and in his gaze I saw complete understanding, a sympathy of spirit which did nothing to mar the experience which was encompassing me.

At the end of the meeting I felt drained, exhausted; and yet strangely light, somehow filled and strengthened. I walked out into the bright sunshine, blinking my eyes, feeling disoriented. Again I felt the pressure of a warm hand on my arm, the firm, purposeful guidance. I found myself seated on a cool spot of grass beneath a tree whose black branches were stripped nearly bare. I saw Penelope reach over and hand me a sandwich.

"It was a wonderful meeting, wasn't it?" she asked. I thought her face looked beautiful, shining. I nodded my head and smiled back at her.

Dr. Bekker was sitting beside me. He handed me a carton of milk. I ate and drank mechanically. I felt a calm peace inside myself, and at the same time a sense of excitement, a sense of spiritual pleasure, altogether a new sensation. When the conversation around me turned to common, everyday matters I felt my mind shut it out, protecting the impressions and feelings that were so precious to me. Then Hans Bekker bent toward me.

"The first time I saw Temple Square I had just received my master's degree from Harvard. I had been attending school in the East ever since my arrival in this country from Germany."

"How old were you then?"

"When I came to America? Seventeen." He smiled, and his smile was not for me. It was a very sad smile, and I believe it belonged to his memories.

"I think I had forgotten what life was all about, what purpose there might possibly be to all the suffering and struggle. But this place changed that. This place—" he paused and hesitated. "This place awakened my soul again."

So he was telling me he understood what I had felt in there, what was happening to me. His eyes said it, too. Everything pure and beautiful in him reached out and touched me. I did not know how to respond. I dropped my gaze and said nothing.

"It is all right, Augustine." His voice was so soft that I was not sure he had spoken.

"Thank you." My own voice was scarcely more than a whisper. But I knew that he heard.

The afternoon meeting was just as outstanding, as clear and sweet as the first had been. I was afraid that it might, somehow, fail to measure up, that I might lose this beautiful feeling that was singing through me. But the feeling stayed. Even when we went all together and ate a meal at a noisy, crowded restaurant, the gentle feeling lingered, like a protecting and soothing aura around me. Is this what my mother had felt when she embraced Mormonism? Is this why she read scriptures and attended meetings? Could one glean such feelings from these things, too?

The temple itself was the first architectural example we considered, learning that it is often described as being a modification of the Round Gothic, but that Joseph Young, one of the architects on the building, called it Romanesque, modified by the Castellated style. It was one of the rare buildings I had seen which reminded me of those graceful edifices around which I had grown up. But now we saw others: Brigham Young's Beehive House, in the Greek Revival style; the Catholic and Presbyterian cathedrals on North Temple, the Masonic Hall, and some of the old mansions built along that same street. I was riding with Penelope in her jalopy, studying the printed guide we had been given, finding myself a little confused as I searched for Doric or Ionic columns, pointed Gothic towers, Roman arches, and Baroque curves and swirls. Penelope was more adept than I, for I had a hard time concentrating, switching both my mind and spirit from where they had happily been.

We left the others a little early and drove back to Martha's, where I picked up my things, introduced my two friends, and kissed the children good-bye.

"Call if you need me—if you need anything," Martha reiterated. "And come whenever you like." She blew us a kiss from her fingertips, then added, calling after us, "Bring Penelope. I'll get a baby-sitter and we three can go out on the town."

"I'd like to do what your friend suggested," Penelope said, once we were well started. "She seems awfully friendly and down to earth. I think we three could have a good time."

I thought uncomfortably of my early prejudices and resentments against this meddling lady missionary. How harshly I had judged her, how unfavorably I had pictured her in my mind. I suppose fear, more than anything else, had been my motivator. But inwardly I felt terribly ashamed of myself.

"Emory missed a great day, didn't he?" Penelope said, unable to keep a note of smugness from her voice. She knew I had invited him and he had declined, using for an excuse his "Bricker" initiation activities. He was president of the most socially elite social club on campus; or so he regarded it. But most students thought of the Brickers as snobs. And Penelope was definitely among that group.

"I'm glad Emory wasn't with us," I retorted, and I meant it. How could I explain that he would have spoiled things, that what happened to me inside the Tabernacle probably would not have happened if he had been there—to distract me, to alter my impressions, my inner responses?

"Well, you had enough attention as it was," Penelope replied, with a twinkle in her eye and the smugness still in her voice.

"I don't know what you mean."

"Oh, yes, you do. Dr. Bekker likes you, Augustine. There's nothing *wrong* with that."

"Well, I do not wish to talk about it."

"All right—all right!"

I knew Penelope thought me a bit strange where the man was concerned. But I could not help it. I felt such mixed reactions toward him. And always, no matter what I was feeling, an underlying sense of unease. I remembered my earlier resolve to ignore him altogether. That would be difficult for me, I knew, because something within him drew me toward him, as a kindred spirit, as a friend. So then, why did I not feel I could trust him?

I fought against the confusion which began to churn in my insides, wishing fervently that Penelope had not brought up the subject. I wanted the light, peaceful feeling of joy to stay with me. I wanted it as much as I had ever wanted anything in my life.

Chapter

6

*M*onday, as soon as my classes for the day were over, I wrote a long letter to my mother, trying to describe what I had experienced, trying to explain to her what I had felt. As difficult as this was, I thought she had a right to know. I realized what it would mean to her, especially in view of the sacrifices she was making, willingly, for my sake. I also enclosed a small sum of money. My earnings had always helped to support us, yet she had stubbornly refused to point this out to our benefactress, back when Martha's offer first came. And she forbade me as well to get a job while I was going to school.

"I know you will work hard for high marks," she had said. "And if you have a job, too, then you will have no good times at all."

You mean I will not find a husband! I had thought at first, bitterly. I could almost smile, thinking of how my outlook had changed. I *could* smile when I thought of how impossible Emory made it for me to avoid having good times, having all the "fun" I could handle! Perhaps when my mother learned about Emory she would not be too angry about the job.

That day I also wrote letters to my niece and nephew and sent off the package for Raymond, with a little something for Elise also tucked inside. I liked imagining their excitement as they tore open the package with the American postmark. I felt like a fairy god-mother, and savored this opportunity to bring pleasure and happiness into their lives.

I worked at the bookstore until six. Emory picked me up there and drove me home in his car.

"Honey-dear," he crooned, as he pulled into our parking lot and cut the car's engine. "Ah've got something to show you."

He sidled closer, drawing a large envelope from his inside jacket pocket. "Ah had my picture made last week for the year-book and an article they're doing in the campus news." He grinned. "You know, president of Brickers and all that."

I nodded. "Well, let me see it."

He kept his hand over mine as he gave me the photograph. I was very aware of his closeness.

"This is *so* nice, Emory," I said, "very impressive."

He laughed lightly. "Ah am a handsome devil, aren't I?"

It was a shame that he knew it, because it was so painfully true.

"I'm afraid you are," I responded, sliding a little away from him and handing the photograph back.

"That one's for you, Snow White. Ah want you to have it."

And why? I thought.

"Keep it someplace close to you," he murmured, and I felt the warmth of his breath on my neck.

"You just want me to be taken in by you, fall madly in love with you," I replied, purposefully keeping my tone light, almost teasing.

"That's right, honey, Ah do."

His voice was very low, very serious. He pressed his lips to the back of my neck, then brushed them against my cheek. A pleasurable flush of warmth spread through me.

"Emory, stop that."

He knew I meant it and drew back, a bit puzzled.

"Ah've never met any woman like you, Augustine. Ah care about you—" He hazarded enough to lift a lock of my hair, twisting and curling it with his fingers. "Oh, Ah've had girlfriends in plenty before, course Ah have. But that was all just in *fun*. With you it's different—with you Ah feel—"

"Emory, no! I do not want to hear this."

He drew away with a sigh and his face was clouded. "You're a hard one, you know."

He came round and opened the door for me. As I stepped out he moved close to me and put his hands on my shoulders.

"Must you play hard to get, Augustine?"

His little-boy pout was appealing—his nearness, everything about him—and he knew it! He was using it purposefully, using it against me!

With some difficulty I broke away from him and began walking toward the dorm. He followed at a leisurely pace. As I stood finding my key in the messy cavern of my purse he came up, hands in his pockets.

"I'm sorry, Emory," I said. "There are plenty of girls, as you know better than I do, who would do anything to hear what you said to me. I'm just not one of them."

"Ah'm tired of those kinds of girls," he said, and his voice sounded so unaffected, so sincere, that I looked up, and met his steady gaze watching me. "Ah told you that you are different," he said.

I felt my pulse beginning to beat in my temples. I felt that softening inside which his nearness could always do to me.

"Ah'll wait," he said. "Ah'll be patient. You are worth it, honey-dear . . ." Each word was measured, each word was as tender as a physical touch would be. He bent his head and pressed his lips to my forehead. I prayed he could not feel my trembling.

"Ah'll be here, quarter to ten in the morning, honey."

He turned and ambled slowly away. It was a pleasure simply to watch his movements and the sway of his dark hair, so thick, so shining. I wanted to reach out and touch him, I wanted to call out and bring him back—I wanted his nearness, the touch of his lips again. Thank heaven he didn't know! Thank heaven!

You must be careful, I told myself. *Nothing foolish must happen here, nothing that you would regret.*

I walked into the apartment. I still had his photograph, stuck inside one of my school books. I took it into my room with me and slipped it inside my top dresser drawer, face down. After a moment

I got it back out and propped it on top of my dresser, just beneath the framed painting Armand had given to me.

I cannot run away from him, I told myself fiercely. *Let his face, with that cocky grin, be a reminder so that I do not forget.*

Something must have really changed in me. I went to my Book of Mormon class Tuesday morning, expecting nothing in particular. We had been talking about the early days of the Nephite settlement in America, the death of Lehi, and Nephi's writings concerning the last days. Suddenly it all meant something. Suddenly prophecy concerning the choice land which had been kept, by God's wisdom, as an inheritance for the righteous, a place where his gospel might be restored, sent an electric thrill through me. I was here in this choice land, I was here on the spot where many of the great events of the latter days had taken place. Nephi's words penetrated my understanding and became precious to me. I found myself marking passages I wished to remember, to perhaps memorize. I realized that I was feeling something very akin to that wonderful feeling I had known Sunday on Temple Square. I walked out of the class almost singing—humming out loud under my breath. This class would be enjoyable from now on, it would mean something to me. In fact, it seemed that everything in my life had taken on new meaning and new color.

Wednesday morning while several of us were still getting ready for classes, our dorm mother came into the apartment. She used her key—hoping to surprise us for some reason of her own? As it turned out, she wished to question us about last weekend.

"It has been reported to me," she informed us, in a most serious manner, "that there has been a serious breach of dorm rules taking place. One of the girls in your apartment has been seen, on more than one occasion, sneaking in during the wee hours of the morning."

Anja, Nancy, and myself, the only ones still home, looked back at her solemnly. *For heaven's sake,* I thought, *get to the point, woman. And be decent enough to name the culprit.* Though I had a very good idea who the culprit was.

"At such a very late hour," Nancy asked, "who else was up and about to catch this offender?"

A good question, I thought. The dorm mother raised her head a bit and coughed into her hand. "A girl in one of the apartments is troubled with asthma and doesn't sleep well. There was no purposeful spying here, mind you, just unavoidable discovery."

"Is this person certain the offender was from our apartment?" Nancy persisted.

Judy Craig hedged a little. "She is not positively certain. That is why I require your cooperation." She paused meaningfully, glancing at us each in turn. "Were any of you girls out past dorm hours last Friday night?"

We all shook our heads. I thought her gaze, with a bit of a glare in it, rested longer on Anja, but I couldn't be sure.

"Did any of you notice anything unusual, anything that ought to be reported?" She spoke each of our names in turn. Anja shook her head; Nancy replied, "Certainly not," and, taking her response as dismissal, went back into the bathroom to finish her hair. When Mrs. Craig looked at me and said, "Augustine?" I could feel Anja's eyes boring holes in me. "Nothing to report," I said.

She was not happy. After uttering a few dire warnings, she went out again. Nancy came briskly from her bedroom, checking her wristwatch.

"If I'm late to class because of her—" she bristled, sweeping out with no further farewell.

The room was as still as a stone. "Why did you cover for me?" Anja asked bluntly.

I gathered my books and papers from the kitchen table. "I'm not sure," I said, honestly.

"What do you want for it?"

"Heavens, I don't want anything!" I replied, taken aback. "What you do with your life is your own business, I believe."

She was watching me closely, surprised, I suppose, at how liberal and enlightened I was sounding.

"I only hope you don't sell yourself short." I made her meet my eyes for a moment. "I think that would be a pity."

I turned and walked out of the room. On and off during the day I thought about what had happened, wondering if I had done the wrong thing. Perhaps nipping her deceptive tendencies in the beginning might prevent her from involvement in something more serious later on. Perhaps I was abetting something terrible. But I didn't think so. I do not often lie, or deceive in even small ways, as

I had done this morning. Some inner sixth sense had told me that loyalty to Anja right now was crucial. And that feeling made no sense. I was not close to the girl; I scarcely liked her. So why should such a premonition come over me? I did not know. But one thing struck me, as I continued thinking about it. Anja had said nothing that could be construed as kind or grateful. But there had been a subtle difference there. The hard glaze had been gone from her eyes. In her moment of amazement she had appeared briefly open and unguarded. *That's at least something,* I told myself. *A beginning, at least.*

⁂

In fact, I was thinking about Anja during my shift at the bookstore, straightening shelves, concentrating on my own matters, and I ran headlong into Dr. Bekker. Literally ran into him. I was flushed with embarrassment. But he covered the awkwardness by holding out the book he was carrying.

"Look what treasure I have found," he said. His voice was low, with a musical quality to it and, right now, a note of obvious enthusiasm.

I read the title out loud: "*Hermann Hesse, Reflections.* I do not know him or his writings."

"I did not expect you should," he responded. "He is a German writer. But you would like him, nevertheless." He smiled ever so slightly. He had a way of meeting your eyes when he spoke to you, making you feel that his words and ideas were very important, and that he meant them for you, alone. "He looks at life much the way you do."

"And how is that?" I asked. "How do you know the way I think, the way I look at life?"

"Augustine!" he said. And I could not read the expression in the word, and he gave me no further answer.

But I found, in a few moments, that he had drawn me into a very pleasant discussion of writers and writing, and I was telling him some of my favorites, sharing thoughts and opinions I did not usually share. He made it such an easy, natural thing, drawing people out the way he did, yet never going too far, never prying, never forcing. And today, aware that my time here was not my own, he cut the discussion short and took a courteous farewell of me, leaving me with a warm, pleasant feeling. But also leaving me thinking about him, which was not a good thing to do.

∞

"Love me tender, love me true, take me to your heart, for my darling, I love you, and we'll never part. . . ."

Elvis Presley's voice came over the loud speaker, sweet and seductive: "Love me tender, love me true, all my dreams fulfill, for my darling, I love you, and I always will. . . ."

The slow dance was ending. Emory had been holding me much too close. I was sure he could feel my heart beating a quick little rat-a-tat pattern, giving my feelings away. As the music stopped I saw Leroy's pale, freckled face only inches away from mine. He was grinning from ear to ear.

"Sorry, old man," he said to Emory. "Snow White promised me the next dance."

I admitted that I had, and Emory handed me over with good grace. It pleased and surprised me that some of his friends had taken to calling me "Snow White," and the name had stuck. Leroy was tall and skinny, and he was a very good dancer. He swept me across the floor with such agile ease that I had to concentrate to keep up with him. Nancy, after meeting him, had called him a hayseed, and I suppose he was one, at least if looks mean anything. But he was such a nice boy, always smiling and enthusiastic, always willing to help. I smiled at him now. "I can't keep up with you," I admitted.

He grinned and slowed down a little.

"Our boy is really taken with you, Augustine."

"Our boy" is what Leroy called Emory. I shook my head at his words. "I'm a bit of a novelty, that's all. You know Emory—what it would mean to him to say he is dating a French woman."

"I know all that," Leroy argued. "And you're right, as far as it goes." His grin widened. "In fact, you've got Emory figured better than most girls do. But with you it goes deeper—I can tell."

I lifted an eyebrow, hoping to look dubious. "You can tell."

"I've known Emory since we were kids, Snow White. You can see yourself I'm not part of his crowd." Despite himself, there was an emphasis of contempt in his voice when Leroy said "his crowd." "He keeps me around partly out of loyalty—" he shrugged his shoulders. "Partly 'cause I'm the only real friend he's got, and he knows it."

That made sense to me. The song ended, and I thanked Leroy, squeezing his hand a little before I let go. I would have to think about what he had told me. But the rest of the night was a whirl of music and lights and laughter. And, surprisingly, I enjoyed it, though I knew part of the pleasure and part of the ease I felt were due to the fact that I was at Emory's side. He was aggressive enough and polished enough for both of us. And some of his aura attached itself naturally to me. I could not help enjoying that, shy and reticent as I usually was in new situations. And I'll admit that pride, too, was a factor. I drew a certain vain satisfaction from the envying glances that were so often and so obviously directed my way. Being the center of attention, for any reason, was a heady sensation for me. And knowing how firm was my hold on Emory, how he was the pursuer and not the pursued, I could smile at the giddy girls who openly flirted with him. I knew I was playing a game. And if I felt somewhat uneasy at times, I put such qualms from me. I was determined to enjoy myself thoroughly, be young— yes, perhaps even a bit foolish. I had never done that before.

Chapter

———————

7

"ou've got yourself a job," Clara said, reaching for the last crêpe on the plate.

Sally rolled her eyes at me and moaned. "Why did you make that last batch? I'm so full I can't move."

"I had no idea what we were missing," Clara mused. "What else can you cook?"

"We eat lots of fish where I come from," I told them, "and we cook with herbs. I have an especially good recipe for sole in butter sauce. And *potage cultivateur*—a soup with potatoes and leeks, string beans and carrots."

"I've never tasted leeks before." Sally wrinkled her nose, as though in distaste.

"I've been thinking about baking bread once a week," I admitted.

"Don't you dare," Nancy threatened, pushing her chair back from the table. "I don't intend to add an extra inch to my waistline this year."

Penelope smiled at me. "Come on, I'll help you with the dishes. Don't you have to work this afternoon?"

"That's right, I do."

"Let's get going, you guys," Penelope goaded. "The head chef shouldn't have to do duty as dishwasher, too."

"Absolutely! We don't want to discourage you from cooking, Augustine," Clara added, with a smile.

I was pleased. It had taken me a while to work up the nerve to show my preference for French food by cooking my own. I hadn't wanted my roommates to think I put myself above or apart from them in any way. But it would be a great pleasure to work up some of my mother's recipes and to smell the fragrance of fresh bread again. I had missed that more than I liked to think about. There was no sense of "home" in an apartment of hodge-podge young women. There was no peace, no sense of welcome and solace when I walked in the door. The adjustment had not been as terrible as I had feared; but still, there was so much to miss.

Work seemed to go slowly that afternoon. Perhaps because the day outside the window was so mellow, with a golden autumn hush sifting over everything. Mike Allen was working with me, though, and that made the time pass more pleasantly. We always spoke French to one another, as a matter of course; though he had said last Wednesday, with some surprise, "Your English is improving, Augustine. You never seem to hesitate any more. You speak just like a native, except for that beautiful accent of yours." He had smiled at me then in open admiration. "Don't ever lose that."

I walked home leisurely, as was my custom, enjoying the solitude and the various sensations around me. Squaw Peak looked close today, its granite edgings finely etched against a blue sky. At this hour before sunset the mountains seemed lit from within, glowing golden, almost throbbing with light. The array of colors that stained their flanks had faded during the past week, but the leaves sifting to the ground as I walked still splashed bright spots of red and yellow upon the gray dusty pavement. I could smell rain in the air, and see a gray stretch of clouds building up in the west. I hoped a storm would come, a dark storm, wild and wind-ridden. Something restless in my spirit craved it. Emory was busy tonight with his Bricker friends, and I felt content to spend a quiet evening by myself—a cozy evening if the storm broke. Perhaps later I could take a walk in the rain.

When I entered the apartment it was silent and appeared deserted. Good. I wouldn't mind having the whole place to myself. But Penelope burst out of the bedroom, looking distressed.

"Where have you been, Augustine? I thought you'd be here fifteen minutes ago."

"I took my time walking home," I admitted.

"Of all nights! Dr. Bekker will be here in less than half an hour."

"What are you talking about?"

"He called earlier saying he has two extra tickets to the play tonight, and would you and I like to take them."

"Go with him?"

"Yes. But not alone, at least I don't think so. Anyway, the play is *Blithe Spirit*. I know you'll just love it, Augustine. So I said yes."

"You said yes for me as well as yourself?"

"Well, I had to do something." Penelope was getting a little put out. "I thought you'd be happy. I knew you didn't have any other plans."

"I'm sorry, you're right. It ought to be wonderful. It's just—well, I wasn't expecting—I thought I'd spend a quiet night—I—" She was blinking her eyes at my verbal reflections. "It doesn't matter. I'll be ready."

"Really?"

"Yes. That is, if you'll put my hair up for me."

"Done." Penelope was beaming. "I'm nearly ready myself. So I can do anything to help that you need."

We made it in record time. I chose my gray suit to wear; it makes me look slender and sophisticated; I felt I needed that tonight. I put mascara on my long lashes and applied a little more shadow to my eyes than I usually wear. The effect was stunning. It made me realize that I had not dressed up much since I had come here. I knew I looked good even before Penelope's low exclamation of approval.

"You're an absolute knockout, Augustine."

I smiled uneasily, and jumped nervously when I heard the front bell ring. But Penelope seemed to have no such qualms. She opened the door and said brightly, "We're ready."

But when I heard Hans Bekker's voice something inside me tightened uncomfortably. He looked past Penelope and saw me, and for a brief moment his blue eyes registered surprise, perhaps even alarm. Then he smiled and said, with practiced ease, "You girls look lovely tonight."

We filed out into the parking lot, Penelope chattering, blessedly—

for I could not utter a word. When I saw the shape of another person sitting in the front seat of his car I know I let my breath out in a sigh, I was so relieved. Penelope and I climbed into the back. The other person was Miss Barnes, a professor in the English department. She weighed close to two hundred pounds and looked to be in her forties, but I didn't care. She was another person, another adult, and that changed things completely.

All was confusion for a while, hurrying from the car to the theatre, locating our seats and getting settled. Miss Barnes, discovering that we possessed an aisle seat, requested it for herself and thus, as things turned out, Penelope sat four seats in, then myself, next Dr. Bekker, and finally our oversized friend. So I was beside him again, in the close, dimming theatre. His presence was too powerful to ignore—leaning close to point something out on the program, explain a bit of action, tell something of interest concerning one of the actors. Yet, he seemed at ease; they all did, all but myself.

Brenda Barnes was a delightful person, as funny at times as the play was. During the intermission between acts she kept us all in stitches. I discovered I liked her immensely, and wondered if any problems I felt existed were not solely in my own mind. After all, Dr. Bekker had never behaved unseemly to me. He was sensitive and sincere, and therefore more real in his relationships than most people are. But he always behaved like a gentleman. Perhaps I was imagining things. Perhaps my own fears and insecurities—if he were just not so handsome! That alone would have helped.

None of us was ready to call it quits when the curtain fell for the last time. We had too much to say still. To my surprise, Miss Barnes invited us to her place for ice cream sundaes. And, as I helped her get out the dishes, the nuts, and toppings, she asked me about myself, with real interest. And she was a very good listener. At last I began to relax. When the ice cream and the talk had both dribbled away to nothing, I was still reluctant to leave. I thanked her sincerely. And when Dr. Bekker walked Penelope and myself to the door of our apartment, I tried to thank him as well. But he would have none of it.

"The pleasure was all mine," he insisted. "I've not had such a thoroughly enjoyable evening for a long time."

His voice was relaxed and happy. But, no matter what the

tone, his voice was as thrilling to listen to as a resonant, finely-tuned instrument.

"Miss Barnes made the difference," I reminded him.

"Not the only difference," he replied, and he spoke the words slowly, looking straight into my eyes.

So, despite everything, I was trembling inside when the apartment door closed behind him, fighting sensations I wanted no part of. And, though it was late when at last I climbed into bed, and I was more tired than usual, I tossed and turned and was unable to sleep. In the deepest, darkest hour of the night the storm broke, loud and terrible. I awoke with a start, the dream that had been troubling me vivid in my mind still. I pulled the covers around me and listened to the steady, relentless driving of the night rain. Why should this old dream haunt me now—and with such intensified vigor and force? Would this vague, half-remembered past ever leave me in peace? I had been a very small girl when the war came, and long years had passed since then. Green grass grew in the scar-line of trenches and covered the graves. New buildings had been built out of rubble. There was industry and prosperity and growth, and the Seine wound its way through a quiet, contented countryside. So why could not I put the monsters and the shadows of my childhood to rest?

I lay in a tense and frustrated weariness until the rain softened into a steady pattern, quiet and reassuring, and my exhaustion was greater than my fear, and I slept.

My surprises were not over. The next day in Sunday School I found myself enjoying the lesson more than I ever had. Questions came into my mind—questions that I wanted answered! And that same feeling of excitement, of intensified interest, altered every impression, every experience.

Perhaps the new-washed day helped, the Sabbath morning feeling of hallowed wonder when one considered God's splendors on every hand. I had always been susceptible to the influence of beauty. And here, where the mountains rose, gray towers and castle turrets, into a pearl-blue sky that still wore a faint blush of rose—here where the air smelled of rain and fresh earth, and birds sang from the trees—here it was easy to believe in the sweetness and goodness of life.

Clara had cooked a pot roast for our dinner, and I went back to the apartment with the others, despite Emory's importunings. He wanted a ride in the mountains, and perhaps a picnic, but I knew he would not consider it essential that we make it back in time for sacrament meeting. And that disturbed me a little. I told him, "Come by this evening, and you can have me all to yourself. I promise."

He held me to the bargain. Our meeting had been well worth attending, and I had walked home humming "The Spirit of God like a fire is burning . . ." The song described so perfectly the feelings I had experienced on Temple Square a week ago. Had that been only a week ago? Things seemed different since then; I seemed different, and it appeared that much more time had passed in the interim than six short days.

Emory did not understand that, and I suppose I should not have expected him to. But he seemed particularly restless that evening, in an amorous mood, and in a worldly state of mind.

"Don't you like going to church?" I asked him suddenly.

He blinked back at me. "That's a strange thing to ask, Augustine. Yeah, church is all right."

"I thought you went on a mission."

"Ah surely did, honey-dear. Two whole years in Great Britain. Don't think Ah ever got warm."

His lopsided smile was meant to charm me, but I persisted. "Aren't you glad that you went?"

"Glad isn't the word, Snow White. Let's put it this way: since Ah was a small tyke Ah had known Ah would go on a mission. It was expected of me. It was not something one questioned, at least not in my family."

"So that's why you went?"

"In the first place. But, of course, that changes. If you try to do a good job—and Ah did—then as a matter of course you get acquainted with the Spirit, you have what we call 'choice experiences,' the kind you come back and talk about at your homecoming."

He was warming to his subject without knowing it.

"So you are glad that you went?"

"Heavens yes, for half a dozen good reasons—and personal spirituality *is* one of them." He purposefully scowled at me, his dark brow wrinkling. "But not the only one, my sweet little Puritan."

He swooped close suddenly, without warning and kissed my cheeks, then covered my mouth with his lips. I began to struggle a little, but he simply ignored me.

"Ah can love you and the gospel, both at the same time, Snow White. Can you find anything the matter with that?"

He spoke against my skin, against my hair. His voice was honeyed and languid. "Can you, honey-dear?" he persisted.

I knew I could not refute him, at least not on the surface. But, deep inside, what was he thinking, what did he feel? Behind that smooth, polished, polite facade, what was the real Emory like? Did I know the real person, even a little?

"Augustine," he said earnestly. "You promised Ah could have you all to myself tonight, and you're not even here."

I smiled at his little-boy petulance. He had a point.

"I'm sorry, Emory." I placed my hand on his arm. "You're very patient with me."

"My pleasure, ma'am," he smiled. "Your company is worth any price, my dear."

He was dripping with charm and Southern graciousness. But somehow I knew that, beneath the assumed manners, he meant what he had said. He felt it sincerely. He was anxious to please me. There must be something soft and vulnerable inside this charming creature that he was not anxious to show.

Chapter

8

I do not wish to alarm you, Augustine, but since you have been gone, your mother has not appeared well. She does not complain, but she always looks tired, and seems to have no energy"—so Sylvie wrote at the end of a letter thanking me for the gifts I had sent to the children. "I take into account the fact that she is obviously lonely and misses you. Perhaps I am only imagining . . ."

She left the sentence in mid-air, not realizing what a torment her doubts would be to me, thousands of miles from home and helpless to do anything at all about it. And I knew my mother. If she were truly ill, she would never seek a doctor's attention; she had a fear of doctors. And she had always ignored her own needs, a habit which came from the war days, I believe. And nothing could alter it now. I knew that, for in the past I had tried to get her to take care of herself: once when she fell and broke her wrist and insisted on binding it herself and continuing to do all the household work she was used to; and another time when a cold infected her chest, probably her lungs, and she coughed day and night and shivered with fever and chills.

Was my sister-in-law an alarmist? The letter I had received just three days ago from my mother expressed her happiness in such glowing terms that it brought tears to my eyes.

"Every dream I had for you seems to be coming true, my dear daughter. So, you see, sacrifice can lead to blessings . . . My heart rejoices with you, Augustine."

I knew she was referring mainly to the spiritual experiences I had shared, and the changes they had wrought in me. All else would be secondary to that, as far as she was concerned. And, of course, having a boyfriend—"prospects"—that did not hurt, either.

I would somehow find time to write her more often; that would help the loneliness. October was slipping away. I had papers due and big tests this week in two of my classes, and I had taken on extra hours at the bookstore because two of the other girls were ill and unable to work. It seemed I had not a spare moment to fit in anything else, but I would make time for her. And once some of these big things were behind me it would not be so bad.

I went to Dr. Bekker's class with my mother still on my mind, and so it seemed a bit strange that our discussion for the day centered on the ravages and sufferings of war. We had been learning about the Myrmidons, the soldiers of Achilles in the Trojan war. But the discussion meandered of its own will to current times, conflicts that had troubled mankind in our own day. It was an intellectual exercise for most of the students. Oh, some had fathers or uncles or neighbors who had gone off to fight the Germans or the Japanese and had come back with their share of horror stories to relate, but that was the closest any had come to first-hand experience. I was amazed at how open and probing Dr. Bekker was, making the students dig deeper and deeper, forcing their imaginations and their understandings down roads they had never traveled before.

One inane student raised her hand and asked, "You lived in Germany during the war, didn't you? What was it like for you?"

I felt my muscles tense as I awaited his answer, and he took his time.

"My father fought in the German army," he began, "even though he was a peaceable man, a teacher—" he paused briefly— "and a Latter-day Saint. As you have heard, I myself was a member of the Hitler Youth during the last year of the war."

I held my breath. He was really going to talk about this.

"Nothing was easy, nothing was clear-cut. There were too many conflicting emotions and impressions. I was the oldest at home and the only son. We were Germans, true, but because we were Latter-day Saints we had the SS to fear, as well as the enemy."

He gave the word *enemy* a brief emphasis, and for a heartbeat his eyes shifted and sought my face. What he was thinking or feeling inside was not evident. His voice was soft and controlled, but in a way that reminded me of a crouching lion, muscles tensed, ready to uncoil into deadly action.

"Yes, we were hungry." He was answering another inane question. "And frightened. From the very beginning of the war there were long food lines, even essential commodities were rationed. All went for the war effort. The war came before the people."

I wondered how he was able to talk about it.

"Eventually my sister and I went into hiding, as many children did, staying with friends in a small forest village, away from the bombings and . . ." He paused again. "Other things."

"What was it like to watch people you love die?" someone asked; a random question called out from an unidentified source.

I thought I saw him go pale. His fingers did clench the spine of the book he was holding. "I cannot answer that question," he said. He attempted to smile. "Perhaps a poet could, or an insane man, but not I."

The strangeness of his answer, the tense, almost desperate note in its delivery stunned the class enough to allow him to turn their attention into a safer vein. But his face remained pale, his eyes wide and almost empty of expression, as though he had lowered a veil, a protective veil to conceal—to conceal what?

I had slid down in my seat at the beginning of his comments, praying he would not notice me and think to call upon me. The horror of that possibility froze the very blood in my veins: *Miss Mousset is from France, as some of you know. She lived through the war. Perhaps she would share some of her experiences with us.* I trembled at the prospect. When the class at last ended I felt weak and shaky. As I walked to the front of the room to leave through my usual doorway, I heard his voice call my name. Not "Miss Mousset" but "Augustine." Softly spoken, a mere breath, but it froze me where I stood and seemed to pierce to my heart.

He waited to approach me until the classroom was nearly cleared. Then he came close, very close, before speaking, and the mere nearness of him made my trembling increase.

"You were frightened, Augustine, and I'm sorry." His voice was soothing, like a lullaby. "I did not mean to do that, to distress you." He paused, waiting until I looked up and met his eyes. "You can trust me, Augustine, perfectly. I want you to know that, and rest in the fact."

"No one in this room understood what you were talking about," I blurted, surprised at my outburst and the anger my words and voice were revealing. "Why did you vulgarize your sufferings, personal and terrible, for them to see?"

He put his hand on my arm and the touch seemed to burn. "When we suffer something that is terrible, overwhelming, almost unbearable, we tend to think that Life has put her mark upon us, set us apart from all others . . ."

I was holding by breath, listening to every word as it fell; not on my ears, but my heart. "We feel that no one could ever have suffered as we have, and we build a lonely isolation around our being." He sighed, and the sound was so full of sorrow that it brought tears to my eyes. "The truth is . . ." he put a finger on my chin and lifted my face so that our eyes met squarely. "The truth is that many people carry hidden sorrows." His mouth twisted into a wry, bitter shape. "We humans are master deceivers. Look into the faces of the people you pass on campus, Augustine. You see nothing at all—vague expressions, empty eyes, thoughtless laughter. Do you think you see into their souls?"

His voice was resonant and intense, but low still. "Does anyone here see your soul, Augustine? Can anyone guess what you have been through?"

He moved his finger and brushed it across my cheek lightly before dropping it. "Never judge the hearts of others, Augustine." My name, in his mouth, was a caress. Why did I shrink from his kindness? Why did I tremble before him?

"Are you all right, my dear?" He leaned even closer. I nodded, unable to speak. His hair fell over his forehead. It looked like a shock of ripe wheat beneath a blue Burgundian sky. Suddenly a longing for home overcame me, a flood of bitter-sweet memories and sensations. I leaned my head against his shoulder and stood there and wept.

⌀

Minutes later, hours later, I drew back, his man's handkerchief, large and square and utilitarian, clutched in my hand. He folded his arms and stood regarding me with a tender yet enigmatic expression. "You needed that. And I am glad it came now, with me here."

A strange thing to say. I wished to ask why, but was afraid to.

"We must meet. We must talk some time. It would be good for you—for both of us." He spoke as if he were musing out loud. "I know a little grocery in Salt Lake that carries foreign foods. Would you have dinner with me some evening? I will cook German dishes, and you may cook something French for me?"

He was watching me, with those beautiful, piercing blue eyes. "Yes, I should like that," I said. And, though something still frightened me, I felt strangely drawn to him, longing for the safety he promised me, longing for things I could not put a name to.

He walked with me out to the hall. Then we parted, each going in opposite directions. But the sensation of his presence stayed with me, powerful and soothing, for hours, until at last it faded away.

⌀

There was a Halloween dance the last week of October. I told Emory I would go with him, but he must drive me to Salt Lake afterward, for I wished to spend a night with Martha and the children. I had never celebrated this holiday before. I found myself fascinated, somewhat amused by the plastic skeletons, the black cats and green-faced witches. I liked the jack-o'-lanterns best. Penelope and I drove out in her jalopy to a farmer's field on the outskirts of Provo and bought three golden-yellow pumpkins. It took us an entire evening to carve them, even with everyone helping. But they looked delightful lined up on our window ledge. I bought Halloween cards at the bookstore and sent one to my mother, one to each of the children, one to Sylvie and Jean-Paul, and one to Armand. They would be confused and delighted; I wished I could see their expressions, hear their laughter. Armand was a man, and men are seldom good correspondents; in six weeks he had written me once. He could not imagine the experiences I was going through.

Life was the same for him, basically, as it had been for his father, and for his father's father before him. And he would keep it so, despite the changes that come with progress. He respected the old ways, as did I; that was one of the things we shared. I could not expect him to understand things that were foreign and unknown to him. He was my touchstone with all that was loved and solid, and would not change.

The dance was a costume dance. Emory arranged for costumes. I should have known what was in his mind.

"Snow White," he said. "Who else, honey-dear?" He had found a gathered skirt with a white country-style blouse overlaid with a laced red vest, much like a German folk costume. Sally painted bright rouge spots on my cheeks, applied dark red lipstick, and pulled my hair back into a ribbon. The effect pleased everyone, even Emory, but I felt uncomfortable and conspicuous. Emory was a prince charming of some sort, from one of the fairy tales, it did not matter which one; he looked the part of every girl's dream man: tall, broad-shouldered, wavy black hair and bold, flirting eyes. He did flirt, too, once we made our way into the crowded dance room. It was too much in his nature; he simply could not help himself. I did not mind much, because he stuck close to me, my hand looped through his arm, his eyes turning to appraise me with glowing admiration every now and again.

I was pleased to see faces I recognized from some of my classes. My social activities were limited to Emory's group, or to private tête-a-têtes with just the two of us. It pleased me when a boy from my geology class came up and asked me to dance. Emory let go of my hand with a look of puzzled reluctance. Ten minutes after I was returned to him another boy did the same thing. His name was Doug and he had served a mission to Italy. It piqued Emory no end to have him approach me and begin speaking Italian. But we took that class together, which I explained laughingly as I went off on his arm. He was quite a charming boy, actually, and I enjoyed his company and his gentle teasing. "You speak Italian with an enchanting French accent," he said.

I had wondered if Emory would grow disgusted and go off with one of the many girls who were making eyes at him. But he vented his jealousy in the opposite way.

"This is worse than Ah feared," he said, after Doug left us alone together. "Ah've got to keep more of an eye on you in the future." He put his arm around my waist and pulled me close to him. "These lads are treading on thin ice, Augustine. You are *my girl*." He pressed his lips to my cheek in a long, lingering kiss. "Ah wish there was some way Ah could make that clear to them."

I did not like his assumption of ownership. I replied, with an edge to my voice, "They were merely being friendly, Emory. They meant nothing, and you have no right to feel threatened."

At that moment my first partner returned to ask for another dance. Emory took a step or two in front of me, shielding me with his body. "The young lady is *with me*," he said, "and I do not wish to share her."

My friend stood blinking for a moment or two, and then turned away. My cheeks, beneath the bright rouge, were red with anger and embarrassment. Emory turned to me, his eyes warm with satisfaction. "You are so naive, honey-dear. You don't know your own powers." He pulled at the full sleeve of my blouse, drawing me closer to him. "Men want you, Augustine, and all the more because of your innocence."

I wondered, with a slight, unpleasant sensation, if he was describing himself. I pulled away from him. "I do not belong to you, Emory. I can speak for myself. If I—"

He placed his finger against my lips. "You're a feisty one, Snow White, but Ah don't mind that. Southern men like their women to have spirit." He pulled me close to him again, a little roughly. "You are so beautiful. Can you blame me for wanting you all to myself?"

Without warning he pressed his lips over mine. I could not work free from him! I wondered frantically who might be watching. How dare he? I struggled against him, all the more angry because of the pleasurable sensations his touch sent coursing through me. I felt I must be both weak and wicked to enjoy his insolent kiss so much that I secretly regretted it when he drew away, leaving me breathless and trembling, and confused inside.

Chapter

9

*E*mory was pleasant on the way to Salt Lake, working hard to be agreeable, and he really was good company when he wanted to be. I brought him into the house with me and introduced him to Martha.

"Hey," he said, looking up from under long lashes, a slow smile spreading over his face. "Pleased to meet you, ma'am."

Martha was charmed. After he left, she sank against the sofa with a long sigh. "He's a dreamboat," she said. "And he's smitten, dear Augustine. It's easy to see he cares for you."

I replied cautiously. "I don't know. He's a ladies' man from way back, and he has courting down to an art."

"He can't help that," she defended. "He sees you're different; I can tell he does."

"So he tells me," I admitted. "But he's very possessive."

She waved that away, too. Emory could do that to women. Besides, she was so glad to have me there. Although it was late, we talked for hours, catching up on things, then slept in the next morning as long as Roger and Ellen would endure being ignored. This was actually Halloween day. Martha made pumpkin pies and chili, neither of which I had ever tasted, while I helped the children carve their pumpkins. Despite my previous experience, it was a struggle for me. I looked up at one point to see Roger smiling at me, his little eyes brimming with merriment.

"Go ahead, laugh out loud," I told him, laughing, too. He was so adorable. Without thinking, I said, "Martha, he looks just like that picture of his father you have upstairs on your dresser."

She turned sad eyes upon me; yet they held a soft satisfaction that was comforting. "Yes," she responded, "he looks very much like his father. It's uncanny at times."

"It's a blessing," I said firmly. As long as I had broached the delicate subject I might as well try to make the most of it.

She smiled then and squeezed my shoulder. "Yes, many times it is a comfort to me."

After the pies were out of the oven and cooling safely on the ledge, Martha turned the chili to simmer and we all piled into the car, in search of adventure. We found squirrels in the park, a dead robin under a pile of rotting leaves, an adorable stray kitten, and Roger discovered a penny as we walked through the cluttered parking lot.

"Your lucky day," Martha smiled.

There was a slow, quiet pleasure in being with this young mother and her two children. It soothed all that was frazzled or anxious inside me. How did she come by such peace? The respect I felt for her increased each time I was with her. I feared to think of the mess I would be if I were in her shoes, facing the lonely realities she faced, day after day.

By late afternoon both children were so excited they couldn't stand still. I helped Martha dress them in their costumes: Ellen was a kitty cat with long black whiskers and black pointed ears lined with soft pink felt in the center; Roger was a fearsome pirate with a sword in his belt and a black patch over his eye. We took so many pictures that the children were next to tears, Roger at last threatening to take his trick-or-treat bag and go off by himself.

"I know everybody in the neighborhood," he said, "and I'm not scared of the dark."

"Aren't you scared of the witches and goblins?" his mother teased. He merely rolled his eyes at her.

I took his hand. "This is all new to me, Roger," I said.

He took my lead. "I'll help you," he offered. "Just stay close to me."

I was happy to do so. I had never gone trick-or-treating before in my life. I was delighted by the hordes of costume-clad children who ran, giggling and screaming, from door to door. I had never seen so many different kinds of candies and suckers and gum. "I'll share mine with you," Roger whispered. I gave his hand a squeeze, feeling a surge of overwhelming tenderness for him.

We tramped the neighborhood streets for over an hour. My toes and fingers were numb with cold and the children's sacks were sagging with goodies, but they would not call it quits. At last Martha and I half-bullied, half-cajoled them inside, with promises of hot chili, and pumpkin pie piled with whipped cream. We burst through the door shivering and red-nosed, bringing in the sharp taste of cold air and the pungent odors of wet leaves, scorched pumpkins, and ripe apples.

As soon as coats and mittens were tugged off, the children sat on the floor, poring over their goodies, offering pieces now and again to their mother or me.

"Try this—and this," Roger said, making a face. "I don't like them, but you might." Then, after a moment, his sticky fist opened to reveal two fat tootsie rolls, tied in brown and white paper. "Try these, too," he said, "they're my favorites."

I gave him a quick hug; I couldn't help myself. I loved everything: the chili, the pie, even the over-sweet, brightly-wrapped candies. The sense of excitement had hold of me; I still felt its pleasant tingle after Martha and I had scrubbed the two tired children and tucked them safely in bed.

"I could get spoiled, having you here to help at weekends," she smiled.

"That was great fun," I admitted. "I've never done anything I've enjoyed more; it makes me feel like a child myself."

She grinned at my enthusiasm. "I know."

We collapsed in the front room, which Americans call a living room, relaxing with cups of hot spicy cider. A few stragglers still rang the bell or pounded on the door, and Martha let me go and hand out the candies, sending the cold little ghosts and pumpkins and witches scurrying on to the next house. The porch lights and the dusky glow of jack-o'-lanterns perched on porches or window ledges lent an eerie sense of excitement to an otherwise ordinary landscape. But things were slowing down as the hour grew later and the night colder.

It was a little before nine when the doorbell rang for the last time. I jumped to my feet, and had the door flung wide and a handful of candy thrust out before my eyes and mind adjusted. There were no grinning, red-cheeked children jostling each other on the doorstep, bags open and waiting in anticipation. A solitary figure stood there, dressed in a long formal overcoat. He carried a package in his hand. The night wind had tousled his hair, and it shone like a wild gold crown beneath the bright light. He ran his fingers through it and stood staring back at me.

"Who's at the door, honey?" Martha called.

"Augustine." He spoke only my name, in the clear music of his voice. The sound seemed to reverberate on the night air. I was trembling inside; his presence had that effect on me.

"Hans!" Martha's voice was pleased. "I'm so glad to see you!" She had come up behind me and stood rubbing her bare arms. "Hurry inside, for heaven's sake, or we'll all freeze to death."

There was a certain confused bustle as he came in, took off his coat, and gave her the gifts he had brought, little goodies for herself and the children. I trailed after them into the kitchen, where she dished him a big bowl of chili, cut bread and pie, poured cider, chattering happily all the while, then pulling chairs out for me and herself at the square kitchen table.

"We'll keep you company while you eat," she said.

"I did not expect such a feast," he answered, gratitude warm in his voice.

Martha waved her hand in the air, as though to dismiss any protestations. "Goodness, I haven't introduced you to Augustine."

She turned to me, and so did Hans Bekker's eyes, briefly. "I know Augustine," he said quietly. Her face registered surprise. "She is a student of mine."

"Why didn't you tell me you have a class from Dr. Bekker?" Martha cried. "How lucky for you, Augustine!"

Why not, indeed? I asked myself. I had thought several times of telling her about this man who had such a strange influence upon me. But I was never sure of what to say or how to say it, and my feelings about him were so conflicting, so intense—I believe I feared that Martha, in her quick discernment, might discover something, something—

His voice brought me back with a start. What was he saying?

"Augustine is not certain yet what she thinks of me."

He had spoken the truth, but so kindly, so matter-of-factly that I was able to conceal my shocked response at his statement. But I found myself blowing between my teeth, making the faint, hissing sound that always expressed my uncertainty or confusion.

Martha was smiling at him. "I find that hard to believe, Hans. I have never met a person, man, woman, or child, who has not fallen immediately in love with you."

She was only half-teasing him. My eyes widened as I listened. He glanced toward me again, and I sensed an underlying sympathy in his manner.

He shook his head. "It is difficult for someone as open and guileless in nature as yourself to understand some of the things Augustine struggles with." Again he spoke the words gently; there was no offense in them. Martha nodded her head, understanding what he was saying. "I have told Augustine she can trust me . . ." He paused ever so slightly. "Perhaps in time she will."

I was churning inside; I was very uncomfortable. "How do you two know each other?" I blurted, a demanding note in my voice. Hans Bekker looked up and smiled.

To my amazement, he answered in French, telling me that he and Martha's husband, Heber, had gone to school together in the East. "He had a great effect upon my life," he said. "He helped me understand things at a time when I needed help." His eyes said, "As I am trying to do now, my young friend, for you." I was sure of that when he continued, "In fact, it was Heber Pratt who brought me to Salt Lake for the first time—"

"And took you to Temple Square?" I guessed.

"Hold on," Martha protested. "Slow down a little. I hate to admit it, but I'm not keeping up."

Hans Bekker was relaxing. I could see that. He leaned back in his chair, his face turned away from me, and rattled off something to Martha, very quickly, that made her giggle like a girl and put her hands to her cheeks.

"Don't tease me, Hans," she laughed. "You have an unfair advantage."

He smiled and changed the subject, asking her about the children, listening intently to all she told him. It was easy to see that he sincerely cared for them. But what about her? The wife of his best friend, a man he had loved—what were his feelings for Martha?

Suddenly, deliberately, he turned his attention to me, as though aware that I stood, awkwardly, a little outside. "We are well met, as they used to say, Augustine."

Why did he use my name so frequently, so freely? The sound of it always disturbed me, trembling through me like a strong current.

"I have a bratwurst and red cabbage out in the car," he said. "And, let me see, what else? Hot potato salad, and Black Forest cake—for our feast," he cried, seeing my blank expression.

"What is this?" Martha wanted to know.

He explained. She thought it a grand idea. "Perhaps tomorrow, after sacrament meeting?" he asked, turning his eyes to me.

I nodded. "That should be fine. I do not have anything else planned." Though, as I spoke, I thought of Emory's parting words. "Call me the minute you arrive, honey-dear, especially if you stay until Sunday. I don't like going too long without seeing you."

Once that was decided we removed to the living room with mugs of cider. Dr. Bekker settled in comfortably. I thought to myself, *He is used to this. He feels comfortable in Martha's house. How often does he come here?*

We talked, in an easy, rambling way, letting our words find their own course, though I noticed that no one brought up politics or the state of society. Rather we discussed places we had seen, great pieces of music we shared a love for, films and books we had found especially interesting. I learned that Hans Bekker loved Tennyson, Yeats, and Byron, as I did. He also loved the writings of the American philosopher, Emerson, which I did not know.

"You would like the American poet, Edna Millay—wouldn't she, Martha?"

Martha agreed with him.

"There is so much to show you, to share with you, Augustine," he cried, in sudden enthusiasm. Martha looked at him oddly, and I laughed to cover the awkwardness. Why did this strange, fascinating man single me out? Why was he interested in me?

The hour was very late when he rose to go, but even then a shared reluctance tinged his departure with an emotion very much like sadness. When the door closed upon him the room seemed empty, lifeless, and the sudden silence chilled and strained.

"Will he be safe driving back to Provo so late?" I asked, making conversation, really.

Martha seemed unconcerned. "I believe he's used to it," she answered.

I drew a deep breath and asked, "Does he visit you often?"

She looked at me with the same strange expression she had turned upon him earlier. "Not really. He's a busy man. But our friendship goes back a long way." She hesitated, then decided to say what she was thinking. "Sometimes I think he comes out of a sense of responsibility. He *was* very fond of Heber, and the thought of his widow and children pains him, I know."

"I think it is more than that," I forced myself to say. "It is obvious that he cares for"—I chose my words carefully—"all of you."

A smile entered her eyes, but she kept it there, guardedly. And then she replied, "It's obvious that he cares for you, too. And that is unusual for Hans. He's cautious with people—" The smile left her eyes. "Most especially with young girls."

My tired mind was in a whirl of confusion. What did all this mean? I knew one thing: Martha and I were wary of one another; something about Hans Bekker had made us so. I abhorred the mere idea of such an impediment existing between us, and felt a vague resentment for whatever conditions may have caused it.

We were both exhausted. Bed was an easy excuse to dismiss the matter. When we awoke the following morning our attentions were immediately claimed by the children and the Sabbath morning tasks to be performed. I attended Martha's Sunday School with her, and we ate a light brunch and then left immediately for the drive to Provo. The day was cold and a bit overcast; droopy, as though played out by the intense scenes and emotions of the Halloween celebration. The sense of deflation hung over us, subduing even the children's natural enthusiasm.

We all rallied a bit when I showed them round my apartment and introduced them to Clara and Nancy, my only roommates who happened to be at home at the time. Ellen was adorable; shy and yet curious; she very soon won their hearts. Roger kept his grasp on my hand and examined everything he saw with a cautious and serious air.

"I bet this is nothing like the house you lived in in France," he said.

"You are right," I smiled. "That is a wise observation, Roger."

"Are you happy here? Are the other girls nice to you?" His concern brought tears to my eyes. Happiness should not be a worry to a small boy of his age. I hugged him close for a moment. "I do just fine here," I assured him. "But it helps knowing that *you* care; it truly does."

He could not help smiling then. But he let go of my hand reluctantly. Martha hugged me for a moment and kissed my cheek before herding the children out the door.

"Have a good week," she said. "Don't go too long without calling."

But I thought it a bit strange that she made no mention at all of Dr. Bekker and our proposed dinner that evening. If things were all right, as they should be, it would have been the most natural thing in the world for her to say, "Have a wonderful time tonight, and give Hans my love." But she said nothing. I waved good-bye with a very uneasy sensation building in the pit of my stomach and a feeling as though a heavy hand had laid its weight on my heart.

I came very close to phoning Dr. Bekker and calling off the engagement; in fact I tried once or twice, picking up the phone and dialing a number or two, but always losing my courage. I would have been nervous and unsure enough of myself without this further, rather baffling development. But I knew I must brave it through.

I had hoped to sneak away without saying much of anything to anyone. But less than twenty minutes after Penelope entered the apartment the phone rang and she answered it. Dr. Bekker was on the other end, giving her the message that he would come in his car to get me at six-thirty. I was immediately beset by questions, followed by exaggerated reactions and heartless teasing. I would have liked to be able to take it in the same light vein in which it was given, but that was impossible. I harbored too much uncertainty to relax in the slightest.

I have to admit that sacrament meeting that afternoon was not much more than a grueling ordeal to be got through. Anticipation was the worst torment of all. The encounter could not be over with until it had fairly begun, and thinking about it was terrible, but I could find no way to put it out of my mind. I had also avoided Emory altogether, hoping that if I did not call him he wouldn't call me. Although he at times attended meetings with me, he did not belong to our branch. Perhaps he would get involved with some of his friends and forget, at least until I was safely gone. Somehow I felt he would be easier to deal with after the fact than before.

The reprieve was granted me. At exactly half past six Dr. Bekker knocked on the door. I was waiting, and slipped out quickly, much to Penelope's frustration. The gray day had grown colder and the air had a bite to it that made me shiver. It was not far to his apartment, and vague pleasantries punctuated the awkward silences that fell between us. I had never been alone with him before. I was painfully aware of him, unable to relax, wishing I could regain the camaraderie we had enjoyed at Martha's house.

Once inside, I looked around his apartment with unavoidable curiosity. He lived in half of an old house which had been split into a duplex. The floors were hard wood, covered with oriental rugs, old and worn comfortable. Wood trimmed the doorways and the windows, which were also hung with lace curtains. The main impression I got was of books: one of the shorter walls was lined entirely with bookcases which stretched almost to the ceiling; there was a desk in one of the corners, nearly covered with books; a stack of books on the floor; books on both the end tables; and one lying open upon the cushion of a comfortable over-stuffed chair.

He must have been following my gaze, because he laughed, a bit self-consciously. "It is disgraceful. Yes, I know."

"It is wonderful," I replied. "It makes one itch just to touch them." I walked over and lifted one from the top of the floor stack. It was a life story of George Washington. I looked up in surprise.

"I am tortured with a wide range of interests," he admitted, as though confessing to a vice of some sort. "History of all kinds, art, literature, biography, poetry—" his voice trailed into a sigh.

"Your entire life exists within these walls, doesn't it?" I replaced the book and looked up to see him watching me with a keen gaze.

"I teach. I sit on many committees. I have many important responsibilities."

"You love your work, and you are a brilliant teacher," I agreed, "and absolutely everyone sees that. But here, here is the real you."

He nodded. "You speak truly. But so few people know that." He moved closer to me. "Let me take your coat, Augustine." He remained thoughtful as I removed my coat and scarf and handed them to him. Our hands brushed in the exchange. His was warm, pulsing with the same intense life which lit his eyes and fired his intellect. "You sense this about me because life has dealt harshly with you, too. Made you suffer, made you dig deep." I met his gaze. "Set you apart."

I laughed at him. "Are you putting the lie to that little lecture you gave me?" I tried to quote him. "Many people carry hidden sorrows. You cannot judge the human heart, Augustine."

For some reason my contentious attitude seemed to please him. I could not insult or provoke him. "Yes, Augustine, yes," he said, and his eyes were a deep, friendly blue and almost sparkling with pleasure. "But you and I are in an environment which is not native to us, among people who have had virtually no experience with the kinds of things we have suffered."

I took his meaning immediately and could not be mean enough to disagree with him. "Something within you understands something within me." He shrugged his shoulders again and smiled gently, withdrawing purposefully the intense seriousness of the discussion. "It is that simple." He reached out his hand to me. "Come, the food is ready and waiting."

The room we ate in—part kitchen, part dining room—was light and airy. Several house plants, full and green and obviously healthy, sat about on ledge and table. The food was rich and delicious, reminding me of how impoverished my diet had been since I came to America. When I remarked upon this he did not laugh, but with an earnest, regretful expression agreed.

"Yes, it is true." Then, leaning close and placing his hand over mine, he added, "I shall have to cook for you, Augustine. In self-defense, I have become quite good at it."

He was at ease, sincere and gentle, yet still I trembled inside, still something in me drew back from him. So for now I concentrated on the tender red cabbage, the sizzling brat, the thick brown bread spread with real butter, thick and creamy. I had not enjoyed such a feast for a long time, and I savored each bite, as only a Burgundian who appreciates the true value of good food can. It was not until he was cutting the cake and setting it before us that the realization came over me. I sat back in my chair with the impact and must have assumed a thoughtful expression. Dr. Bekker noticed the change at once. He looked down at me and said indulgently, "Does German food stick in your throat, Augustine? It did not seem to a few moments ago."

"I was too overwhelmed a few moments ago," I replied honestly. "And how can you tell so easily what it is I am thinking?"

He did not answer my question; in a way forcing me to continue. But I could not, and I looked down at my plate, feeling frustrated and miserable.

"I am not the enemy, Augustine." He said the words firmly. But they gave me the opening I needed.

"I have been taught my whole life to look upon the Germans as enemies." I let my anger show, not caring what he might think of me. "It was German soldiers who occupied my country, who took our food, who destroyed our buildings . . ."

He sat listening to me, not protesting, not trying to stop me.

"It was German soldiers who shot my brother when he was fighting with our troops in Belgium!" My voice was rising. It had taken on an ugly note, which I did not want there, but could not control. "It was German soldiers who forced their way into our house, and murdered my father—in his own home!"

I was shaking almost uncontrollably. Hans Bekker made no move. His face was almost devoid of expression. He sat calmly and silently facing me across the table. Yet his sympathy reached out and enfolded me, with a warmth and strength that was palpable.

"You were there, Augustine." It was a statement, not a question. "How old were you? Five, six years?"

"Four," I corrected him. "Not quite five years yet."

The muscles of his face and the lines about his eyes twitched, as if in pain.

"I see. That is very young. Well, such agony as yours cannot be reasoned away, can it? At least not easily . . . at least not all at once."

What did he have in mind? I could see that his eyes were full, but I could not read what they held. Only the sympathy, the steady, quiet sympathy; that was all I could feel.

※

We ate in silence for a few moments; or rather, he took a bite or two and I toyed with my food. He was thinking still. Behind his fine forehead I could almost see his mind working. When he glanced up the steady serenity I had felt looked out from his eyes, deep-set, and so startlingly blue that the very color in them seemed to pulse.

"Augustine, let me help you in the only way I can right now: by being your friend."

What could I say? I felt a panic rise in me, and at the same time a longing for the comfort and strength he could give me. Watching me, his eyes mirrored confusion and a sudden distress that I felt with a sharp misery and regret.

"What is it, Augustine? Why do you draw back from me, why do you seem to fear me? *Why*, when I know in my heart that your spirit responds to mine, is like me, is—"

"Stop it!" I cried. "I don't know, I don't know! I don't know any better than you do!"

He sighed deeply. "I'll accept that, for now." He seemed at once to relax. Then he began asking me about the French writers I liked best, and had I ever read George Sand? He was the most interesting of people to talk with: knowledge flowed from him, yet he was never pedantic, and all that he said reflected excitement or love for his subject. He was a good listener as well. I relaxed. Time ceased to exist. The feast we shared was more delicious even than the food had been. I could feel renewal, I could feel the beauty and calm of his spirit, like a current, coursing through me, and I was immersed, mind and spirit, in the moment and the sweet nourishment it gave.

Chapter

10

I awoke in a cold sweat, at first unaware of time or place; for a few confused moments I thought I was home, with the sagging springs and the song of the wind in the old tree outside my window. I lay tense and trembling, listening for the sounds of an autumn night, expecting or hoping to hear my mother's light step on the creaking floorboards; but all was still. I could not remember where I was—nothing seemed real or familiar. The dream loomed too large, pushing out all other realities to give it room.

I dared not shut my eyes, for the colors of the dream still pulsed there. Red, bursts of red; and shouting; and my mother's terrified eyes; and my father, reaching his hand out, as if in entreaty; and someone crying, a high, piercing wail. I knew that someone was me. Every time the dream came I *was* that little girl again, and her frantic screams tore through me again and again, leaving me weak and trembling, and so terribly frightened! But this time there was more. This time I was aware of the shape and color of the German soldiers, and the terror was so heavy and dark that I feared it would choke me.

I switched on the lamp beside my bed. The clock read 3:30. I got up, poured a glass of cold tap water, and curled up in the corner of the sofa, cold and exhausted, the pulse in my temples pounding. I don't know how long I sat there before drowsiness overtook me, nor how long I dozed before a sharp sound woke me with a start. I opened my eyes to see Anja staring down at me.

"Are you the self-appointed mother hen of this apartment, Augustine?" she goaded. But I must have stared back with a blank gaze, for she added, "How kind of you to wait up for me."

"I have more important things to worry about than you," I replied.

"Like the handsome Hans Bekker? I understand you're now one of the privileged few to have been invited to his house for dinner."

The sarcasm in her voice stung me, but I would not let her see that.

"Go to bed," she said. "You look like you're freezing." Then she turned, walked into her own room and shut the door.

I forced myself to get up and go back to bed. I was still trembling inside, but the fatigue was stronger than the residue of feelings, drugged and dull, that still clung to me. I drew the covers up to my chin and closed my eyes, but I left the bedside lamp on. I was not ready to plunge myself again into the black, swirling darkness where memory and imagination could play havoc with me.

❦

"Mash that window button, will you, honey-dear? It's a bit airish in here."

As he spoke Emory leaned across me and pushed the automatic window button himself, and it rose with scarcely a whisper. He saw my smile, and one corner of his own mouth curled in anticipation.

"Just what are you laughin' at, Snow White?"

He spoke in a soft, unhurried drawl that delighted me, and somehow had a calming effect on my spirit.

"I have a difficult enough time learning American idioms," I teased, "without throwing your southern ways in to confuse things."

"It is a cryin' shame that they don't teach you the right way to speak here, that *is* for certain." He touched my cheek with his lips, just briefly. But how pleasant the sensation was! I leaned back against the comfortable seat cushion with a sigh.

He could feel my contentment, and I think it pleased him. He drove to campus slowly and took the long route to the building where he would be dropping me off.

"Ah missed you last night. Is it true what Penelope said, that you were working on a project with your humanities teacher?"

So that's what she had told him! Close enough to the truth, I suppose. While my mind scrambled to think of ways to amend the explanation, I muttered, "I'm sorry, Emory," and that seemed to do.

"What is it about you, Augustine?" he drawled. "Your pretty nose, your silky black hair, the way your voice sounds like music when you speak—there's never been anyone like you in my life, never before."

He stopped the car gently, moved the lever to park, and turned to face me, bending close enough that I could catch the scent of cologne on his golden, tanned skin. His brown eyes were serious. "Ah like being with you, simply bein' with you, and Ah've never felt that way about any other person."

I did not know what to say. I touched his hand where it rested on the leather seat. "I'll be late to class," I murmured.

His slow smile started. "All right, all right," he conceded, shaking his head, but getting out and coming round to open my door for me. "You do not make things easy for a man, honey-dear," he said, lifting a lock of my hair and letting it run through his fingers. "See you for dinner?"

I nodded. The mid-day meal for Americans is lunch, the evening meal dinner. For Southerners, lunch is dinner and dinner is supper. It was all very confusing to me. I walked to the building knowing his eyes were watching me, feeling a tenderness for him that surprised me a little. He was simple-hearted and well-meaning, and devotion of his sort, I realized, could be a very attractive thing.

That week went quickly. Once or twice I thought of calling Martha, but I never quite got around to it. I saw Emory every day, either in the mornings or the evenings, even on the days I worked.

I saw Hans Bekker only in class and we spoke hardly at all. Indian summer, as the Americans call it, wove a hovering spell of warmth and golden beauty, and autumn lingered, making winter feel like a meaningless threat that would never come true. I finished my papers and got through my tests, earning scores that pleased me. But each day was full and demanding, and scheduled to the point of confinement. And I felt a restlessness building in me.

Near the middle of the month I received a letter from my mother. It was long, filled with local news and tidbits, and somewhere among it all she slipped the reassurance I was hoping for: "Pay no attention to Sylvie's ravings," she wrote. "Of course I miss you and, from time to time, am under the weather. But Sylvie watches for the sensational, partly just for something to do. My health is no different now than when you left me." Thank heaven for that!

One afternoon at the bookstore, Michael Allen surprised me by coming up to the poetry section where I was shelving new acquisitions and asking me boldly, with no warning or preliminaries, if I would go out with him. At first my heart caught in my throat and I thought only *Emory!* and could see his dark face brooding above me. But then, as Mike explained, I relaxed. There was a French film at International Cinema, one he had heard was particularly good—had I seen it before? I had, but I did not want to tell him. I blew through my teeth, trying to make a decision. Emory had been very demanding of late; no, not demanding, proprietary, possessive. But this was a casual sort of outing, and Michael and I were good friends.

"I'd love to go," I said. "Tomorrow night, is it?"

We made arrangements, and I went home feeling good about it. I usually went to the foreign films on campus with Penelope; Emory had no patience for such things. But to see a French film again, with someone who understood the language—and, yes, even loved French, and would speak my native tongue with me— where could the harm be in that?

When I got to the apartment I discovered a letter with a French postmark waiting for me. It was a note from Armand. I considered it a good omen. I felt like talking to someone, so I called Martha. I had things to tell her, and that would make it easier. We had not spoken since that Halloween weekend.

I asked her about the children and told her what my mother

had written, which pleased her, as I knew it would. Then I told her about the letter from Armand and the date I had made with Mike Allen. Her reaction took me somewhat by surprise.

"What about that handsome boy you introduced me to—the Southerner? Aren't you still dating him?"

"Yes, I am," I answered. "In fact, I see him almost every day."

"Well, be careful," she admonished. "You don't want to mess up something good with a casual flirtation."

"Martha, this is just a friendly date, and, and—" I took a breath and said it: "I do not want Emory thinking he owns me."

She neither laughed nor responded with sympathy. "Well, you don't want to lose him, do you? It seems to me he's too good a thing to take chances with."

Feeling a little dismayed, I agreed with her and changed the subject. *As if you know anything about it,* I thought to myself. *You don't know the boy himself, only the fact that he's dreamy to look at and knows how to flatter a woman.* Why was Martha so keen on my relationship with Emory, anyway?

After I hung up the receiver I realized that, again, she had not mentioned Hans Bekker, and the question struck me with real force: Did they keep company with one another? Had he been up to her house to visit since the last time I had seen her, or seen him, for that matter, except in class? Is that why she wished to see me keep on good terms with Emory? I brushed the terrible thoughts from my mind: I was imagining things! I was making mountains out of molehills! I tried to put the whole conversation aside.

The next day, when Emory was driving me home, I decided to level with him, as Americans say. I told him I was going to see a French film with one of the boys from the bookstore. We were approaching an intersection. He slammed on the brakes and jerked the car to the side of the street, stopping it so suddenly that it sat there and shuddered, much as I was doing. I put my hand on his arm, but he shook it off.

"Emory, what's gotten into you? You are behaving like a child. Michael and I are just friends—*you* won't go to the foreign films with me . . ."

The light at the intersection turned green. Emory squealed onto the street, his tires skidding along the pavement, and darted back into the traffic. I looked down; he had ground the gas pedal against the floor and the big Oldsmobile engine leaped forward in response. I opened my mouth to speak to him, but thought better of it and sat back against the seat. Let him wear out his anger, if he wished to be childish about it.

But I did not realize what I was in for. The road we were on kept rising toward the low foothills, and I realized he was steering the red convertible away from the last steep streets of neighborhood houses toward the open hillside beyond. He was driving recklessly now, the car careening around corners, spitting gravel and blowing up clouds of loose dirt. I tightened my lips and said nothing. His face was set and he did not look at me or in any way acknowledge my presence. I slipped my fingers securely into the hand-hold above my door and watched our progress with a bit of a detached air.

Climbing the steep, unpaved road, with the lights of the houses below us, there was little to see, only occasional vague outlines of trees and bushes in the murky blackness, or a sudden outcropping of rock, bare and jagged, looming up suddenly in front of us. With an unexpected jerk of the wheel Emory turned off the path into the unmarked dirt and sagebrush. I leaned forward as the car bolted to a stop. We rested on some kind of an outcropping of land. Below us spread the lights of the city. I had never seen it from up this high. I could easily identify the university buildings and, far out beyond the clusters and strings of glittering gemstones, the line of the lake, dark and uneven, marked only intermittently with thin edgings of light. I let my breath out in relief, prepared to enjoy the view below, when I felt Emory near to me, his hands pulling me roughly closer. Before I could protest, his mouth covered mine and he kissed me as I had never been kissed before in my life. When at last I worked free of him I drew back weak and trembling, and we sat staring at one another, unable to speak.

"This is where guys bring their dates to make out, did you know that?"

I shook my head in reply, thinking that a strange thing for him to be saying.

"Ah never brought you here, Ah wouldn't think of it," Emory continued. "You're different . . ." He ran his fingers distractedly through the tangled curls of his dark hair. "You're above all that." He doubled his hand into a fist and pounded the cushioned seat in frustration. "Snow White, what are you tryin' to do to me?"

"Emory." I spoke his name gently, confused and concerned suddenly. "I did not mean to hurt you. I had no idea—"

"No idea! No idea how deeply Ah care for you!" His voice was tight with pain, somehow more poignant because of the soft drawl that prolonged the emotion of each word piteously. "Ah believed Ah had made that most clear."

His eyes held a longing that made me shiver. "Emory, please," I stammered.

"Please what?" He was relentless. "Please stop loving you, honey-dear?"

I placed my finger against his lips. "Do not use that word," I pleaded.

"It is the proper word, Augustine," he replied, with a sudden dignity. "It is the only word Ah am able to use."

He laid his hand against my cheek and then lifted a lock of my hair as he liked to do, letting it run through his fingers. "Ah am nearly twenty-five years old, Ah've served a mission, Ah have nearly completed my education, and this spring when Ah go home Ah wish to bring a wife with me, and Ah wish that wife to be you."

He had spoken with such straightforward simplicity that the words sounded sane and reasonable, but I knew they were not. I said nothing. I could feel the trembling intensity of his feelings reaching out to me, demanding a response of some kind.

"What cruel injustice," he cried, but his voice was no more than a low moan. "Do you know how many girls there are who would jump at the chance Ah am giving you? And Ah have to fall in love with the one girl in the world who does not want me!"

"That is not true!" I returned. "I care for you, Emory, but you are going too fast. Would you wish me to lie and tell you what you want to hear? I do not love you, not now, not . . ."

"Not yet!" He whispered the words against my hair, and the feel of them tingled through me. "Then Ah shall have to work harder, honey-dear, shan't Ah?" The words were wooing, honeyed, seductive.

"Are you sure, Emory?" I murmured.

For answer he bent close and kissed me, and then whispered against my lips, "Ah've always known what Ah want, Augustine, but Ah have not found it . . . till you."

I was no match for his tenacious powers, for his florid emotions, and I think he knew it; he relaxed and turned gentle, even admitting, as he drove down the mountain, "Ah broke bad tonight, and there's no excuse for that, frightenin' you and everything, honey-dear."

Broke bad, I had learned, meant to behave badly or shamefully, and I was touched that he would apologize. Yet still I said, shaking as I spoke the words, "I will not stand my friend up tomorrow night, Emory. He would not understand, and I would feel ashamed of myself."

He studied me closely for a moment and then replied, "You're too sweet for your own good, honey-dear." He pulled into our parking area and shut off the engine. In the sudden stillness I could hear my own heartbeat.

"*Awraht*, we'll let it stand this once, but remember one thing, Augustine." He tucked his finger under my chin and turned me to face him. "You may not have any romantic intentions toward this young man, but there is not a male bein' who knows you who does not harbor the most serious of romantic intentions towards you."

I wanted to laugh off his remark, but could not. "I will remember that, Emory," I replied, in a manner solemn enough to appease him. He walked me to my door, and I thought all the way, *He has a stranglehold on me, he wants to dictate my life, he wants to make me docile and obedient!*

He kissed me once more at the door and, despite all, the physical touch of him melted me. When I was safe in my own room again I stared at his photograph, perched haughtily on my bureau top.

"So you think you're in love with me," I told the picture. The deep, liquid eyes smiled back at me. "So you think you can order my life."

I turned the image to the wall, resenting the confusing, unidentifiable emotions he had set into play. And the last thought that came to me was the most disconcerting: *Can it be true what Emory said? Do other men desire me?* I almost laughed at how he had put it: all males who know you. Indulging my fancies for a moment, I let myself imagine that his words could be true. And, if they were, would that include Dr. Hans Bekker? Could he, as well as the younger male students, desire me?

I felt immediately ashamed of myself. With resolution I dragged out my schoolbooks and began doing my lessons for the night.

Oh Mother! I agonized. *Have you forgotten what all this is like? You really wish me to fall in love, to find someone I can marry, and to get good grades as well?* I was worn out, and for the moment despaired that I could do a good job of either, much less of both.

Chapter

11

I went with Michael as I had promised, but I was a bit uneasy most of the evening; looking over my shoulder, listening for unusual noises. I would not have put it past Emory to do something illogical and crazy, and I had vague images of him showing up and confronting the poor boy, or planting some friend of his to play terrible tricks on us. There *were* times when I forgot Emory altogether and enjoyed the company of this good friend, who was such a kind, intelligent, uncomplicated companion. We went out for ice cream after the movie and spoke only French the entire evening, laughing at the attention we attracted and the reactions we drew. Michael was good sport enough to laugh at the mistakes he made, trying to remember how to say words he had not spoken or thought about for over a year. I could not help wondering if Emory would ever do that; he avoided anything that made him appear in an unfavorable light.

Just as we left the ice cream parlor I saw the face of a boy I thought I recognized as one of Emory's crowd. And whenever I glanced in his direction, his eyes seemed to be watching me. I said nothing to Michael, but I was sure that he followed us to my apartment. I was jittery until I had sent Michael safely on his way, though I closed the door behind him with some regret. It was not even eleven, and the night felt young and unfulfilled to me.

Clara was home; she did not date much that I knew of. So we decided to make some popcorn and play a round of Monopoly. Popcorn was a very American food, but I was growing used to it. I had never played this game before, but Clara assured me that there was nothing to it. Just as we were opening the game board and getting settled, Anja burst in the door, and close on her heels another girl, a stranger to both of us.

"All right, so I'm sorry," the girl said. "Who else could I turn to?"

She actually screamed the words in a high, distraught voice. Her long hair looked tangled and uncombed and her face, devoid of all makeup, looked white, almost sickly. Clara, with natural instinct, peered at her closely.

"Are you all right?" she asked. "Are you ill?"

"She's fine," Anja snapped. "I just have to get something and then we'll be out of here."

"Aren't you going to introduce us to your friend?" I asked.

Anja glared at me with a look so close to hatred that it stunned me, like a blow.

"Your uncle had no right! Who does he think he is—the wise and almighty—"

Anja's friend's voice was hard and laced with venom. But Anja turned round on her before she could finish, her face dark with suppressed anger. "Shut up, you little fool! I said you were not to mention him here! Can't you do anything right?"

She grabbed the girl's arm roughly and marched her out the front door, without a word to us or a backward glance. Clara and I blinked at one another. "I wonder what that was all about," she mused.

"Nothing good," I assured her, thinking of Anja's late, mysterious nights, and the air of secrecy about her.

"Anja is certainly not a happy girl," Clara said. "Anyone can see that. And her friend"—she screwed her face up in what was her expression of concern, and it made her look half like a wise little gnome and half like an innocent child. "Her friend is even more miserable than Anja, don't you think?" She sighed.

"Explain these rules to me," I urged her. "Otherwise I'll think better of all this and go to bed."

"Chicken out and leave me to eat all this popcorn myself?" She pursed her mouth into a smile and proceeded, and I did my best to concentrate. But the scene with Anja had had its effect on my spirits. Everything about me seemed in turmoil lately, and the restlessness I had been feeling stirred uneasily within me.

∞

Perhaps that is why I accepted the unusual invitation that came the following morning. It was a Thursday, and therefore I had no classes until one o'clock. Shortly after eight-thirty I heard a knock at the door and opened it to see Hans Bekker standing there.

"Good morning!" he said, smiling in a boyish way, his eyes shining as if the whole world were filled with beauty, and all the beauty had been created for his pleasure.

"I hoped you would be home, Augustine. You must come with me." He seemed almost to dance where he stood. "On such a morning as this—hurry! Can you come this moment?"

I stammered a little. "I . . . but . . . yes, I suppose. Where are we going?"

"You will see!"

His pleasure danced along my skin. I grabbed a jacket and went with him, out into the still, frosty morning. The restless feeling inside me was spilling over. We got into his car and headed out the long road that led up to the canyon. The black tree branches were coated with a layer of stiff, sparkling jewels; even the broad flanks of the steep rocks were crusted and glittering. We climbed into the silent wonderland, leaving the clutter and racket of civilization behind us. Nothing else existed but ourselves and this breathless moment.

All at once I realized that a soft snow was falling, coating the road, coating the car, coming thicker and thicker, until at last it threatened to blot out the sky. Yet I was not frightened, not even anxious. The excitement within me seemed like a strain of music, thin and sustaining. I leaned back and relaxed. The car seemed no barrier, no impediment; I could almost feel the soft caress of the wet flakes against my skin. I was hardly aware that Hans had slowed the car and turned off the main road. But before me opened a deep, open meadow, fringed with willows and slender white aspens. And behind them, like a magnificent backdrop, an endless expanse of pine, thick and green against the steep cliffside, sprinkled now with a gossamer mantle of white. The sun, in thick yellow streaks, played across the landscape, errantly highlighting a tangled brown thicket, a streak of gray creek water, a cluster of rough, moss-green stones. Every place my eyes fell appeared some new, quiet beauty to please them. I gazed and gazed, letting the peace and beauty seep into me, fill me.

At last, with a sigh, I glanced at the man beside me. He, too, was lost in the vision before us, but I felt his awareness of me, gentle and undemanding. He sat silent for a few moments longer and then said, "I knew what this would mean to you, and I thought you might need it."

One of the bright fingers of sunlight had found his gold head and was playing in the tawny softness of his hair. I felt my fingers aching to reach out and touch the thick folds of it. Just then he turned his eyes to me, and I feared what he might read in my face.

"Are you content, Augustine?" he asked.

"Content," I confirmed, "yet with this small point of throbbing agony that beauty always creates deep within me."

"Joy so intense, so impassioned, that it feels like pain."

He understood, then. Of course, of course.

I do not know how much longer we sat there. But we drove back down the mountain in a silence so perfect that nothing could penetrate it. Inescapably we reached the city streets, and I experienced a dark shock, a deflation of spirit, much as a disappointed angel would who had been suddenly banished from the bright regions above. He felt it, too. I sighed, and he said, "It is difficult to come back, I know. Except that now we carry those moments with us—they are a part of us from now on, and forever."

His voice, as well as his words, thrilled through me. I blinked back tears, wanting to raise my eyes and smile at him, but hesitant suddenly. When we reached the Heritage Halls he slid his car into a parking slot, turned off the engine, and came around to open my door for me. The silence was with us still. I gave him my hand and he helped me out, but he did not release his hold, and it seemed natural and right, the warm firmness of his hand over mine as we walked to the building. At my doorstep we paused. He was standing very close to me. I wanted to thank him—but what words could express the feelings that yet hovered between us? Without meaning to, I leaned toward him and rested my head against his shoulder. He touched my hair with his outstretched hand. "Yes," he said, "yes."

We stood that way for a few moments. Then, with great effort, I reluctantly moved, entered the apartment, and left him—helpless to do anything else.

❦

Things were different between us after that, they had to be. We needed no spoken word, no sign of any kind, really; the difference was there in the silence that harbored our two spirits and altered all ordinary exchange between us.

I tried not to think about it. I went to class, went to work, did my lessons, cleaned house and cooked meals, and spent more and more of my evenings with Emory. And Emory was skillfully and methodically doing what he had said he would do: try harder, woo me back again. Some days there were flowers waiting at my apartment, or at the bookstore, with a message on the card that would make my cheeks go scarlet. Some mornings when he arrived to take me to class he would have a bag of fresh, warm Spudnuts and a carton of milk. He would find me afternoons where I was studying in the library and sit and rub my shoulders, or quiz me on my Italian verbs. When it was not my night to cook for the apartment and no one else had, he would bring take-out food to me, and then run errands for me—at times even for my roommates.

One afternoon he surprised us and took Penelope's old jalopy to the car wash *and* filled the tank with gasoline—which kindness alone endeared him to my roommates for longer than time and memory will last. I held my breath, waiting for his good intentions to wear thin and his model behavior to become tedious. But he maintained his incredible devotion so thoroughly that I felt myself relaxing, beginning to trust him, beginning to believe his endearments, beginning to soften my resistance when he held me, when he kissed me. Sweet and delicious was the web of his affection, and it was with a sort of relief that I felt myself cease to struggle and give in at last.

❦

Near the end of November came a holiday I was not familiar with—Thanksgiving Day, when the Americans celebrate the first harvests of the early settlers in this country, and count their blessings, as Clara explained it. We were even given vacation days from school, and people traveled to be with their families if they could, and everyone cooked a big feast. Emory and some of his social unit brothers were planning a long, four-day ski trip, and Martha had called and asked me to come spend the day with her. I agreed. Though a faint reservation had invaded our friendship, nothing really had changed, and I looked forward to being with her and the children.

Tuesday evening I received a phone call from Dr. Bekker. "I spoke to Martha," he said, "and told her you may as well ride to Salt Lake with me."

"You are coming, too?" I blurted.

"For my third year in a row," he affirmed.

That changed the face of things, considerably.

"I thought it would be nice to drive up *early* Thursday morning. Could I come by for you as soon as six?"

I swallowed my surprise and agreed.

"Good." He seemed pleased. "That will give us time to take a little detour on the way."

I wondered what he had in mind. I could not help anticipating being with him, yet the nagging insecurity, almost fear, I felt in his presence tainted the prospect. And I wondered if the tension I had felt on Halloween would be a necessary component whenever the three of us were together.

I packed my bags Wednesday night and forced myself to rise in the dark, chill hours of the morning to shower and get ready for the day. Hans Bekker arrived at precisely six by the kitchen clock. Anja had gone off someplace for the long weekend with a group of her friends, Sally and Penelope had gone home, and neither Nancy nor Clara was awake yet. I switched off the light and locked the door behind me.

The morning was very still; gray and unlit yet, trailing the last tattered remnants of night. Dr. Bekker carried my things to the car and held the door for me. I was painfully aware of him: the mass of his fair hair, damp and curling at his temples, the smooth, firm line of his jutting chin, the pressed tidiness of his charcoal pants, and the line of his shoulders beneath a soft, moss-green sweater. There was a sense of solidarity, even safety, in his presence. But his voice and his eyes always carried a strain of expectation, a promise of excitement and pleasure. I settled on the seat beside him, as tense with anticipation as a child.

He did not take the customary streets that led to the highway. Instead he turned up the Provo Canyon road, and we climbed to meet the sun in the high recesses that first stirred to life at its touch. And again there was splendor all around us. He found a classical station on the radio, and the sweet voices of violin, cello, and oboe filtered, gently surrounding us. We drove over the spine of the mountain, hugging the curve of the reservoir, then down and through a sleepy community. On the outskirts, just before the wilderness encroached again, he stopped the car at a small restaurant; cozy, with white curtains at the windows. He ordered what was the specialty of the house and I ate it, and it tasted delicious because I was with him, because the sun, like thick yellow butter now, stained the checkered tablecloth, coated our skin and warmed my hair and shoulders; because his voice, more musical than the violin and oboe, became the instrument of his pleasure and clothed with words the impressions and understandings of his spirit. I listened, I became part of the meaning, and without realizing it reflected back to him the impressions and thoughts of my heart.

We talked, we were in a world of our own. When we went back to the car, he drove with familiarity through what he called the hinterlands, showing me old pioneer houses and landmarks, naming the trees and even some of the peaks that surrounded us, at last clattering through the narrow and twisted lanes of a deserted mining community called Park City, gray and wasted and falling upon itself, but alive still with whispers and memories of what had once been.

"How do you know all these places?" I marveled.

"Heber Pratt. He was a natural outdoorsman and he loved these mountains. There wasn't a place he couldn't find if he wanted to, and I don't remember one time we got lost."

His words reminded me where we were going and what was ahead of us. The fabric of my joy was too fragile. As the road dropped sharply and descended toward the city it disintegrated altogether. And when we pulled up in front of Martha Pratt's house and got out of the car, I was no more than an ordinary schoolgirl coming, in company with her professor, to visit her friend and benefactress.

℀

The smells that greeted us when we entered were succulent enough to have been coming from my mother's kitchen. My uncertainties were put on hold. After a hurried greeting, Martha promptly assigned half a dozen tasks to Hans and as many more to me. I cut celery and carrot sticks and set the table with best china and cloth napkins, Ellen assisting haltingly, hampered more than usual by the excitement she was feeling. We filled tall stemmed glasses with homemade grape juice, frothy and rosy. Then Roger brought out the gumdrop turkeys he and Ellen had made for place markers, and decided with due gravity where each person should sit. I positioned myself purposefully beside Ellen, to assist her during the meal. Dr. Bekker and Martha would naturally take the head and foot of the table, and Roger would be left an entire side to himself.

While Martha stirred gravy, Hans mashed mounds of smooth white potatoes and positioned the large awkward bird onto a platter. I had never eaten turkey before, but I was beginning to look forward to it. Roger and I managed to get the rolls from the oven just when they were nicely browned. Suddenly all was ready, we took our various places, and Martha asked Dr. Bekker to pray. The sincerity and simplicity of his prayer set the mood for the meal, and I enjoyed thoroughly the discovery of so many new taste sensations. When it came time for pumpkin pie we talked Martha into waiting. So she herded the children into their rooms to play and we three did dishes—more dishes than I had seen in my lifetime. When I told her so she smiled, but Hans Bekker laughed gently to himself.

"I remember when we left our home in Berlin. We had packed most of the minimal belongings we were allowed to take with us. I was nervous about leaving my mother behind, but my sister was delighted. 'No more dishes to wash' she sang over and over again, pleased with herself."

I was confused. "Where did you go, then, and how did you eat?"

He laughed again. "We went to a village deep in the forest, where some of my mother's relatives lived. And what my mother had told us was true: we each had a rough wooden set of bowl, plate, and mug. There was very little food to eat, and that was simple and easy to prepare; and there were very few dishes to do." He was talking to us, but a different look had come into his eyes, one I had never seen there before. "The joke came when Constanze realized how many new, backbreaking tasks she now had to replace the simple chore of washing dishes."

I was interested. "Such as?"

"Feeding the goats, gathering eggs, and cleaning the hen house. Hauling water from the well, weeding the garden, churning butter by hand—the tasks were endless, really."

"It sounds to me like you ate well enough," Martha said.

"Bread, milk, and cheese," he replied, "sometimes an occasional chicken, but otherwise no meat. And the portions were small—so small, so carefully meted out." His eyes met mine and in that moment they said, "You would understand, Augustine. You have your own memories."

After the work was done we all piled into Martha's car and took the children to see a Walt Disney movie called *Sleeping Beauty*. I sat beside Roger and he held my hand most of the time. I caught myself nodding several times and was glad when it had ended and we walked back out into the bracing evening air. The mellow glow of twilight had softened the contours of the mountains. They seemed to pulse with some inner light of their own making. I stood gazing at them, unaware that I had stopped altogether, until I felt a touch on my arm and looked up to see Hans Bekker watching me. He smiled. Nothing needed to be spoken between us. I walked beside him back to the car.

But when we got back inside Martha's house the subtle change had already started. She had grown quiet and a little moody. I helped her put the children to bed. I wanted to believe she was struggling with loneliness and longing for the husband who was not with her this day. But I knew it was more than that. I had seen her gentle mourning for Heber; this was different. From time to time she gave me sidelong glances that shivered along my skin and made me feel cold inside.

When we went back to join Dr. Bekker he was immersed in a book. He closed the cover when he saw us, but could not resist sharing tidbits from what he had been reading. I was interested, but Martha, with a brittle gaiety, turned the subject and asked suddenly, "How are things going with that handsome boyfriend of yours, Augustine?"

She smiled brightly, and I blinked back at her. I knew why she was doing this. Hans Bekker was waiting with that controlled air of expectancy, and I should have answered her, for she continued—turning to Dr. Bekker and placing her hand on his knee—"Augustine is dating a boy from the South. He is good-looking and rich, and I think he is falling in love with her."

"Martha—" I began to protest.

She ignored me. "And this is just what her mother wants for her, Hans, to find a husband who will take care of her and give her a good life."

Dr. Bekker's face was impossible to read. I looked at Martha and saw her with unexpected clarity. She was not a particularly pretty woman, and her face right now looked tense and drawn. I felt a twinge of compassion for her, struggling against the anger and sense of betrayal her words had produced in me.

"Are you serious about this young man, Augustine?" Hans Bekker turned to face me, asking the question with gentle gravity. There was a note of concern in his voice.

"He is very persistent," I said, "very charming and attentive, and he thinks—"

"That is not what I asked, Augustine. I asked you how *you* felt."

Suddenly I wanted to shout at both of them. What business of theirs was it, anyway, either of them? He was not my father or my bishop. What right had he to question me? To demand answers and explanations?

"I do not know how I feel." I bit the words off and rose to my feet as I said them. "I'm tired. I think I'll go up to bed."

Martha smiled wanly. "All right, honey. I'll see you in the morning."

I turned and fled the room. I should have thanked her for the good meal, or something of the sort, I thought dimly, but I was close to tears. She had what she wanted; she was alone with Hans Bekker. And more power to her. I wished nothing to do with either of them—or, suddenly, with anything else here. If only I could go home! Run away, be safe and cared for and understood again.

I slid between the cold sheets and closed my eyes, employing all the powers of my mind and memory to call up the faces of my mother and Armand, the smells and sounds of the crowded shops and village streets—the face of the Madonna shining down from her rock sanctuary, smiling into my heart. I was a stranger here. My aching spirit longed for France, for home.

Chapter

12

The sound of my own crying awoke me. I rubbed my eyes, disoriented, and feeling drugged. The dream had been terrible this time, and longer than ever before. I rose, put on my slippers and robe, and padded as silently as I could down the creaky, uncarpeted stairs and into the kitchen. I poured myself a glass of milk, grabbed one of the rolls from the bread box, and groped my way to the living room. I had not turned on a light yet; the kitchen window, with no shade and only a filmy white curtain, had let in enough moonlight to see by. Here there was nothing but hollows and bulky shadows, night counterparts, I thought, of the friendly chintz chairs and flowered sofa that stood here by day.

Carefully I felt my way until my hands touched the solid wood of an end table, then the shape of a lamp, and with one tiny click there was light, strong and golden, and the room as I knew it leapt back into existence.

I lowered myself onto the couch, nearly sitting on top of a book that had been left there—the book Hans Bekker had been reading. I picked it up. It was a novel by the American writer Mark Twain, called *Huckleberry Finn*, the one Hans had talked to

Martha and me about the evening before. He had such an enthusiasm for life. How did he maintain that? I felt ages old and intimidated by life. From what little he had said last night, and now and again during classes, I sensed that he had suffered far more than anyone realized, even myself. But it did not seem to show in him, at least not in any of the negative ways.

I thumbed through the book, aimlessly at first. Then I found myself pausing and reading longer and longer passages. It was over an hour later when I made myself go back upstairs and to bed. I took the book with me. Perhaps I would read more in it later. It comforted me somehow to have it near, but I refused to allow myself to think about or explore any of the reasons why that might be.

I don't know what either Martha or I would have done without the children. Oblivious of adult anxieties, they smoothed over the tension that still existed between us. Hans Bekker's name was not mentioned. I assumed he had driven back to Provo the night before. I thought it a bit childish to ignore his very existence, but it was not my place to alter conditions Martha had set in her own home. Besides, I had begun to feel painfully aware of the debt I owed her—all the effort, all the dollars and cents spent on my account. I felt uneasy, because I wondered if Martha had begun to regret her generous impulse and perhaps even to wish she could undo what she had impulsively done. I did not like owing anything to anyone; this had been her idea and my mother's, not mine. But I was the one on the firing line, so to speak, which had made me feel awkward and apologetic from the beginning, but which made me feel downright miserable now.

We made it through the day, but I dreaded an evening along with her. I was literally praying that something would happen, so when the phone rang and Martha said it was for me I jumped, and must have looked guilty. It was Emory. One of his friends had broken his leg on the slopes, so they were on their way back home early, and he wondered if he could talk me into coming along? He was here in Salt Lake and could pick me up in a few minutes.

Martha understood. How could she do otherwise, after advocating this relationship so openly and fervently? I had never before been half so glad to see Emory; even he noticed my unusual exuberance when I hugged him at the door and planted a light kiss on his cheek. His presence made the good-byes easier. I thanked Martha sincerely for the delicious meal and the movie and all the trouble she had gone to. Then I kissed the children and skipped out into the cold twilight with Emory, feeling gratefully light and free.

With me sitting in the front beside him and three of his group of friends crowded into the back, we raced to Provo in time to make it to a movie Emory wanted to see. As we traveled he told me of their adventures, pleased to have someone to talk to, someone who was a good listener, I thought. When we filed into the theatre somehow there were nearly a dozen more to the group, and there was a sense of lighthearted, youthful gaiety which I needed. Afterward several of us went to Emory's apartment and played games for hours, munching on potato chips and pretzels, unmindful of time. When I first glanced at a clock it was well past dorm hours, but I had checked out for the entire weekend and no one was expecting me. Emory parked his car and we walked a roundabout way, beneath tree shadows and across grass lots checkered with moonlight, reaching the apartment in safety, breathless and laughing.

I leaned against the door and Emory placed his hands above my shoulders, so he was leaning over me.

"You've been a great sport tonight, Augustine, putting up with the lot of us rowdy boys."

"I enjoyed myself," I replied.

"It beats me," he drawled, "why you make such a difference to me, Snow White." His eyes had gone soft, but his voice was serious and reflective; he was not consciously using it as a means of charming me. "All those people having fun, but Ah'd have been miserable without you there."

I did not know what to say, but he didn't seem to expect anything. I smiled gently, knowing he was going to kiss me, anticipating the touch of his lips upon mine.

"Augustine, Augustine . . ." he whispered against my hair. There was something different, something deeper in the way he touched me. When we drew apart and I let myself into the dark, quiet apartment, I was shaken, afraid of this change in him, wondering where it might lead.

As I flipped on a light I realized there was a glow coming from Anja's room, and thought it strange, since neither she nor Sally was here this weekend. Idly I walked toward the closed door, thinking to switch off the light and save electricity. As I opened it a voice called out to me, "Shut the door and leave me alone," though a rather strong curse was added in with the directive.

I walked into the room. Anja was lying on top of the bed, fully clothed, her arms flung over her head, her blonde hair matted and uncombed and her face red from crying.

"What are you doing here?" she demanded, swearing again. "I thought you went to Salt Lake."

I ignored both her crudeness and her question. "How long have you been crying here alone?" I asked. "Let me help you."

She laughed. "Go to bed, little do-gooder. Girls like you are such a pain, Augustine. There is nothing in the world you could do to help me."

"You're wrong," I said quietly. "And I wish you knew that, because I would like very much to help you."

I turned and went into my own room. All the time I was getting ready for bed I listened to hear the sound of a door opening or footsteps in the hall. But there was nothing. In the silence that now felt empty and lonely I climbed into my cold bed and went to sleep.

The next morning when I stumbled out into the kitchen I found both Anja and Clara eating breakfast. Anja was hunched over a bowl of cereal, morose and silent. But Clara was happy to see me and began to chatter away.

"Oh, Augustine," she moaned, "it was awful yesterday, and when I came home there was no one here to talk to! So I just sat right here at this table and bawled by myself."

"Whatever happened?"

"We lost a baby at the hospital. I was on pediatrics with a couple of other students and having such a grand time cooing over all the *beautiful* babies, rocking them, and feeding them—"

She began to choke just trying to tell it, and her eyes were filling with tears.

"Then they brought in this preemie—a little girl born at seven and a half months, but there was something wrong with her as well, and her lungs weren't properly developed." Clara wiped tears from the corner of her eyes. I noticed that Anja, her head buried in her arms, had raised her eyes and was listening.

"The head nurse and a couple of others whisked her into a special incubator and worked over her for hours. Then one of the nurses walked out, tears rolling down her cheeks and shook her head at us. It was awful, Augustine! I felt so helpless!"

I reached over and stroked her short curly hair, still crushed and rumpled from sleep. "You poor thing. How terrible for someone like you, Clara. But you could not help it."

"But that was part of it," Clara burst out. "I *felt* somehow responsible, as though I should have figured out something to do! The baby fought for her life, Augustine—I watched through the glass! We failed her! And her mother!" Clara's voice was a wail now. "She was young and this was her first child. She cried as though her heart had been broken." Clara's voice trembled and dissolved. "I've never heard anyone cry like that."

From some great distance I heard the sound of my mother crying; a high, thin sound, more animal than human. She sat in a corner, hugging her arms to herself, rocking back and forth. "They have killed him, Giselle; they have killed my good husband. What shall we do? They have killed him, they have killed him." The words a chant, so painful that my sister put her hands over her ears. "Augustine," she whispered to my mother, "she is too little to hear this. *Maman*, please!"

"Stop it!" The words brought me back to the present with a terrible jolt.

"Anja!" Clara was shocked and confused by the venom in Anja's voice and the wild look in her eyes. Suddenly, with a quiet assurance, I knew.

"Your friend who was with you the other night," I said, "you're worried about her, aren't you?" Something came into Anja's eyes to confirm what I was thinking. "She's pregnant, isn't she?"

"Yes."

Anja's voice was miserable. Thank heaven for Clara's sensitive compassion. She sat staring, bug-eyed now and amazed. "Oh dear!" she muttered. "Oh dear! Poor thing."

Anja looked from one to the other of us for a moment. "That in itself would be bad enough," she volunteered. "But I can't help her, at least not openly, because I've been forbidden to have anything to do with her."

She was watching us closely, aware of the vulnerable position she might be placing herself in to be honest with us.

"The university has forbidden you?" Clara asked, her voice reflecting her incredulity.

"In a roundabout way," Anja answered. "Let's just say it like this, *the powers that be* have threatened instant expulsion if I'm caught having the least thing to do with her—if I'm even seen in her company."

I wondered briefly what past behavior on either or both of the girls' parts might have occasioned such a strict edict, but I said, "That is none of our affair. If we can help either one of you, we will do all in our power."

Clara's head bobbed up and down in enthusiastic agreement.

Anja glanced at me, the familiar expression of disdain hardening her features, marring her beauty. "So you say, but if you knew absolutely everything, I wonder how fast you'd play turncoat and change your colors."

I had no idea what she was talking about, or why she seemed to distrust me so deeply, so I let the words slide.

"Another complication," she continued. "My friend—" I noticed she did not wish to name the girl— "has a condition that will make it dangerous for her to be pregnant. She should be under a doctor's care, and she knows it. But, of course, she refuses to do anything about it."

Clara leaned forward. "What is the condition she has?"

"She's a diabetic." Clara drew in her breath. "She must seek attention immediately!"

"That's what I just told you," Anja responded, put out by Clara's plodding nature.

"Does she know who the father is?" I asked.

Anja turned inscrutable eyes on me. "Yes, she knows who the father is, and he's a jerk. So even if she wanted help from him, which she doesn't—"

She left her sentence uncompleted. We both got the message. I wanted to ask, "Do we know this boy?" but thought better of it. "Does he know about the baby?"

"I don't think so. And that's how she wants it."

"Oh dear! oh dear!" Clara muttered.

"Anja, listen," I said, an idea tugging at the back of my mind. "If Clara could arrange something, would your friend let someone in the College of Nursing help her, someone who would allow her anonymity and—"

Clara was shaking her head at me. "We're part of the university, Augustine. The nurses would have no choice but to fill out a report, and then . . ."

I sat back with a sigh. "What about a Salt Lake doctor? Perhaps my friend, Martha, knows a good one."

"Perhaps," Anja considered.

"What about telling her parents? Wouldn't they rally and help her?" Clara's plain face was soft with concern, her eyes dark and troubled. *She will make a wonderful nurse*, I thought.

Anja's face had gone hard again. "Her parents will kick her out the next time she messes up, they've made that more than clear."

I realized I was hissing through my teeth in my frustration.

"We'll think of something," Clara said, obviously trying to convince herself as well as anyone. "Would she let us help her—directly, and keep you out of the picture?"

"I don't know," Anja said bluntly. "But she can't be seen here. This is where *I* live." She glanced plainly at me. "I'm not sure it would be smart for her to be seen with any of my roommates, either—especially you, Augustine." Her eyes had narrowed and grown watchful.

"Why especially me?"

"Good reasons."

Was she testing me or something? I let out my pent-up breath with a sigh. "All right," I agreed. "Your confidence is safe, as far as I'm concerned."

"No one—" She glanced from one to the other of us. "You'll not tell a soul, not even the other girls in the apartment?"

"You have our word," Clara assured her. "But we must think of something to do, and you must promise to keep us—well, let us know what's happening."

Anja nodded. "That's fair," she said. "Thank you. I don't know about my friend, but at least I can deal with this better after talking to you."

Clara smiled sweetly, as though she were some ministering angel and her kindness and good intentions could solve anything. I knew better. I thought the prospects looked gloomy, and I had no intention of forgetting Anja and the miserable, frightened girl who felt she had nowhere to turn. As Anja got up from the table and went back to her own room, I wondered if she remembered our encounter last night. I wondered if this morning had altered her opinion about me, even a little. I hoped that it might. Anja was far from affectionate and far from demonstrative, but I knew she needed a friend. And I found myself wanting to help her, though I could not have told anyone why.

Chapter

13

$\mathcal{D}$ecember was a messy month. The first few days were dreary, with a slate sky spitting snow that swirled over a dull, dirty landscape and left no mark, only an awareness of something harsh and inhospitable to come. I was ill with the beginnings of a cold, working more hours than usual, because of some vague, prideful determination to pay Martha back, at least in part, the investment she had made in me—if it ever came to that between us.

I was worried about Anja and her unnamed friend. Nearly two weeks had passed since our breakfast table conversation, and Clara and I had been of no use at all. I was homesick. With Christmas approaching I longed more than ever for the comfort and familiarity of home. And I had vague misgivings about my mother. How could she endure a Christmas separated from one another any better than I could? Loneliness was as painful as any physical ailment, I thought.

Then there was Dr. Bekker. I had not spoken to him on any sort of a personal level since that Thursday night when I had stomped up to my bedroom in Martha's house, fighting tears. What did he think? Why did he say nothing to me? Discontent and discouragement seemed everywhere about me, with one very obvious exception: Emory.

One night he announced out of nowhere that he was taking me out on the town, so I should find the best thing I had in my wardrobe to wear. When he picked me up we drove to Salt Lake and attended the opera *Tales of Hoffman*, at the University of Utah, then had dinner by candlelight at a charming Italian restaurant with homemade breads and a man dressed in costume who went from table to table singing, or at times playing a melancholy tune on the violin, provoking vague images of crossed lovers, tragic and trembling with emotion.

In this setting and atmosphere he leaned across the table, which was already small and intimate, and drew my hand close to him, stroking it as he spoke.

"Snow White, don't fault me, but Ah cannot live without you. Ah didn't dare speak to you before . . ." His southern speech was accented and honeyed. His dark hair fell over his forehead. He had never looked more handsome and beguiling.

"But lately Ah have come to b'leeve there is hope." He drew a small velvet box from his pocket. "Ah do love you truly, Augustine. Will you marry me? Will you be my wife?"

I gasped. The room around me had grown dim and indistinct. As he opened the box and began to draw out the ring I shook my head and drew back from the glittering sparkle of it that seemed to reflect off the silver, the glasses, the softness in Emory's eyes. I wanted to weep.

"Emory, Emory," I murmured, "I care for you very much, but I cannot say it is love yet—I cannot say you are the man I wish to spend the rest of my life with."

"You're jest frightened, honey-dear." His voice was gentle, but his eyes were terrible. He held the ring to the light, turning it round and round, so the reflections from it danced and spun out in all directions. "Say yes, Augustine! It might help you know if you make a commitment in one direction or the other." He drew my hand up and pressed it to his lips. "You care for me more than you know! And Ah love you enough for both of us! *Augustine!*"

I drew my hand away. I did not realize I was crying. "I cannot, Emory. It has to be right—I have to *know!* I'm sorry, so sorry . . ."

He slipped the sparkling jewel back into the dark case and

snapped the lid shut. "Stop cryin', Snow White, it'll be fine, you wait and see, jest fine."

We rode most of the way home in silence; not companionable, but not hostile. His pain was real, and I felt it. When we reached my apartment and he turned off the car engine he said, out of the clear blue, "Ah wanted to take you home with me and show you to my mommy and daddy."

I had destroyed a bright day-dream for him. He came around to my side and helped me out of the car. "Where else will you spend Christmas, honey-dear! It's magical in the South. You'd love it, and everyone there'd love you."

He drew me into his arms and kissed me, with just the right mingling of passion and tenderness. He walked me to my door and did nothing more in those last minutes than brush my cheek with his lips and murmur, "Ah love you, Augustine, Ah love you . . . Ah'll make you happy . . . Ah promise . . ."

I was shaken. Yet, from my own dull misery came the aware-ness that Emory had simply not taken *no* for an answer; at least not yet.

ॐ

The following day I was working in the fiction area when I saw Dr. Bekker approaching. My first impulse was to duck into the next aisle and avoid him. Whenever I went long periods of time without talking to him on a personal level I grew shy and uncer-tain in his presence. Besides, I was still tender from last night's scene with Emory and felt, illogically, that everyone who looked at me must be able to read in my face what had happened; especially someone like Hans Bekker, whose gaze pierced so deeply. And . . . perhaps I was a little put out with him for the long silent spell be-tween us, which I deemed was his fault.

I was a little cool, or at least withdrawn, when he approached me.

"You did exceptionally well on Friday's paper," he said.

I glanced up. His fine voice was warm with praise, but his eyes were cautious.

"An A was all I could give you, but for the record, it was the highest grade I have ever given a student paper."

I was flattered; no, not flattered; delighted and proud. I hesitated in my response, and he added, "You *should* be proud of yourself, Augustine. You have a fine mind, tempered by experience and the insight . . ." He hesitated. "The insight your life has given you."

Suddenly he angered me. "All your fine reasoning, all your high talk, what good is it in the long run? Where does it get you?"

He did not answer me, and I felt I had wounded him.

"I want to be happy!" I exploded. "And what do your grand theories have to do with that?"

"You want someone mindless and charming, like Emory Tuckett, to take care of you—the way Martha said? I don't believe that!" He stepped closer to me and lowered his voice. "You and I don't talk theory, Augustine. We talk truth and beauty, the things that feed man's spirit, that keep him sane through life's experiences!"

Why did his words anger me? Because they were vague and led nowhere? "What do you know of Emory?" I demanded.

"Enough." He spoke the one word with a wry twist to his voice and a secretive air that made me feel uncomfortable. From the corner of my eye I saw Anja's friend walking toward us. I called out to her, wishing I knew her name.

"Hello! Do you remember me?" I waved and smiled as I spoke. "I met you—"

As she looked up and caught my gaze her eyes flooded with horror. She quickly darted into a crowded aisle and walked swiftly away. My thoughts followed her; she had looked so frightened, like a small, trapped animal.

Suddenly I realized that Hans Bekker had his hand on my arm and was shaking me gently. "Augustine, listen to me!"

"Why? What have you and I to do with one another? You are a mature, educated man, a professor. I am a child yet. We do not belong to the same worlds—I don't even know what to call you!"

He could see my dilemma, I knew he could. He watched me with smoldering eyes, but before he could respond a customer, noting the name tag I wore on my blouse, came up and asked me a question. I went off with him and was busy for some time. When I came back Dr. Bekker was gone. A hollow ache gnawed at my stomach the remainder of the afternoon and a gloomy feeling that was only increased by the events of the evening.

I accompanied Emory to a Bricker Christmas party that evening. I did not particularly enjoy such occasions where there was a concentration of the rich and beautiful and the veneer was so thin one could scratch a nail across it and what was pathetic and real would show through. The girls in Emory's crowd had never accepted me; he was still top of the heap as far as they were concerned, and I was still an intruder. He had seated me at our table and run off to take care of some business when two of his friends, walking along together, paused to lean against one of the pillars, less than two feet away from me. I could not help overhearing their conversation, and what they said made me sick. When Emory returned it was with two other couples, and no opportunity presented itself for me to question him until the night's celebrations had worn down and people were disbursing in groups and in couples.

"There's a little get-together at Larry's place," Emory said, draping his arm casually over my shoulder. "You want to go for a while?"

I shuddered visibly. "Absolutely not," I said. "In fact, I want to talk to you about Lawrence."

He grinned. He was in high spirits because the evening had been successful and he had been at the center of everyone's attention.

"Has ol' Lawrence been breakin' bad again?" He made a clucking, scolding sound far back in his throat.

"It's nothing to joke about," I persisted. "Do you know anything about the girl he's been dating?"

"That hot little California number? Cain't say that Ah do."

"What's happened to her? She isn't with him tonight. Have you heard anything?"

"Why this sudden interest, honey-dear?" He stroked my cheek, his smile warm and suggestive. "This is a night to celebrate and be happy."

"Have you heard that she's in trouble? What does she look like, Emory?"

He sighed in resignation, having come to know me pretty well by now.

"It might hep if Ah knew what you're so stirred up about."

"Emory, please!"

"Awraht, Ah have heard rumors that the girl is . . . well . . . you know . . ."

"Yes, I know. And what is Lawrence doing about it?"

Emory blinked his beautiful, empty eyes at me. "How should Ah know what the boy's doing about it, honey-dear?"

I turned away in disgust. "Take me home, Emory. Please."

He drove the short distance to my apartment in a pout, but I didn't care. "How can you be so unconcerned, Emory? Think what this poor girl is suffering, while Lawrence goes his merry way—"

I had not meant to lecture him, I knew he disliked it. He held his hand out as if to stop me. "This *is* none of my affair, Snow White. You think Ah can control what my friends do?"

"Yes, I believe you can, to a degree—" I leaned toward him in my earnestness. "These are Mormon kids we're talking about, Emory—returned missionaries!"

He shook his head at me. "Few are as naive and pure of heart as you are, Augustine."

I found myself hissing through my teeth, though he had said the words in a kindly way.

"Ah know a good thing when Ah see it, Ah know my mama's got to meet you, honey-dear." He drew the car to a stop and leaned back to survey me with pleasure. "You were the prettiest girl there tonight."

I was not comfortable with direct compliments, especially the lingering, suggestive kind Emory usually resorted to. I smiled half-heartedly.

"Please come home with me, please . . ." He wound his fingers through my hair. I was getting nowhere at all. Not until I was in my apartment did I realize how thoroughly the subject of Lawrence and his "little indiscretions" had been avoided, or conveniently dropped. My anger increased, and an unpleasant sense of betrayal played around the tattered edges of my consciousness.

When the phone rang I snatched it up and nearly snarled into the receiver.

"Are you all right, Augustine?"

It was Martha. I calmed right down and soothed her.

"I'm calling because I thought of the name of a doctor here who is very good, but also discreet, and he has connections with LDS social services."

"That might be just what we're looking for," I responded with enthusiasm, and wrote down the information she gave me. Then, for conversation's sake, I told her how Emory wanted me to spend the holidays in the South with him.

"That's a lovely idea," she said, adding hastily, "not that I don't want you here. I do! And the children would be disappointed. But what an adventure for you. And an opportunity. If you think you may be getting serious about this guy, now's a good time to check out the family."

Her voice was light, with an air of casual intimacy. *If you think you're getting serious about this guy*—I had never indicated anything of the sort to Martha. This was wishful thinking, to be sure, on her part. What would she do if she knew the whole story, if I told her of Emory's proposal?

By the time I hung up I was as mad as a hornet, but at least there was one piece of good news. Anja thought so, too, when she came in and I told her of the doctor Martha had located.

"This might help, she might go for this." Anja looked up and actually smiled at me. Encouraged, I said, "This boy she's involved with is one of Emory's friends, isn't he?" Her widened eyes gave me my answer. "Lawrence Ward."

"How do you know?"

"I heard him talking at the party tonight, he and one of his friends. They didn't know I was listening."

Anja swore under her breath.

"Calling him names won't help. Why didn't you tell me?"

"Why should I have?"

I sighed. The situation, with all its implications, made me feel ill.

"Thanks," Anja said. "I'll see what I can do with this."

I worked on lessons until I could not hold my eyes open, then crawled into bed. But the last thought I had, despite the fog of exhaustion that was dulling my senses, concerned the pain and irony of my circumstances. *Emory wants me*, I thought, *and I'm not sure that I trust him, not sure I could spend my whole life with him. But how quickly Martha spoke up to get rid of me, to get me out of the way!* I assumed Hans Bekker would be spending at least part of the holidays at Martha's house. Was that in the back of her mind when she responded so eagerly?

Fine! I thought, with sleepy stubbornness. *I'll let her think I'm going with Emory. So much the better. Let her do what she likes then, and I'll be rid of the whole mess of them, and have Christmas to myself.* I slept, holding the thought—half-promise, half-threat—in my mind.

Chapter

14

$\mathcal{I}$n truth, I might have weakened and given in and gone with Emory, but bad grew to worse. It was happenstance, really, a mere accident of fate that brought to me a piece of knowledge that I would never have anticipated, that made me think Emory's pronouncement of me as *naive* was more than accurate.

I was just getting off one of my shifts at the bookstore when Leroy Blount, Emory's freckled friend from back home, came in to buy some notebooks he needed. He waited for me and we walked to the library together, a biting wind nipping at our ankles and urging us on.

"So our boy has gone and asked you to marry him."

I blinked up at him in surprise. "Who told you that?"

"The great man himself. Who else?"

"And did he tell you I refused him?"

Leroy grinned. "Well, he showed me the ring." He whistled through his teeth. "Don't know how any girl could keep her head and think clearly after seein' a rock o' that size."

I could not resist, and I asked him, "Did Emory seem despondent, upset when he told you?"

"He didn't want to let on, but Ah think he was mighty low, Snow White." Leroy scratched under the rim of the rumpled old cap he was wearing. "Ah told him, 'This one be too smart for you, boy, as well as too good for you.'" He grinned again. "Course, he didn't like that much."

We walked along in silence for a few moments, the cold air taking our breath away. When we reached the warmth of the building he said, in a much more serious manner, "Our boy'll keep persistin', he's like that. And who knows, maybe he is more serious this time."

"This time?" I kept my face carefully free of expression.

"He's been engaged two, three times before. You know how Emory is with the ladies, or Ah could say it the other way around, couldn't I?"

I smiled, but the muscles of my face felt stiff.

"Anyhow, Ah think he really cares for you. But Ah still b'lieve you're too good for him."

After a few tortured minutes he took his leave of me, and I made my way shakily to a chair and sat down. So that was the way of it! What a fool I was!

I stomped resolutely to the little cubicle where it was my custom to study and slid into my seat. *I will not think about this right now!* I told myself sternly. *What does this change, after all? I have not said yes to the boy. And, if I'd thought about it, I would have supposed this could never be the first time Emory had thought himself to be madly in love.*

In love . . . What a strange, vague phrase! What an elusive, vague concept. I opened my Italian book and began on the exercises the professor had assigned. But I could not keep my mind on the subject. My head and throat hurt and I felt suddenly hot and unable to breathe well. I fidgeted in my seat, rummaged through my purse for a throat lozenge, then a pencil with a sharper point. It was hopeless. Penelope would be here in half an hour to drive me home in her car. I did not dare attempt walking, not in this bitter weather and feeling the way that I felt.

But I was unable to concentrate on anything to any purpose. At last I took out pen and paper and wrote a long letter to Armand. I had gifts for him and my mother, for Sylvie and Jean-Paul and the children; carefully-chosen gifts that I was pleased with. In fact, they were already on their way *home*. I swallowed a different kind of ache in my throat. *Don't be childish*, I scolded myself. What would Armand say? *Learn something new. You've been here all your life, Augustine. Nothing here changes. You change, you grow, you have a right to.* And Sylvie? Sylvie had already written, "Christmas in America sounds terribly romantic to me, cherie. Such different customs, so much money spent, so much fuss and glitter." She had no more than the picture-book concept of this country. Mormons in Utah were not exactly New York City!

I sighed. In three more days classes would be over and the campus would clear as if a great vacuum had sucked all the noisy, two-legged creatures from off the surface, leaving it cold, clean-swept, and silent. That thought appealed to me. When Penelope and I arrived at the apartment we found a large, elegant vase filled with white roses, spilling over with fragrance and loveliness, so that they brought tears to my eyes. The card tucked in among them was addressed to me. "Snow White," it read, "you are my happiness. Please say yes."

Penelope raised her eyebrows at me but said nothing. She thought I should go. Everyone who knew Emory had asked me to go with him for Christmas felt the same way.

"He's not exactly a knight in shining armor, no matter how he may look," I bit back at Penelope.

She glanced up and her eyes narrowed. "You don't look well, Augustine," she said. "I think you should go to the health center tomorrow and get something to take."

I smiled weakly. "I suppose I should," I agreed. I knew Emory had meant *yes* not only to the Christmas plans, but to the marriage proposal. Others didn't know about that. What in the world would they say if they did? Suddenly I wished I knew, suddenly I no longer wanted to carry the burdens and decisions of my life all alone.

I will say for Martha that she called and checked on my plans. My head felt all muddled, and I had not made up my mind yet. But, as it turned out, I did not have to lie to her, not directly. She asked, "Would you be able to make a Christmas concert on Temple Square the twenty-first?"

"I'm afraid not," I replied.

"That's what I thought. When will you be returning?"

"I'm not certain yet."

"Well, let me know, will you? I'd like us to spend some time to-gether. Roger is feeling terribly cheated and gets grumpy every time your name comes up."

In what ways did my name come up, I wondered. She rang off with many bright wishes for success on my "venture," as she put it. I wondered what she would think if I told her I was not the first woman Emory had asked to marry him. She would probably laugh it off and say, "What would you expect from a boy as handsome as Emory?" It was not merely the knowledge that he had been en-gaged before which disturbed me, it was a feeling of duplicity and manipulation, something I had felt from him often: he should have been honest with me. He should have . . .

My head was aching terribly. I turned away from the silent telephone. I *must* get some homework done, no matter how I was feeling. This would keep. The inner life often bears neglect, even starvation. It is the outer life which demands so much of our time and energies.

I saw Emory the following morning and thanked him for the flowers. I had tossed and turned in my bed the night before, trying to decide what to do. I had even climbed back out of bed and onto my knees to pray about it. I had done more praying since that weekend in the Tabernacle than ever before in my life. I knew my mother was a praying woman. I had always wondered how she could be, seeing all God had taken from her and all he had allowed her to suffer. I was beginning to see that the gospel the Mormon missionaries taught had given her answers, had helped her see suf-fering in an altogether different light. *Life* had brought loss and suffering to her, not a capricious god. Men, with their agency, had brought to pass horrors and indignities nearly beyond comprehen-sion. It was God who sanctified these things to the spirit's growth and understanding. I was beginning to perceive this in a vague sort of way, but I knew my mother—and Hans Bekker, for that mat-ter—lived by these truths.

I had decided last night to confront Emory with my new knowledge of his past life and loves; that would be the safest, most dignified course. But he kept pressing me.

"Time's runnin' out, Augustine. Come south with me, it will be good for you. You work too hard, you are too serious about life. Let Mama and me spoil you a little . . ." His honeyed speech, his languid eyes . . . I shook my head. "You have my answer," I told him. "Wait. We'll see what happens when you come back."

He drew the ring out from some inner pocket and held it out to me. "Ah love you, Augustine. Ah want to take care of you, give you the good things of life. Can't you trust me?"

"No!"

He grew angry for the first time. "And what am Ah to do with this?" He brandished the ring like a small, gleaming weapon.

"Try some of the other girls who've refused you. Maybe one of them will stick it out this time."

I stumbled from the car and began walking toward the new McKay building. He let me go. I did not look back, and he did not follow me. I went through the day not in a haze, really, but with a black veil draped over my mind and my spirits.

That afternoon, after the bookstore closed, we had an employees' Christmas party. We had drawn names and, as we were passing round gifts, I saw Michael approach me, a package tucked under his arm.

"Don't tell me you drew my name, fair and square," I teased, as he handed me the present.

"I'll confess to a little contriving," he grinned, "but I had to give you this."

I tore away the wrappings and pulled out a slim volume: the poetry of Edna St. Vincent Millay translated into French.

"Where did you find this?" I was stunned. He knew I had been entranced by the few things of hers I had read in English.

He smiled gently, well satisfied. "Sent off for it," he said.

I hugged it in my pleasure. "You are too good to me," I murmured.

"Nonsense." He bent close, and his look was concerned. "Just because that southern hunk of conceit is doing his best to monopolize you, doesn't mean the rest of us need to stop caring—or have any reason to," he added, planting a kiss on my cheek.

Of course, somebody saw him, and then the teasing and catcalls began, and the moment was lost. I blinked back tears and wished I had some way to thank him.

I did let him drive me home, though the Heritage Halls were

embarrassingly close to campus. But the evening was cold, with a thin, icy snow falling, and I felt hot and dizzy and quite unwell, really. He walked to the door with me.

"If I don't get snowed in up in Idaho," he said, "I'll see you after the holidays." He leaned close and kissed my cheek as he had before. His lips were cool and his skin carried the faint scent of a very nice men's cologne. "Maybe that little book will help you to be not *quite* so homesick." There was such tender understanding in his eyes that it brought tears to my own again.

He ran off toward the parking lot, turning and kissing his hand to me. I entered the apartment both warmed and shaken. Emory sat on the sagging sofa, waiting for me.

℃

My roommates had discreetly ensured that no one else was in the room when I entered. Emory looked up at me, but the customary light was not in his eyes. I was seeing him discouraged and unsure of himself for the first time. I sat on the edge of the chair opposite him.

"Can we go someplace and talk, Snow White?"

"I don't feel well, Emory, and I've got so much to do. Besides, what is there to say?"

"You could let me try to explain."

I sighed. I suppose he had a right to that. With effort I rose again, glancing down at my wristwatch. "Half an hour," I said.

We went out to his car and drove ten minutes up to the foot of Squaw Peak. All was quiet and deserted. He left the engine running and the heater blowing.

"It's natural for a guy to look for someone to marry, Augustine," he began. "Back when those girls were a part of my life Ah didn't even know you existed—Ah didn't know there was something so much better out there."

"You should have told me."

"Why, to hurt you? Give you doubts you have no cause for?"

My head was pounding and I couldn't think clearly. "It's a pretty serious step to ask a girl to be your wife, Emory. How could you have been wrong about something so important—three different times?"

"Ah don't know!" He was uncomfortable. He ran his hand through the black thickness of his hair. "Ah was young and impulsive." He leaned toward me. "This is different! You are different! How many times have Ah told you that, Augustine?"

We were going round and round in the same patterns we always had. Some things he just wasn't capable of understanding.

"Go home for Christmas, Emory," I said, as gently as I could. "Have a good time with your family. We'll try to put this all together, see what happens when you get back."

He looked miserable. Emory crushed and unsure of himself was a very different creature from the one I was used to. He played the role of big man on campus and charming ladies' man to much greater advantage.

"If you mean what you say, if you truly care for me," I began, feeling awkward, feeling as though I were quoting lines from a novel, "if I am worth marrying, then I'm worth waiting for and making sure of."

I suppose I really left him nowhere to go. We drove back in silence. He walked me to my apartment. Still nothing was said between us. As I closed my hand over the doorknob, he covered it with his—so warm, so throbbing with the inner vitality he was now checking.

"Ah love you, Ah do love you, Augustine." The words were a measured, sober statement. He bent and kissed me. Not an overhasty kiss, but too short; I felt myself shiver when he drew away.

He turned his back to me and I watched him walk into the darkness, the mere impression of him tall and handsome, even confident, in the obscuring shadows. An overwhelming urge to call after him flooded through me. How easy it would be, how easy it would be to . . .

But he had opened the car door, slid into the seat and turned on the engine. I watched the long elegant Oldsmobile pull onto the street, merge, and lose itself in the traffic. I stood watching after it a long time, until I realized I was shaking with the cold. Then I opened the door to the apartment and went inside.

Chapter

15

*T*hursday morning Penelope insisted upon driving me to the health center, where a doctor examined me, shaking his head and writing half a dozen prescriptions.

"You have what we call walking pneumonia, young lady," he scolded. "But we've caught it in time. You take these antibiotics and medications exactly as I've instructed, go to bed for three days and take care of yourself, and you should be all right for Christmas."

We went straight to a pharmacy and I reluctantly spent an alarming percentage of my hoarded money on medicine.

"I feel much better," Penelope stated, as she dropped me off at the library. "Martha will take good care of you—if you'll let her!" She gave me a hug. "I'll see you early," she promised. "I'm coming back for a ski day the weekend before school starts."

I hardly heard what she said. My head was ringing and it hurt my throat every time I swallowed, and it hurt my chest every time I breathed. When I staggered back home, dizzy and weak, the apartment was empty, cleared of all signs of life or habitation. I *felt* the emptiness; dull, with no air of expectancy. I poured some juice, took the pills I had been given, and went to bed.

I do not know how much later it was that I awoke. I crawled out of bed, surprised to see that the windows were light still. I ate some cheese and crackers and curled up on the corner of the couch with a book I had been wanting to read for the past month. But my head kept nodding, and finally I shut it and went back to the dark, cheerless bedroom, aware at first of my troubling cough and the ache in my back muscles. Then sleep stole my consciousness, and the next time I awoke everything about me was dark as pitch.

Even after I turned on a few lights and warmed some soup, the sense of desolation clung to me, worse by far than mere loneliness. I had no taste buds, I had no energy, my mind was too muddled to think. I opened the book again and forced myself to read a few pages, but the effort made my eyes ache. I swallowed more pills and fell asleep on the sofa, to awaken with my muscles cramped and feeling chilled to the bone.

I was groggily aware that a new day had arrived. But life had become a meaningless routine to me of sleep and waking, forcing myself to eat something and take the pills the doctor had given me, forcing myself to crawl back into my crumpled, pain-ridden cavern, which seemed to sink deeper and deeper into isolation each time I succumbed to it.

❦

The hours were passing. I was aware that I had slept again, and for some reason I was struggling to open my eyes and wake up. Perhaps it was the fragrance, delicious and familiar, that tickled my nose. Mushrooms . . . and warm tomatoes?

With my newly-learned caution I lifted myself slowly to a sitting position and remained still while the room steadied itself. Even yet, I swore I could smell food cooking.

"You are awake. Good! I have a nice treat ready for you."

I heard the voice before I saw its possessor, and I had my hand up to my mouth and was heartbeats away from screaming when he walked into the little square of my vision, standing just outside my doorway. He wore a man's apron of a gray herringbone pattern. His blue eyes smiled. They were as clear and deep as a summer lake stained pure indigo.

"What are you doing here?" My voice as well as my face must have expressed my stunned bewilderment.

"Let me try to explain," Hans Bekker replied, still not venturing further than my open doorway.

⚘

I pushed my hair back from my face, wondering what in the world I must look like, and tried to listen.

"Augustine—" He held his hands out, as though not knowing how to alter or embellish the truth. "Anja was worried about you, and so she called and asked if I would check up on you."

I sat up straighter, feeling a warmth of interest and emotion course through me. "Why would Anja be concerned about me, and why in the world would she telephone you?"

He took a step or two into the room and leaned against the side of the bureau. "I think she suspected what you were doing, and—" He paused and cleared his throat. "Anja is my niece, her mother is my oldest sister." He paused again. "But the most amazing part is that she would contact me, for in doing so she gave up her sacred privacy."

"What do you mean?"

"She most emphatically did not wish me to know where she lived or anything she was doing with her life. She views me as cold, didactic, and meddling—to use the kindest terms possible." He knit his fine brow, his expression reflecting a mingling of amusement and pain. "You must have made quite an impression on her. Anja does not like very many people. But then, you probably know that, having lived with her these past months."

"I certainly never thought I was on the list of the favored few," I replied, with grateful honesty.

"She is difficult to figure out. No one ever knows what she is thinking or feeling. She has kept it that way since she was a very small child." He shook his head and smiled upon me, a slow, gentle smile. "Whatever it was that moved Anja, I am here now, Augustine." He clucked his tongue at me in a scolding manner, but the sound was as kindly as his smile. "Did you intend to pine away here during the whole of the Christmas season?"

I looked down, refusing to answer him. "How did you get in here?"

"I went to the dorm mother's apartment and spoke with her. She let me in about an hour ago, and will probably be checking back soon. You were sleeping so soundly . . .” His sentence trailed off. He stood upright, abruptly, and rubbed his hands together. “Wait just a moment.”

He disappeared into the kitchen and returned very shortly with a tray of food. “Eat this while we are talking,” he said, settling it on my lap.

There was an omelet cooked with cheese and mushrooms and tomatoes, a hot cereal of some kind, and a hot drink that looked like molasses.

“Postum,” he laughed, “it’s a cereal drink and will be good for you.”

It all tasted delicious. But in between bites I realized I was answering his questions.

“Martha thought, I suppose everyone thought, you were going with this—” he fumbled a little—”Emory fellow to spend the holiday in South Carolina—”

“Martha wanted to believe that. She made it plain that it pleased her to have me—” I almost snarled “out of the way,” but caught myself and said only “gone!”

He raised his fine eyebrows, but did not contradict or scold me. “Were you ever really planning to go with him?”

“I told him *no* from the beginning.”

I saw the pleasure he could not contain seep into his eyes and tug at the curve of his mouth.

“Well. But why did you let everyone believe that was what you were doing?”

“I have my reasons,” I replied, aware of how stubborn my voice sounded, and how illogical my words were. But I refused to say more.

He took the tray from me. “I’ll be back tomorrow, in the afternoon, to check on you. Mrs. Craig said that I might.” He stood looking down at me, blonde and slender, achingly healthy and alive. “I thought if you’re feeling good enough I might read to you for a while.”

I said nothing.

“Sunday morning I’ll be back to take you to Martha’s.”

I opened my mouth to protest, but he was more nimble than I.

“I will be here, and you will come with me, and that is all there is to it. Do not waste your strength by trying to argue.”

“I do not wish to go—I have a right . . .”

He waved his hand at me, brushing aside my futile emotions. "It would be morbid for you to stay in this room over Christmas, and you know it." He took a few steps closer to me and his eyes narrowed, holding my reluctant gaze. "Martha needs you, and that is a fact. And so—you are going to go."

He turned and left the room. I could hear him rattling around in the kitchen for what seemed like a long time. Then his voice called out of the emptiness, "See you tomorrow afternoon, Augustine. I will lock the door when I leave. Try to get some sleep . . ."

His voice trailed off. I heard the click of the front door, then the heavy, unpleasant silence of an empty apartment. I sank back against the rumpled sheets. I did not know what I felt. I could not isolate or identify any of the many emotions churning inside me. I closed my eyes and buried my face into the pillow. My head was still too tired and fuzzy to think about Hans Bekker and what had happened. I would rest, only for a little while. The food had made me feel stronger, I could tell. After just a few minutes I would sort things, face things. That was the last thought that came to me before sleep blacked everything out.

I awoke to the sound of someone calling my name, insistently, over and over again. I struggled to answer, fighting a heavy gray torpor that would not allow my eyes to open. When at last my conscious self emerged, I blinked a few times and realized I was staring up into the plain, almost expressionless face of Mrs. Craig, the dorm mother, who had never bothered much with any of us except to reprimand one or another who had broken some rule. She put on a weak smile, like something she had selected from a box marked "Appropriate Expressions" which she kept in her drawer.

"I think you were dreaming," she said.

I nodded and rubbed my eyes. I certainly *had* been dreaming, and the dream had drained me more than any fever could.

"Are you feeling any better?"

"I think I am," I mumbled. And it was true.

"Well, good." She stood back on her heels and folded her arms across her chest. "It's a new day, did you know it? You've slept straight through the night."

"Have you been here before?" I asked.

"Half a dozen times or more, checking in on you, but you never moved a hair, even once when I turned the light on."

"I'm sorry to be so much trouble," I mumbled.

The stiff smile softened. "Goodness, I don't mind. Most times the girls can do well, and better, without me—and are happy to let me know it. It isn't often I have a chance to do something for one of you."

I swallowed a sudden lump in my throat. Why was I always so quick to judge people, to shut myself off from them? I returned her smile. "Thank you," I said. "Then, is it Saturday?"

"Yes, but Dr. Bekker won't be here for a few more hours, and I'll tell him not to come if you'd rather not have him." She leaned a bit forward, arms folded still, and regarded me with care. "Hans Bekker's a good man, and my family knows him personally, but, he hasn't done anything . . . inappropriate, has he? You would tell me?"

I nodded. "I would tell you," I promised. "He has always behaved like a gentleman with me—nothing improper, nothing . . ."

She nodded, satisfied. "He's a bit of an idol on campus, isn't he? But that can't be helped. He's a great man, a rare man, that's all there is to it."

"Do you know much about his life?"

She shook her head. "He's close-mouthed when it comes to what he suffered in Germany. I know his childhood sweetheart was killed in a bombing, and I think his father was shot by the Russians. I guess it was a miracle the way his family got out of the country." Her eyes were gentle with sympathy, but she wasn't much help.

"I'd like to take a shower," I said.

"Fine. I'll have some breakfast ready for you by the time you're out."

"No, please don't trouble yourself, I—"

"It's done," she said, "and no trouble. I'll be back in forty-five minutes." She swept out of the room, shutting the door of the apartment firmly. I leaned back and sighed.

"You never let people help you," Armand used to say to me. "And that is not good. You believe it is pride or independence which prevents you, but it is fear, my little one, fear left over from the war days."

It was a reprimand, but he would always kiss my cheek when he said it, and then end with a tease. "When are you going to grow up, *ma chérie?* You pout and look just like the little four-year-old with chubby legs I carried on my back up the hill."

I looked up at his picture of the Seine, green and gray and golden against my wall, and did not even try to hold back the tears.

∾

When Dr. Bekker came I was dressed and waiting, and looking human again.

"You're looking much brighter," he said, and his pleasure was obvious. Judy Craig let him in with her key. "Would you like to stay for the story?" he asked her. "I'm reading the Christmas scene from *Little Women.*"

She was obviously surprised at his choice.

"I am sure Augustine has never read Louisa May Alcott before," he reminded her.

"Yes, and it is a heart-warming story," she remembered.

I wondered if Dr. Bekker thought my heart needed warming. It was a strange thing he had said: "Martha needs you, and so you are going."

Sister Craig decided to stay, and I wasn't sorry. My dream of the hard-faced German soldiers had a strange effect upon me where he was concerned. I felt not shy of him, but actually wary, distrustful in some deep, intuitive sense which I knew was absurd, and which I knew also distressed him. But when I looked upon his gentle, finely-moulded face I saw the taut, coarse lines of those German faces that had burst into my home, bringing red snarling fire and the sharp taste of mindless, covetous anger, fed by hatred and rage.

"Here, Augustine, tuck this around your legs." Sister Craig, in her narrow, efficient way was mothering me. I smiled my thanks, aware that *he* was watching me, and sensing something.

I settled in. "Thank you. Well . . ." I turned my eyes briefly toward Hans Bekker. "We're ready."

He opened the book and began reading the hilarious scene in which the four sisters gather and share their hopes and complaints with each other. Jo quickly became my favorite: wanting to be the man of the house and go off to the army, acting brusque and undignified to hide the gentler emotions within her. I understood that. With the cadence of Hans Bekker's voice enhancing the tone of the story, we all three fell under the spell. I forgot my own sufferings as I yearned over theirs, touched to tears by their desire to please Marmee before themselves. But when she gathered her daughters around her and read the letter written by their father—lonely and miserable, beset by suffering and the cruelties of war—I thought my heart would break, and I had to fight hard to keep back the tears.

This was too close to home for me, and Hans Bekker knew it. I looked up once and met his eyes and saw such tenderness there, such unmitigated compassion, that something inside me melted and relaxed into peace. "Tell them I think of them by day, pray for them by night, and find my best comfort in their affection at all times," the loving father wrote. And his little women were moved to do all in their power to warrant his love, to overcome any petty, selfish weaknesses which kept them from being all he would wish them to be. When I saw Sister Craig wipe unashamedly at her eyes, I was relieved to be able to do the same.

"There are more parallels in this, more symbolism than one would imagine," Hans Bekker said quietly, as he closed the cover on the book. He knew I would think about that, try to put it all together in my mind; I could see in his eyes that he did.

It was with many a sigh and kindly word that the two rose and left me. But for the first time since Thursday morning when I arrived home sick to an empty apartment I did not feel alone. And for the first time the coming of Christmas seemed a reality, and something to look forward to. A gentle spirit lingered with me, soothed me, upheld me. And I knew, though I did not wish to acknowledge it, that it was not only the spirit of Josephine March and her sisters that spoke to my heart.

Chapter

16

It was a frosty afternoon when we drove to Salt Lake, with a new layer of snow, like a clean white eiderdown, spread over everything. The sun, weak and pale after a long day of battling against wind and ice, sank with a thin rosy shiver along the horizon, and the night shadows stirred. Twilight had always created a deep, empty loneliness within me, and I felt it now, and was grateful for the warm safety of the car, that could move through the gloom unscathed, and for the calm strength of the man who sat silent beside me.

At length I broke the silence and said, "Tell me more about Anja."

He did not even glance at me as he began to speak, yet I knew that his thoughts and feelings were trained upon my heart with the same intense light that his eyes reflected when he looked into mine.

"My older sister, Gudrun, is Anja's mother. Actually, she is my half-sister. My father was married to her mother when he was a very young man, and that wife died of complications shortly after Gudrun's birth. I was the eldest of my mother and father's children—"

"And how much later did they marry?" I interrupted.

"Six years later. Gudrun is nine years older than I." He paused, and I had the feeling he was recalling places and experiences he had not thought about for a long time.

"When she was just seventeen, Gudrun went to stay with friends of her mother who lived in the United States. She attended school in Boston, met a young man named Douglas Bates, and married him early in 1939. It was impossible at that time for any of us to come here and be with her. My father was in the army, Germany had already seized Austria and Czechoslovakia, and we were on the verge of war with France and Britain."

He threw me a sideward glance. "You know all that. But, back to Anja. Her father went with the Allied forces to Italy in 1943, was at Normandy in '44, and thence to Germany, where he was made a prisoner of war until Germany's surrender to the Allies in May of '45. He hated the German people. When he went back home, wounded, emaciated, worn down in spirit, he taught that hatred to his little six-year-old daughter."

"But her mother was German," I exploded.

"He did not see it that way." Hans Bekker's shoulders seemed to sag and droop as he continued. "He had met her at an American university; to him she was a bright, pretty American student with the added allure of a charming accent."

"And how did Gudrun handle all of this?"

"With patience and wisdom. She loved him very much. She was ashamed of what the Nazis had done, not only to other countries, but to her own. She realized that it was best and safest for her to be thought of as an American. A few years after the war Douglas was offered a good job in California and the family moved west. And all Anja learned as she grew up was the self-indulgence of the monied class, the California fun ethic, and this old hatred for the country which was her fatherland."

His words held a quiet, matter-of-fact sorrow, as though he had gazed unflinchingly at every harsh, ugly truth and come to terms with it, somehow maintaining his own faith, somehow never succumbing to either bitterness or self-pity.

"So you are her uncle," I thought out loud, "and you come from Germany and carry the taint." Then it struck me, all of a sudden. "You are *the* uncle, the one she refers to with such spite, but refuses to talk about." I was astonished. "She knew all the time—

when Penelope and I went to the play with you and Professor Barnes. It seems strange that she would never let on at all."

We were approaching the city, and I noticed that he did not move the car in the direction of Martha's house; but I held my peace, not wanting to jeopardize the conversation we were having.

"Anja has further reason for . . . for hating me. She was not qualified academically to get into the Y, nor were her standards of behavior above suspicion." He was speaking carefully, choosing his words. "I intervened for her, though I was far from comfortable in doing so." He hazarded a real look at me now, wishing me to understand, I knew, what he was trying to say to me. "I have a sterling reputation here, hard-won, and of great value to me. I am still a single man, and that is a somewhat uncomfortable thing to be in our LDS society." His mouth twisted into a wry half-smile. "But I intervened, just the same. With conditions."

I put my hand up to my mouth. "Then you are the one who forbade her to associate with certain of her old friends."

"For her own protection—she has handicaps enough."

I nodded. "I know. But . . ."

"But what?" He was sharp, he could always sense things in me.

We turned the corner onto North Temple and he slowed the car and eased it into an empty parking space.

"What are we doing?" I asked, grateful for the interruption.

"There is a concert here which begins—" He glanced at his wristwatch, "in less than ten minutes. I thought you would enjoy it—just an hour or so, then we'll go on to Martha's."

We walked briskly to the silver-domed building, catching fleeting glimpses of black tree branches, some wearing strings of lights, through the mottled movement of crowds of people, all solemn and reverent. There was no time for conversation. We slid into a seat and gave ourselves up to the pure beauty of the music as the choir sang carol after carol. I was transported by some to times in my childhood, memories and feelings that were mine alone but in some sense universal; for nothing unites mankind as does the life of the Man who is Savior of all. Near the end of the program they sang a selection in German, O *du fröhliche*, both joyful and dignified, surprising me by its power to move me. Glancing at Dr. Bekker I could see there were tears in his eyes, and the intensity of his emotion brought tears to my own.

When we walked back onto the square the hush of peace and

wonder was still upon us. We walked in silence, stood before the statues of Joseph and Hyrum, paused to gaze at the life-sized crèche set under the cold stars, drawn to ponder upon the humble infant as the shepherds and wise men had been.

We drove to Martha's in silence too precious to destroy with a return to common conversation. And, as before, I felt a reluctance to sacrifice this rare pleasure of spirit for the inevitable let-down of ordinary and mundane things.

∞

It was all right. Martha was truly happy to see me. I had not mustered up enough courage to ask Hans Bekker what he had meant when he said, "Martha needs you," but that, in itself, strengthened me now. The children tugged me away, as soon as we entered, to show me the tree and the wrapped gifts beneath it, and to see what I had brought. Martha never scolded me, nor even questioned me; I was here, and I was getting better, and both things were good. Hans Bekker spent the night at the home of friends he had, somewhere up by the University of Utah, and Martha put me to bed early. The next morning was Christmas Eve Day! We were caught up in last-minute baking and wrapping of presents, and neighbors stopping in with small offerings and staying to talk. It was very pleasant for me: warmth and kindness, fragrant smells, beautiful things to look at, the sense of anticipation, against a background of Christmas music on the hi-fi and children's excited voices and laughter.

We ate a large Christmas Eve dinner by candlelight: Martha, Ellen, Roger, Hans Bekker, and myself. Then we retired to the living room and sat round the shining tree singing carols and reading the story of the Christ child from the scriptures.

Martha seemed more quiet than usual, but I had thought nothing of that, until suddenly, as Hans Bekker read the words, "But Mary kept all these things and pondered them in her heart," she burst into tears, covering her face with her hands and running out of the room. Hans stopped in mid-word and for a moment her cry trembled almost palpably in the air around us. Ellen had tears in her eyes. Roger gazed at me solemnly, his own eyes wide and dark.

"It's Daddy," he explained, in his little man's voice. "She misses Daddy. She does this when she can't stand it any more."

"I understand, Roger," I said, pulling him close to me. Hans Bekker moved his hand in a motioning gesture and Ellen flew to him, settling herself on his lap. Then we proceeded, slowly, achingly—for what other choice had we but to succumb, each one of us, to loneliness and pain. Bit by bit the former spirit returned, sweet and soothing, and we relaxed under its influence and gained the strength to go on. When we knelt in prayer I felt strongly that the poor young man, deprived of living day to day with his beautiful children and watching them grow, was near—yearning tenderly over them, loving them with a purity we could not understand.

Hans helped me settle Ellen and Roger into their beds. The door to Martha's room remained closed. As he took his leave of me and went out into the night, he caught up both my hands and held them gently in his. "Help her, Augustine," he said.

"I don't know how," I protested, feeling a panic inside. "I do not know what she needs."

His eyes grew wide and wondering. "She needs the one thing that can do any good, Augustine. She needs love." The word as he spoke it, in all its purity and power, surged through me, filling my whole being with light. "And you know more of love than you realize."

He let go of my hands and opened the door. The frosty stillness of the night poured over us, cleansing, almost hallowed.

"Good night, and God bless you, Augustine."

He turned and walked to his car. I closed the door upon him, turned and walked up the stairs, pausing briefly before the shut door before I knocked, waited a moment longer, and then walked quietly in.

Christmas morning is for children. Hans arrived early, just as Ellen and Roger were waking, and led them blindfolded in to the tree to see the things Santa had brought them. The American Santa Claus is very different from the Saint who visits the children of Europe, and the effusion of store-bought toys, bright and expensive, overwhelmed my vision and imagination as much as it did theirs. While they were still squealing in delight over new wonders and discoveries, Hans Bekker led me into the kitchen and, with a nod of his head, indicated the telephone where it hung, black and gleaming, against the wall.

"Phone your mother," he said, "My gift to you."

I looked down, too overcome to meet his gaze, knowing protest would not avail me. He put his hand on my shoulder. "In France the day is growing old," he said. "Your mother is thinking of you. Hurry." He turned and left the room, shutting the door behind him. With trembling fingers I reached for the phone.

⚮

The day went quickly. Happy hours always seem shorter and more compressed. I felt a bit weak and light in the head, but not ill still. But it seemed something inside me had changed. My experience with Hans Bekker on Temple Square, my conversation with Martha, the precious moments spent listening again to my mother's thin, tender voice—all had their part in breaking down what was petty and selfish, blind and unfeeling within me. My own spirit had expanded, somehow, and I felt stronger and wiser and humbler, all at the same time. I could not explain how I felt, but I cherished the rare gifts the last hours had given me.

I spent the next two days with Martha. We were able to speak more freely to each other again. We never discussed Hans Bekker directly, never mentioned his name. We did not mention directly the man she had loved who had died and left her. We spoke instead about fear and pain and a woman's lonely suffering, and the ways of a woman's needs. And at last of love. And, in the end, without saying it, each of us knew the commitment of friendship and love and loyalty the other had made.

On Wednesday morning when Martha answered the phone and handed it to me with a grin, I was not altogether surprised to hear a familiar voice drawl, "Hey"—the Southern greeting for the usual American "Hi." "How are you this morning, honey-dear?"

Smooth as new cream was Emory's voice. I laughed back at him, amazed to realize I could miss him, and happy to listen to his cajoling chatter. "See what you'ar missin', Snow White?" he would interject now and again. I looked up horrified when Martha pointed at the clock. We had been talking for over an hour. Humoring my concern as he would that of a charming but unschooled child, he stretched the conversation out another fifteen minutes before, with half a dozen tender, somewhat outlandish endearments, he said good-bye. Was I foolish enough to anticipate seeing

him again? I laughed at my own pleasure, enjoying his devotion
and flattery even if I did choose to take them more lightly than
other girls might.

Friday morning Martha drove me back to Provo. I spent a few
hours straightening the apartment, even doing a little light house-
work. Near evening Penelope arrived. We sat up much later than
we ought to have talking about our holiday experiences and giggling over the attentions of an old boyfriend she had run into at
home. The next morning we would leave early for Timphaven and
a day of skiing. Hans Bekker had been a bit reluctant in allowing
me to participate. But I had promised to spend only an hour or two
on the slopes, not letting myself get over tired or fevered, or ex-
posed to too much bright sunlight.

"I'll spend most of the day in the lodge," I cajoled him, "finishing *Little Women* and writing letters; safe, domestic activities."

With a strangely endearing grin which I could not interpret,
he had permitted me to go.

Chapter

17

"Augustine, don't leave yet!" Penelope called to me.

I looked over my shoulder and waited for her to ski over to where I stood, reluctantly turned back toward the tram. It was mid-afternoon. The sky had lost the warm blue of morning, but the air was only brisk, not bitter. After a break for lunch when we all ate soup and hot bread, I had stayed in the lodge until I could no longer bear it. My morning foray on the slopes had been only sufficient to whet my appetite, so Penelope and I had talked Dr. Bekker into a second session, which was dragging out longer and longer.

I turned my skis. "Once more."

Penelope grinned. "Follow me."

She was not easy to follow, and I could soon see she was heading for the most difficult slope I had attempted that day. She skied often, and I had only done so several times over the past few years. I would take it slowly, let her fly down at her practiced pace and laugh at me a little for my caution.

My full concentration was claimed by controlling my own progress, avoiding grooves cut in the packed powder, watching for rocks and moguls and other skiers. It all happened too fast; I could never have told anyone afterward just what happened. At one point I curved round a stump and looked up to see a jumble of skis and boots and bodies only feet away from me, right in my path. I veered instinctively, and I nearly made it around. But I think the tip of one of my skis caught the edge of a pole or boot or something, and I went down—in a slow motion dive that left me breathless and choking and tangled.

I lifted my head, struggling to untwist the awkward angles of my body. From close by I could hear cries and a muffled scream and the terrible sounds of panic and confusion. Straight in my line of vision I recognized Penelope's scarlet ski cap, then her face, looking white and pinched into tight painful lines. "I think her leg's broken!" someone shouted. I could hear her moaning; a soft, pitiful sound. My head felt dizzy and my ears were ringing. A terrible panic rose in my throat, and I choked it down, struggling to rise again.

Then came the howl of a siren, high-pitched and eerie, and more voices, masculine voices, loud and urgent. And the snow was cold and I was trembling, and it was dark under the trees here, but in the small room there were explosions of light and sound, and men shouting terrible things at us, and suddenly *he* was bent over me, the muscles of his face tight and drawn, his eyes narrow and angry, his blond disheveled hair brushing my forehead. He reached out to touch me and I screamed. I screamed with the agonizing release of seventeen years of pent-up terror, a child's uncomprehending encounter with brutality and evil.

"Don't touch me! Don't touch me!" I screamed it again and again. I could see my father slumped over in his chair and there was blood on his face. I saw my mother go down onto her knees as a soldier struck her. "Don't let him touch me! Don't let him hurt me! Please! Please!" I whimpered the words like a helpless and overwrought child. I writhed and struggled, trying to escape the nightmare.

The face of the German soldier drew back. Someone else lifted me, wrapped me in blankets. Someone was lifting my father's body, limp as a rag doll, and my mother clung to him, brushing his hair back from his forehead, kissing his frozen face. I was crying, sobbing pitifully like a child. I was lost, engulfed in the desolation of a reality that would no longer stay hidden. All I can remember is that as they carried me down the mountain I was calling for my mother over and over again.

❧

They took any of us who had more than a scratch all the way down the mountain to the hospital. I lay on a white bed like a table in an examining room in the emergency section. It took hours, it took years, it took a lifetime, unreal and suspended. They covered me with a blanket and said something about shock. I remember repeating one thing again and again, "Don't let him in, don't let anyone in!" The faces of the nurses and doctors wore worried expressions. They monitored my vital signs for several hours. But all that was really the matter with me that could be measured by medical wisdom was a sprained wrist. And even that, happily, was my left wrist, so I could still brush my hair, put on my makeup, write my school lessons.

When they released me from the hospital my dorm mother was there to drive me back to the apartment. She spoke very little, but I felt she was watching me closely. She confirmed what my tortured mind had heard: Penelope's leg was broken in the mash-up, which was caused in part by a hidden mogul, in part by some amateurs attempting a slope that was beyond them—in part, I wondered, by Penelope's going too fast. It did not matter. It had happened. For everyone involved it was a small, exciting trauma which would make wonderful telling for the rest of their lives. Penelope's injury was apparently the worst one sustained, though Judy Craig thought there had been a couple of broken arms mixed in there somewhere. It had happened. For me it meant the harsh and sudden falling away of a terrible, confusing darkness, and the revelation of a tortured truth, ugly and terrible to dwell upon.

When Sister Craig finally left me alone in the apartment I took the phone off the hook. Penelope would not be home until tomorrow and, since school did not start until Tuesday, the rest of the girls would most likely not straggle in until Monday night. Hopefully, Martha had heard nothing of this. I was alone and safe. At least for the time being, at least long enough to—long enough to what? Is this what I really wanted? In this intimate, lonely seclusion could I bear the weight of what I had learned?

I slept, watched the little cracker box television that belonged to Sally, and tried to read, and let the pain pills dull my awareness. Once or twice I let my mind stop and dwell upon that day in my childhood, but I could not stay there for long. Not now. Not yet.

It was a shock when Penelope arrived with Sister Craig late Sunday afternoon. She was breathless and shining, though a little pale yet, and complaining good-naturedly about the cast on her leg.

"I believe all the students who are on campus for whatever reason heard about what happened," she said, lowering herself onto the sofa with Mrs. Craig's help. "We had a constant stream of visitors, some with cards and candy."

Sister Craig smiled indulgently. "Well, you'll have to rest up, now you're home." She turned and glanced at me, and her brow furrowed into lines of concern. "You and Augustine can help one another." She took a step or two closer. "You don't look well, my dear."

"Oh, it's my fault!" Penelope wailed. "No one knows it, but *I* talked her into going down one more slope with me. You probably have double pneumonia after lying up there on the ice! I'm sorry, Augustine!"

I shook my head at her and tried to smile. "Don't be silly, I'm fine."

"Maybe you bumped your head or something when you fell," she persisted. "The doctors were worried about shock. Are you sure you're all right?"

"Well, I suggest both of you take it easy until classes begin," Sister Craig said. "No more excitement, Penelope."

Penelope nodded her head obediently.

"I'll bring a meal in to you tonight, and—"

"That's not necessary," I protested, but she more or less ignored me.

"I'll see you about seven. And it wouldn't bother me to find you both sleeping."

She smiled as she left, and Penelope sighed as she shut the door. "Sister Craig is much nicer than I ever thought," she confessed.

"Yes, I know," I agreed.

"I'm sorry you've been here all alone," she continued, then bent down and began digging through the big hospital bag she had brought in with her. "Look, I've got something here for you."

She pulled out a package wrapped in paper and tied with a bow. A card was taped on the outside. I took it gingerly.

"It's from Dr. Bekker," Penelope cried. "He's very worried about you."

I removed the card and handed the package back to her. "Open it for me," I asked. "You have two good hands."

My fingers were trembling; I rested my hands in my lap, beneath the folds of my skirt, and waited.

"It's a book," she said, "of course." Then, "Oh, how very lovely."

She held it out to me. It was a hardbound copy of *Little Women*, beautifully illustrated. I had been reading Hans Bekker's book, the one he had read from right here in this room only days ago—but that was *before*, and all was different now.

We thumbed through it together, exclaiming over the pictures. "Look, he's signed it," she said.

The inscription, in his precise, recognizable handwriting, was simple: "To Augustine, who shares and understands . . . Hans Bekker, December 1957."

Penelope glanced up at me. "You look pale, Augustine."

"I'm all right." I took the book and stood up.

"I think you ought to lie down. Go on, now! I'm fine here on this couch, if you'll just hand me that book from my bag."

I did as she urged. Once the door closed behind me the hot tears spilled down my cheeks. Holding the envelope steady with my bandaged hand I worked out the card with my good hand and opened it. "What is it, Augustine?" Dr. Bekker had written. "The things I saw in your face have disturbed me deeply, have frightened me. Please talk to me! Please let me help you!"

I put the card away from me and drew a ragged breath. I knew I must sometime confront him, but I did not know how I could do it, could ever bear to be in his presence, to look upon his fair, Aryan features again!

I threw myself upon the bed and lay there, trembling and fevered, but I did not sleep.

ജ

"Thanks for not telling my uncle our little secret," Anja said, pouring milk over my cereal for me. It was Tuesday morning and we were all late and hurried, trying to get back into the routine of school days again.

"Coming back to two handicapped roommates doesn't help," Clara complained. But her eyes were sparkling and it was easy to see she loved to have someone so close at hand to fuss over and care for. Nancy merely worked around this new encumbrance, in her usual brisk and efficient manner.

I blinked up at Anja, surprised by her sudden, blunt statement.

"Why did you call him, Anja?" I had to ask, now that she had brought up the matter. "Why did you risk so much?"

"I knew he was the only one who could get through to you." Blunt and straightforward again, but her eyes held much more that remained unsaid. I wondered what she would think if I told her what had happened to me, what I suspected. She would be my advocate in a way no one else could be. For a moment or two I was tempted, but the weakness passed.

There was an energetic knocking at the door, and I knew it was Emory come to drive both myself and Penelope to campus. His gallant services would be a godsend now. He had called very late the night before, having just dragged in, tired from driving sixteen straight hours on the last leg of his trip. He was somewhat amused by the story of our mishap.

"If you'd come with me, where you belonged," he scolded smugly, "this would not have happened, Snow White."

It was an innocent tease on his part, but it distressed me. *Much more* had happened than anyone knew. Was it meant to be, or had I disturbed what ought to have remained hidden by my pride and my insufferable standards?

"Well, Ah'm here to take care of you now," he had crooned, and I could tell that the prospect pleased him.

When I opened the door he pulled me into his arms and kissed me—right there with the whole apartment watching.

"Do that again," Sally cooed, and at the same time Clara scolded, "You stop that right now, Emory!" And everyone laughed.

"How Ah've missed you—how Ah've missed this," Emory whispered.

The depth of my response to him took my breath away. He looked so handsome, so big, so alive! There was nothing of mystery about him, nothing of pain and suffering, nothing dark or hidden. He was overwhelmingly male, overwhelmingly appealing, and overwhelmingly in love with me. I pressed my lips against his cheek.

"I'm glad you're here, Emory," I murmured. "I'm glad that you love me still."

⁂

All day while I was on campus I felt tense and nervous, glancing over my shoulder to see if anyone followed me, or peering intently into the crowds of students and teachers crossing and crisscrossing my path. I was terrified at the prospect of running into *him*. I could not face him; yet something in me longed to confront him! I needed *answers*, no matter how painful I might find them.

Wednesday I did not go to class, giving Penelope the excuse that Tuesday had worn me out, and I intended to sleep in.

"I'll explain to Dr. Bekker," she said, but she looked at me strangely. Even the sound of his name spoken out loud made me shudder, and I turned quickly away.

When we met at the library that afternoon she gave me the day's assignment and caught me up on the things that had been covered during class time. "There's this, too," she said, and handed me a note, folded over, with my name written on it. I slipped it into my book and did not read it until later that evening. "You are torturing yourself, Augustine," it said. "No matter what this is, come to me. You cannot keep running away."

I sat holding the paper, feeling sick inside. Of course he was right. But could I do it? I recoiled from the encounter, knowing beforehand the inevitable pain and anger and remembrance that would be an unavoidable part of it. I felt weak just thinking about it.

I was contemplating missing Friday's class, too, but Penelope was ahead of me.

"Tomorrow he's outlining the term paper we have to write," she said, as we were getting ready for bed the night before. "And there will be a penalty for anyone who misses class without the most ironclad excuse."

I have that, I thought. *And he knows it.*

"Please come, Augustine," she said, touching my shoulder. "You don't want to get behind and mess up your grade and make everything harder."

She left me no choice. Emory drove us to campus early, and I helped Penelope walk up the path, which was rough with patches of ice and crusted, uneven snow. As we entered the building she said, "I've been sitting in the front where I can stretch out my leg and lay down my crutches without tripping anybody."

I had no logical reason to object. We had sat near the front since the beginning, ensuring ourselves a good view of the handsome Hans Bekker. I sat down beside her. My hands felt cold and clammy. I rubbed them along my skirt and fidgeted nervously with my books and papers. When he entered the room my eyes looked up at him, automatically, of their own accord. My head went hot and the room felt suddenly so close and stuffy that I could not breathe. He launched right into an explanation and discussion of the topics we could write on and how our papers should be organized, and I kept busy taking notes. But the sense of suffocation did not leave me, and I began to fear that I would faint—right there in front of him and everyone else.

Suddenly he shut his book and said, "That will do for today. You have more than enough to keep yourselves occupied. Class dismissed early." There began an immediate rustling of papers and shuffling of feet. He coughed into the microphone. "I would like Miss Mousset to remain for a few moments."

He had made the announcement so everyone could hear it, and I was trapped. Penelope began gathering her things together. "I'll manage just fine," she assured me. "I did this without you Wednesday, remember?" It was an ordinary enough request to make and would excite no special interest. Many of the students knew of the accident on the mountain and perhaps had noticed my earlier absence from class.

The room emptied slowly. I sat with my head down, ostensibly glancing through papers. I could feel the rapid, almost painful pounding of my heart. As the last stragglers filed off, he walked casually behind, holding the door for the last of them, then carefully pushing the lock into place as he closed it securely.

He returned slowly. I listened as his footsteps approached me, still not looking up. He stopped while he was yet some distance off.

"Whatever this is," he began, "I know it is going to be most painful for you. You have been suffering so terribly already that I dismissed the class early in fear for you."

I should have known!

"Augustine," he said, "tell me."

"I don't know if I can," I said, still not looking at him. "I do not know how to begin."

He drew a deep breath, and it sounded ragged and painful. "Begin by telling me what it was you remembered that caused you to look up into my face with such terror and loathing."

His words threw open the floodgates.

"*It was your face!*" I cried. "It was the face of the German soldier! I had never remembered before—the dream always stopped short of what really happened. But when you reached to touch me I remembered the German soldier who grabbed me and hurt me . . ." Tears were choking my throat and making speech impossible. I gulped them down, determined to go on. "The German soldier who killed my father—I saw him plainly. He looked exactly like you!"

The silence that followed was worse than the most terrible screaming, worse than oaths and recriminations and wild, angry words.

"Merciful heaven!" he muttered suddenly. "I knew it would be something horrible, perhaps unthinkable, that had happened, but I never imagined this!"

He stood where he was, perfectly straight, unmoving. I lifted my eyes and looked at him, though not meeting his gaze. With great effort he moved, drew his wallet from his pocket, and took out a small photograph, which he held out to me. As I took it I noticed that his whole hand was trembling. I held it up to my gaze and uttered a low, anguished cry. The man in the picture was tall and thin. He wore a trimmed moustache, and his lean face was handsome. He stood to attention, straight as a ramrod, in the starched, impeccable uniform of a German soldier.

"My father," he said. "There has always been a most remarkable resemblance between us."

I drew in my breath, and it burned into my lungs. He was right. I would have sworn it was Hans Bekker himself staring at me so solemnly out of the frozen photograph.

"I have no record of my father's precise movements," he continued with painful exactness, "but he did enter France during the blitzkrieg—at the time you speak of—at the time . . ." He could go no further. He covered his face with his hands. As he slowly removed them he dropped down onto his knees, so that his face was on a level with mine. He was still at a long, safe distance from me, yet his pain reached out and touched me like a scorch of flame searing clear through me.

"No! It is of no use!" I cried. "I saw what I saw."

He began despite me, slowly, carefully. "To believe that my father could have been in your village, could have entered your house—" he paused, as though readjusting the weight of what he was thinking, what he was saying—"seems incredible, yet conceivable. But to believe that he could have harmed you, an innocent child! could have killed a fellowman within the sacred walls of his own home!" His voice was rising, strive as he might to control it. *"No! This could not have been!"*

I shook my head, denying his words, denying the pain, the fervent conviction in them.

"I knew my father!" he cried. "What you say is impossible."

I rose, clutching my books to me. I must somehow get past him.

"Augustine, please! There must be some other explanation, there must—"

I looked upon him with a growing horror. "How could I have cared for you, how could I have been drawn to a man in whose veins runs the blood of a vile and heartless murderer!"

As I spoke the word he reached out and grabbed my wrist. "My father was never a murderer!" His voice was trembling, seething with anger, abhorrence, entreaty. "He was a soldier, just as your brothers were soldiers, just as the fathers of France were soldiers."

I pulled away from him, biting back the scream that quivered on my lips. "It happened—I was there! No matter what you think, no matter what you wish, *it is true!*" I pushed up the sleeve of my blouse to reveal the scar which ran along the inside of my arm. "I have the mark of his bullet," I said, "to remind me for the rest of my life how true it is!"

He rose to his feet. He drew back from me, as though I had struck him a death blow. He seemed to shrink where he stood.

"Let me go!" I cried.

He turned and walked to the door and unlocked it and stood aside for me to pass.

"I cannot leave you to yourself in such anguish, Augustine," he cried out as I approached him.

But I could not bear a nearness to him; something inside me went crazy. "You cannot help me," I stammered. "Don't you see? You will never be able to help me again!"

I stumbled into the hall, down the stairs, and out of the building, refusing to look back, refusing to acknowledge the terrible pain that reached after me.

Chapter

18

For the next few weeks I lived in some kind of a twilight between both worlds: the realities of my childhood that were more literal and powerful now than they ever had been; and the commonplace, nagging demands of a life that did not seem to belong to me, that seemed incompatible with all that mattered most deeply; immaterial, of little consequence now.

I could not have made it through that time without Emory. His sane, uncomplicated normalcy was the one life-line I could cling to as I struggled to restore my own balance. No one knew what I was going through; not even him. He would not have been any greater help for the knowing; perhaps even less. Penelope had been too close to it all; she sensed that something was happening, and I believe Hans Bekker had told her to be especially kind and watchful of me, but no more. And I don't believe he told Martha even that much. Her concern, when she learned of the accident, reflected nothing more than was common. I was grateful for that. Only *he* knew, and in almost every way I was able to avoid him, to put him out of my mind.

I had taken to sitting in the back of his classroom now. Penelope, confused and begrudging, sat with me. Many days I could avoid seeing his face altogether, positioning myself so that other students blocked my view. One thing only I could not avoid or escape: the sound of his voice. And even though at times it grated along the unprotected surface of my spirit, abrasive and painful, it still held a strange attraction for me, a power over my consciousness and emotions.

Each day was a struggle. But some time in each day I would spend with Emory—be soothed by him, spoiled by him, admired by him. And so, day by day, I got through.

One strange thing happened which was inexplicable to me. After that day on the mountain my nightmare never returned again. At first I had many nights been reluctant to fall asleep, fearful of what might happen; but no dreams disturbed my peace. My waking hours had become nightmarish now, haunted as they were by phantoms of the past whose cruel, distorting fingers had reached into my present, disordering and entangling the two. My spirit was more bruised and weakened than the hand I had begun to exercise and force back into use again. The spirit does not comply quite so readily to the brain's demands. The spirit is its own substance and breathes and moves on a high plane where human reasoning cannot always follow.

⚭

One morning in late January I awoke to someone shaking me violently. I half-opened my eyes to see Anja bent over my bed, her eyes frightened and swimming with tears.

"Wake up, Augustine!" Her voice was a desperate whisper. "Something's happened. Could you please take me to the hospital?"

I rubbed my eyes and sat up rather abruptly.

"It's my friend. She's gone into insulin shock and they have her at emergency." She pushed back her uncombed hair with a shaking hand.

"We can use Penelope's car," I said. "I know where her keys are and I don't think she'll mind."

"I know it's difficult for you to drive with your hand and all—"

I was mostly dressed by now, pushing my feet into the slip-on shoes I had taken to wearing since my wrist had been sprained. "It's not so bad anymore," I assured her.

We walked out into the moist, close darkness. Though the clock said it was early morning, the sun had not even begun to dissolve the black curtain of midnight and lighten the east. I shivered as I sat down against the cold vinyl seats. Anja hugged her arms to her thin body and said nothing. I eased the car out onto the deserted street. It was not far to the hospital.

"Will you keep me informed? Will you let me know if I can do anything else?" I asked.

"She'll probably lose the baby," was Anja's only answer. I reached across and laid my hand over hers. "She could die herself, you know." A shudder passed through the thin, tense girl. "I can't even imagine how scared she is."

I pulled the car up to the curb by the emergency entrance and watched Anja tug the heavy doors open and disappear into the bright, sightless interior. I drove home in a cocoon as dark and silent as the big, empty night.

All that day I fought a sense of impending doom, a depression of spirit I was certain came only from the dreary and heartless circumstances of Anja's nameless friend and her unborn child. When I had a break in classes I tried calling, but no one could locate Anja. If the girl was still there, they must have moved her from emergency to a regular ward. But I was reluctant to attempt to explain the entanglements of searching for a patient whose name I did not even know.

When I arrived home from classes there was a letter waiting for me, propped against the cookie jar where we always put mail for each other. I saw at once that it had a French postmark, and the writing was Armand's. I snatched it up and took it into my room with me, settling onto my bed and slitting the envelope carefully. What a treat this would be.

At first I read slowly, savoring each word, each small gem of thought or experience, so that it might last all the longer. Then I forgot Armand altogether; forgot everything else in the force of those few simple words—a few marks of ink on a paper that had power to pierce to the very core of my heart: "I fear I must be the one to write and tell you, ma petite, that your mère is much more seriously, much more dangerously ill than anyone knows."

I sat staring at the uniform black marks on the paper, willing myself to read on.

"She has hidden it purposefully, and well, even from Jean-Paul and Sylvie, especially from Jean-Paul and Sylvie since Sylvie began to suspect. But now I am frightened, I think she is using all her willpower just to hold on. But she is only a shadow of herself, Augustine. And—"

I could sense how hard it was for him to write this. He had even scratched a great black slash between the words, and I could see him drawing a deep breath and chewing the end of his pen. "I think you should come home."

I let the letter fall into my lap. I sat there a long time, not thinking, trying to keep the full impact of what was and what might be from invading my heart and becoming real, becoming a part of me. There was a knock on my door, which stood partially open. Clara pushed it a little and poked her head inside.

"I saw Anja at the hospital today," she said. "She asked me to tell you that her friend miscarried the baby this morning—a little girl, perfectly formed."

With great effort I raised my eyes and looked at her.

"It was terrible, Augustine!" Her beautiful eyes were velvet-soft with misery. "Karen—" she half-smiled—"that is her friend's name. Karen is still in very unstable condition. Her pancreas is not functioning as—"

She stopped herself. "Augustine, you look as if you've just seen a ghost." She walked into the room, peering at me in an unconsciously clinical manner. "What is it?"

My mouth was trembling in my effort to hold back the tears, and I could not speak. She came closer and picked up the letter from my lap. "My mother!" I managed. "Armand says she is dying."

"Oh, my poor dear," she murmured, reaching out her arms to me. Then, somehow, she was on the bed beside me, holding me tenderly, as she might hold a small child. I rested my head against her soft rounded shoulder and wept.

It required very little thought to determine that I must go home to my mother. But the question was *how*. To leave in the middle of a school term and throw away all the money and effort that had been expended on my education—I cringed at the thought. To approach Martha and ask for the price of a ticket and in the same breath tell her I was about to squander the investment she had already made in me—I was not able to even contemplate such a thing. I went to Michael and asked him to give me all the hours he could. He did not want to; he said he was worried about me.

"You already look thin and pale," he scolded kindly, "and your eyes have lost that shine I loved to see in them."

"There is no other way," I entreated.

He agreed. But obtaining more hours of work was merely a means of staving off panic, I knew.

The following morning at the close of class Dr. Bekker read off the names of half a dozen students he wished to see briefly up at his desk. Penelope and I were among them. I had every intention of ignoring the summons and leaving the room at once, but Penelope clung tight to my arm and would have made a scene if I'd pressed her. The poor girl could not comprehend the change which had come over me. She was hurt and confused. I was incapable of offering her any explanation, and at times I struggled against a livid and unjust resentment of her concern and consequent meddling in the matter.

As we approached the front of the room I hung back as far as I dared. When he had spoken to all the others, Dr. Bekker turned to us. I remained where I stood, though Penelope moved comfortably closer.

"I have heard of your problem and your mother's illness," he began, addressing me, and I knew that his eyes were upon me, but I dared not look up. I fought a terrible animal urge to fly at Penelope like a cat with her claws out, abandoning all control. How dare she interfere? How dare she expose me in this way—involve this man in my life again? I dug my nails into the soft flesh of my palms and stood still.

"Go now, Augustine, by all means," he continued. His voice was low and painful. "Martha will understand, she loves your mother and will be more than willing—"

"I am handling this my way, thank you, sir." I backed off a step or two.

"There may not be time for your way, Augustine. Go. Your teachers will all work with you."

"I think he's right," Penelope added, and her face was miserable.

I turned away and began walking swiftly down the aisle toward the exit. It would do no good to explain. I *could not* if I wanted to. I was unable to think in his presence, talk in his presence. I stalked out of the building, all too aware of how rude my behavior appeared when judged by ordinary standards, and angry at both of them for manipulating me into a situation in which I had no choice. Now it would be all the more difficult to concentrate my attentions on the tasks at hand, the demands of paying attention and thinking and learning. I felt suddenly weak and overwhelmed by what lay before me. It took all the strength I had to move woodenly, methodically through the rest of the day.

☞

Several more days passed and I noticed that the weather was warming and there was the unaccountable clean, sweet fragrance of spring in the air.

"February thaw," Emory explained. "Usually have one here about this time." He gave me a wide, lopsided grin. "It's what keeps me goin'. Otherwise us Southern boys livin' this long without sunlight would just shrivel up and blow away like dry cornhusks, honey-dear."

He could make me smile, he could make me relax, and certainly nobody else could. I had demurred from telling him about my mother. For some reason it was important for me to keep him separate from all my troubles, untouched and unweakened by them. But I had determined that this night I would tell him. He was picking me up at six, we would have a long evening together, and I would manage to say it, to talk to him somehow. Instinctively I selected a dress to wear that would complement my dark hair and light skin and make me appear feminine and appealing to him.

When we walked out together the air was so mild that I could feel it softening something within me, pushing all my burdens into some far corner to give room to this heady elixir.

He drove the car to campus and parked beside the Maeser building. "Come with me," he said, and led me by the hand along one of the narrow winding paths that spread down the long hill upon which the graceful building stood. The stillness of dusk was just descending. I could hear the high wild cry of rooks overhead. The dry branches of tree and bush rustled faintly as we brushed past. Emory's hand closed around mine was warm; I could feel life pulsing through it. We descended through the sleeping, suspended world of nature, tangled and untended, until we paused upon the arched back of a small stone bridge. He stopped and stood with his arm around me and we looked down at the sluggish remains of the brook that in spring would run free, with the gladness of pure, clear water over the rough mossy stones. I wondered sadly if my winter would end, if I would ever again feel beauty and gladness coursing through me?

I felt Emory turn me slowly to face him. He held the ring in his hand. I had forgotten how big and impressive it was. Even in the dim light of approaching evening, in this darkened spot, it glistened and shimmered with a life of its own.

"Augustine, my gentle, beautiful girl, will you marry me, please?"

He made no move to touch or persuade me. I gazed full upon his strong, firmly drawn features. He looked as splendid and imposing as a young god. Gathering all my strength, all my inner resolve, I gently removed myself from him and stepped a short distance away.

"Before I answer you," I breathed, "there is something I must tell you, something I should have told you before."

He could feel the weight of what was coming, but he had no idea of its content. The muscles in his broad face tightened and his eyes mirrored his confusion. With as few words as I could I told him what was happening with my mother, and of my resolve to go home. He remained tense and his high brow creased into lines of sympathy as he listened, but he did not interrupt me nor distress me with any of the questions and concerns that most surely were troubling his mind.

"This will sound calculated, perhaps even uncaring," I continued, feeling as though I were stumbling over my own words, stumbling headlong down a steep, foolhardy path. "But when I go home I do not know how long necessity will keep me there, and I cannot say for certain how I will feel when I sort things out in my mind."

"How you will feel?" He wanted something more concrete, more detailed.

I drew a deep breath. "How I will feel about returning to America, to school, to this life . . . to you."

He said nothing. This was unlike Emory. He merely stood looking back at me, his shoulders hunched a little, head lowered, his brow furrowed now into a black line over his dark, unhappy eyes. So he would not help me. I must see it out to the end.

"If I come back—if I remain unchanged . . . inside . . ." I wanted him to understand, but how does one clothe the longings and insights of the spirit with mere words? "If so, and if you still want me—then I will marry you, Emory."

His eyes grew soft and liquid. He released his pent-up breath with a long, low whistle. "Things have always come easy for me." An expression of chagrin lifted the corners of his mouth. "Ah've never experienced the like of you, Augustine." He held out his long arm to me. "Come here. Ah'm willing to risk it if you are, honey-dear."

He drew me toward him and slipped the big ring onto my finger. It felt cool and heavy. I gazed down in disbelief. He lifted my face to his then and kissed me, and for the next few minutes, exquisite and blissful, I thought of nothing at all.

⚭

The remainder of the evening would, of necessity, be anti-climactic. We ate a quiet dinner at *Heaps o' Pizza* and considered going to a movie, but made the mistake of stopping off first at Emory's apartment. Of course, all his roommates were there. And, of course, they must see the ring and hear what had happened. I shied away from such blatant attention and the obvious pride Emory took in showing off his "achievement." Only Leroy, grinning so that his freckles danced across the white stretch of his nose, came up and spoke directly to me. He took my hand in his and held it lightly for a moment.

"Ah'm happy for you, Augustine," he said. "If you're sure this is what you really want."

"You still have your doubts?"

"You'll always be too good for him," he grinned. "But you'll make a fine Southern lady, that much is certain. 'Long as our boy treats you the way you deserve." To my surprise he leaned over and kissed my cheek, and I had to blink because my eyes were misting over with tears.

When we reached my door Emory asked, his eyes bubbling with boyish anticipation, "Can Ah come inside for a few moments while you show the girls?"

I could not deny him. Poor boy, it wasn't his fault that my life had turned into a sad-faced tragedy. But a sense of unease was beginning to build in me. This was a "conditional engagement" with some solemn undertones which were being entirely disregarded. That was probably quite natural at such a moment. But as Sally and Penelope, and even Clara, pressed close, oohing and aahing, I could not help wishing that Emory would express some tenderness, some solemn acknowledgment of what all this meant—to *me* a commitment of this nature *was* a solemn and sacred affair, especially colored as it was by the other circumstances of my life right now. I realized that he had not, even when we were alone together, expressed any consideration for what I was going through, nor inquired concerning my mother and conditions at home. I tried to swallow my disappointment as I held my hand out to be admired, and lifted my face to receive Emory's flushed-face kiss.

Chapter

19

Three days later, while we were all bustling about in the morning getting ready for the school day, the telephone rang. I never offered to answer the phone any longer, fearing Dr. Bekker might use that as a means of trying to talk to me, and I do not like phones anyway.

"For you," Nancy said, barely giving me time to grab it before she went on her way. The connection seemed bad, and I ducked into the closet to hear above the noise in the apartment. There in the small dark enclosure I heard Armand's voice speaking my name—such well-remembered, familiar accents that my heart gave a leap. Then, with his words, the darkness thickened and became black and choking.

"Your mother slipped and fell this morning on the ice outside her doorway, and it was hours till anyone found her. She has a fever and a deep cough which may lead to pneumonia, the old doctor thinks. That, along with the cancer that is eating away at her . . ." His voice paused in mid-air, suspended on a note of sympathy, despite the forced even reasoning in his voice. "I think you should come home at once, *ma chérie*."

"I will, Armand!" I choked out the words. "Somehow I will manage it. Hold onto her for me until I can get there." My voice was already shaking with the tears that were thick in my throat. "Tell her I'm coming."

"I will care for her tenderly, day and night, until you arrive," he promised. "And Augustine, try not to worry yourself. Do what you can, and put your trust in God for the rest."

I sat and held the telephone receiver in my hand long after it had gone dead and silent. *Trust in God.* Did Armand even know what the words meant? It is the thing people say when they reach the end of their human resources and do not know where to go, and wish to comfort themselves, like small children. *I* should know what it means. I had learned much this year about God and about myself, and about spiritual power and Heavenly Father's love for his children. I had even learned how to pray. But I felt so desolate now, so alone. Heaven seemed so far from me. Even the physical details of preparing for and enduring such a journey as I faced daunted me. But how to obtain the means for it? I had thought once or twice of Emory. It appeared he had money in plenty, but I did not know for sure. And he seemed so oblivious, and my pride recoiled at the prospect. I could take my small savings and ask Martha for a loan to cover the rest. I would be more than happy to pay off such a debt to her.

A tentative knock against the closet door startled me. I opened it a crack, holding my hand over the phone as though someone still waited on the other line.

"It's me," Penelope whispered. "I have to leave, or I'll be late to my class."

It was Thursday, and I had no classes until one. "Go ahead," I replied, "I'll walk up to campus later."

I drew the door shut again and sat in the cramped darkness, knees hunched, sick and trembling, until I heard the apartment go silent and I knew all the girls had left. Still I came out slowly, blinking as I looked around me. Again, in the deft stroke of a heartbeat, the world had changed, altered irrevocably. I sat on the sofa, longing to be able to sink into oblivion, shrinking from the prospect of what lay before me. At last I rose heavily, finished dressing, made my bed, then walked out to the living room and stood staring at the telephone, where it sat black and mute on the table. I knew I had to call Martha, and the sooner, the better. Yet I made no move.

When I heard a knock at the door I opened it automatically. Dr. Bekker had pushed inside and closed it securely behind him before I had adjusted to the reality of his being there.

"What do you want?" I demanded, backing away from him.

"Something has happened, Augustine. I could not sleep last night, and when I awoke this morning the feeling was so strong that I knew it was something real, something more. Forgive me for coming to you, but how could I ignore—"

He stopped as his voice broke on the word. There were tears in his eyes. Looking closely I could see that his face did appear tired, his skin drawn and ashen.

"My friend Armand called," I began, knowing I must tell him, knowing I could not get rid of him by begging or bullying, or even hysterics. It was easier than I had thought it would be. The fearful words spoken out loud did not become more horrible, but actually loosened their sharp and painful hold on me.

"You must go at once," he said. "I will call Martha and make all the arrangements."

"You do not understand," I protested, my voice rising a little and my breath hissing through my teeth as I stood facing him in weak and angry frustration. "I do not wish to take anything more from Martha."

"How do you wish to arrange it?" he asked. He had been speaking in a calm, measured voice. But now his eyes flashed, and I could see him exerting great effort to maintain his control over himself.

"I wish to merely borrow the money for a plane ticket from her. I have a little of my own saved, and I—"

He waved his hand in the air, interrupting me impatiently. "All this can be worked out at a later date. Now we must get you home at once, no matter what it takes." I could see his face muscles contract as he continued. "You will never forgive yourself if you are too late, Augustine."

I began to tremble inside as his words awoke something within me.

"I will also speak to your various professors," Dr. Bekker continued, "explain what has happened and make any necessary arrangements for you to be permitted to make up your work when you return."

He must have seen something in my eyes. He stopped and merely stood staring at me.

"I may not come back," I said. My voice sounded thin and pathetic, without expression, without conviction. I lifted my hand and brushed the hair back from my eyes.

I watched his face go livid, his eyes narrow and dark. As I dropped my hand I saw the heavy gem on my finger, and knew, and instinctively backed yet further away from him.

"For the love of heaven, Augustine," he said, "what are you doing with that thing? What madness is this?" His voice was no more than a painful rasping.

"Go away," I cried. "Leave me alone! You have no right to question me!" I could hear a note of hysteria in my voice, but I did not care.

"Think, Augustine," he continued, reckless for the first time. "It is your own happiness at question here. He does not love you the way a woman like you needs and deserves to be loved."

Suddenly I saw Leroy's narrow, freckled face in front of me and heard him say, " 'Long as our boy treats you the way you deserve."

I shook my head wildly. "Stop it! I don't want to hear this. You don't know what you're talking about."

"I know, and so do you, Augustine." His voice was deadly calm. "In your heart of hearts you know! He can never understand the refinements of your mind, the perceptions of your inner spirit. He would always leave you lonely and unfulfilled—he is not capable!" I could see reflected on his features the shock and anger that must be playing over my own face. Yet, relentlessly, he continued. "All Emory needs is an adornment—something to show off and brag about to his neighbors. Do you want—"

I put my hands up and covered my face and, with that movement, he stopped, biting his words off in mid-air.

"I will be back in an hour," he said, "hopefully with a ticket which will allow you to fly out of here this very day. Can you begin to get ready?"

I nodded my head, my face still covered.

"Are you sure, Augustine? Will you be all right?"

I nodded again.

"I am sorry, so sorry . . . I had no right to add to your burden . . . no matter, no matter what—"

He left his sentence unfinished. I listened to his footsteps as he crossed the room, I heard the door close gently. I was aware in the sudden stillness that the room held more pain than it had before. I recoiled from his suffering with even greater horror than I felt for my own and struggled, with all my failing strength, to shut it out of my mind.

ℚ

It was closer to two hours later when I heard his knock and, with an effort of self-control that drained me, opened the door to him. He kept his distance, standing ramrod straight, as a German soldier would, to deliver his message.

"There will be a ticket waiting for you at the airport," he said. "The plane leaves for Paris in four and a half hours, and Martha is already well on her way here."

I stood blinking my eyes at him.

"Can you be ready, Augustine?"

I nodded, and tried to swallow. There was no moisture in my mouth, and I coughed a little.

"I could try to find Penelope or Clara, if they might be of help to you—"

I shook my head again. "Saying good-bye would be—no, no, I'll get along fine." I ran distracted fingers through my tangled curls. "I cannot bring everything. If I do decide to stay—"

"Things could be sent to you, Augustine." His voice was ashen; the empty, toneless syllables fell like small stones into an unlit reservoir somewhere inside me.

"I will speak to your teachers, so . . ." His voice hung and trembled. There were things I could see, even glancing at his eyes, that he wanted to say. But he did not wish to distress me, to push me over the steep precipice to which I clung.

"Thank you," I said, though the words clogged in my throat. "You are—I'm sorry that—"

He shrugged his shoulders. "I was here." Then he added, because he had to, "For me it is a pleasure to be able to help you, Augustine."

"Well . . ."

"Yes, this is good-bye then." He stood staring at the floor, knowing how his gaze upset me. "I will pray for you, Augustine. Would to heaven I could do more than that! Would to heaven *you knew!*" A sound escaped him, something between a groan and a cry, and his head jerked up suddenly. "Must I remain forever a villain in your eyes? Must a man who was good and kindly, who was *innocent*—"

"Stop!" I cried. "*Stop!*"

And he did. As I turned away from him he turned to the door, but I heard his words, spoken clearly, with no attempt at apology or disguise. "God go with you, my dearest."

I collapsed onto the couch and sat rocking back and forth, covering my face with my hands, wishing the cleansing release of tears might come to ease the terrible agony that tormented me.

⊱

"Tell me what happened with Anja's friend, Augustine."

Martha asked the question with a tentative air. We had been driving mostly in silence; had already passed the Point of the Mountain and were dropping into the Salt Lake Valley without having spoken more than a dozen words between us. She had called in a woman to sit with Ellen and be there when Roger returned from school. I think I'd have preferred the diversion the child would have created to this strained silence. When Martha first entered the apartment and saw me she had come toward me with a cry and gathered me into her arms. I could tell she had been weeping, and I wondered what she was feeling. I suppose when you help to convert a person to the gospel you give them a little of your own light, watching it ignite the same glow of understanding and faith within their heart; and how that must bind you, one to another, I could only imagine.

"She's doing better," I replied, answering Martha's question. "They had trouble stabilizing her blood sugar, or whatever it is with diabetics. I haven't been paying too much attention—after Armand called—"

"Of course."

"I don't think Karen is taking the loss of the baby well," I added, knowing Martha was sincerely interested, and relieved to be breaking the silence. "Everyone else sees that it will be much easier for her this way—but then, it wasn't everyone else's baby, was it? It was hers."

"That's right." Martha threw me a scrutinizing glance. "No, it would not be easy for the girl, even if it is more 'convenient' in the long run," she agreed. "What about Anja?"

"This has affected Anja, I believe. She isn't as testy, as quick to take offense as she was before. She's been doing some serious thinking lately, it seems to me."

Martha nodded her head as she listened. "That's good. I know it would mean so much to Hans to see her straighten her life out."

At the mention of his name I felt something go cold and hard inside me, as though an icy shadow had passed over my heart. I sank back against the padded back of the car seat.

"I don't know what we'd have done without Hans today," Martha continued blithely. "He's a rare combination—a man who is clear thinking and practical and yet sensitive as well." She sighed, and only glanced at me as she watched the traffic. "Hans Bekker's mother died a terrible death herself, you know. I think that's why he's so concerned now."

"Martha, please," I began. But she didn't hear me.

"She brought her two remaining children to this country at the end of the war, sacrificing every scrap she owned to do so, and she had once been a wealthy woman. Then, against all advice, she returned to try to help her younger sister and her small family. Her husband, too, you see, had been killed in the war. Hans never saw her again. She died in an accident in Leipzig—the explosion of an old war capsule that had not been detonated." Martha shivered, and I said again, "Please, Martha!"

She seemed to feel my words more than hear them. She turned to me briefly. "We're close to the airport now," she said. "I'm sorry. I didn't mean to go on like that, and I suppose it doesn't help much when you're going through something hard to think of someone else suffering."

I don't care, I wanted to say. *Her suffering is nothing to me. My father died because of her husband. All of our lives my mother and I have suffered because of the German people, people like Hans Bekker's father and mother.*

My ears were ringing and my mouth felt dry. Martha got me through all the lines and procedures. I followed her woodenly. Just before I boarded the plane, she pressed an envelope into my grasp, with my mother's name scrawled across it. Clutching that and my ticket tightly with one hand, the cold iron railing with the other, I climbed up into the white-winged vessel that would bear me away from this place. Already, as I walked, my life here seemed to fall away from me, like a discarded coat, bulky and awkward, that I no longer needed.

I settled into a seat. The small square of sky I could see through the window could be anyone's sky, could be the sky over Paris, over the sweet fields of Burgundy. And soon it would be! Soon I would see *home* again! And surely nothing could be too dreadful, too hopeless, if it brought a weary soul home once more to the people she loved.

Chapter

20

$\mathcal{I}$ was wrong, of course. As soon as I saw Jean-Paul's face I knew how wrong I was. Both he and Sylvie met me at the airport. She hugged and kissed me, petting me as she would one of her children. But Jean-Paul hung back. His eyes, usually so open and guileless, looked pale and tainted with fear.

"The children have been ill with bad colds and coughs for a week," Sylvie explained. She herself was coughing, I had noticed. "The fussy old doctor will not let them near *Maman*," she complained.

"Armand is with her," Jean-Paul said quietly. "They are both waiting for you."

He insisted on driving me from Paris to Chatillon. His Citroen was much nicer than a train would be, crowded with other travelers and stopping at every little station along the way. We sped through the countryside, and I watched out the window as the dry fields went past. Their colors were flat and drained and there were no bright poppies to line them. Thin smoke trailed from the chimneys of the scattered farmhouses, diffusing into the broader expanse of a violet-gray sky. Before we reached Troyes the rain began falling. The surface of the Seine gleamed wine dark, and a line of

white poplars skirting the road ahead of us danced like so many silver, loose-jointed ghosts in the wan, gloomy light. I was home.
The bright village roofs told me this, crowded wet and gleaming
beneath the storm. The river, pushing slick and full against its
deep banks, told me. The scent of the air: rain and earth, a moist,
pungent mingling of herbs and breads baking, heavy with yeast. I
rolled my window down and drew in the fragrances as Jean-Paul
negotiated his way through the damp, narrow pathways of Chatillon.

"You are getting wet, Augustine," he observed.

I rubbed tears from my eyes. "I know," I replied.

In a few moments the Citroen shuddered to a stop. Our house,
my own home, stood before me, looking much as it had when I last
left it. I saw with amazing clarity the little things: mud on the
doorstep, the broken hinge on the shutter covering the kitchen
window, scraggly yellow weeds choking the flowers in my mother's
planter boxes, the faded blue paint covering door and shutters.
The house looked so still. I waited for Jean-Paul to come round
and hand me out of the car. A sudden reluctance had come over
me. What would I discover inside? With a momentary strong urge,
almost childishly petulant, I wanted to find my mother standing at
the stove in her kitchen, preparing all the foods I loved best. I
wanted to see her turn, small beads of perspiration dotting the skin
above her top lip, her eyes shining as she called out to me, "The
quiche is baked to perfection, Augustine, the fish tender and flaky.
And, oh the desserts! I have Pêches Cardinal and Tarte a la crème,
and even Croissant aux amande."

"Augustine?"

Jean-Paul had one of my bags in each hand and was waiting by
the front door. "I am afraid to go inside," I confessed to him.

He gazed at me tenderly. His eyes were moist. "It will not be
easy. I have not felt this way since the war."

I reached out and closed my hand around the smooth wooden
doorknob and opened the door. I slipped inside after Jean-Paul and
felt as silent and insubstantial as a wraith. The room was dimly lit
and bore the impress of neglect, or at least of disuse. A dark shape
materialized out of the gloom and started walking toward us. He
began speaking to me in soft, fluid French, and the sound of his
voice loosened the tight control I had clung to so desperately. I felt
the tears run down my cheeks and choke in my throat. Jean-Paul

was family, but he was so much older than I; he belonged to Sylvie and his children and his own life in Paris. But Armand was *home!* He put his arms around me and pulled me close to him, and I buried my head in his chest. There was no hurry. What had any of us to do? When the tears finally stopped and I stood back and blew my nose on Armand's big hanky, I realized that my brother had carried my things back into my old bedroom, and turned on a few lights. And now he beckoned to us from the kitchen, "Come, I have prepared a little something."

"I want to see *Maman* first."

Armand reached out and touched my shoulder. "She is sleeping soundly, Augustine. It would not be good to awaken her. Will you stand just inside the doorway and be very still?"

"You make a fussy old nursemaid," I teased him. "You chose the wrong profession, Armand."

It was a brave attempt, and we both knew it. But I did as he told me. A small lamp burned on her bedside table and she lay, a thin shape beneath the piled, quilted comforters Armand had covered her with. Her face was turned from me. I felt myself sway toward her, but Armand's touch on my arm held me back. "She needs whatever sleep she can get," he whispered. I leaned against the door frame, feeling weak and exhausted.

"You need sleep yourself," Armand said, watching me. "But first, something to eat."

He pushed me gently into the kitchen, *her* kitchen, where Jean-Paul's efforts awaited us. As I sat at the table and forced down cold cheese and fruit and thick chunks of baguette, I was dimly aware of the little things that were my mother, that would always mark this place as my mother's: the blue and white dishes, the stone bowl on the table (now holding apples, not flowers), the old yellow clock on the wall, her blue and white checkered apron hanging on a hook by the sink; and, for the first time, I felt her near.

Between them Jean-Paul and Armand bullied me back to my own room. I crawled into my bed, smelling the familiar scent of the place, feeling the sag of the mattress, looking at the square of green wall where hung the faded print of workers gleaning in a French field. I stared at it—wall and painting, the rounded edge of my old chipped dresser with the limp fall of white curtain above it—until my eyelids drooped and my eyes dimmed into sleep.

❧

Jean-Paul stayed the night, but drove back to Paris before I awakened. When Armand shook me awake I opened my eyes to the bright splashes of a French sun painting bright, errant patterns across my room. Forcing back a yawn I sat up quickly, feeling instantly guilty and selfish for having slept so long. Armand shook his head at me.

"Relax, Augustine. The nurse is with your mother right now, and they are not ready for you."

Jean-Paul had told me, driving down, that he had engaged a professional nurse to bathe and feed my mother and perform all the strenuous duties I would not know how to do.

"Is that not costly?" I had asked.

"I can afford it," he replied quietly. "She will not go to a hospital and I will not make her go. God knows she has earned the right to die in her own home."

And, with those words, I knew. I repeated them now to Armand. His large brown eyes, always so filled with light and laughter, dulled to a somber tone and he drew up my hands and cradled them between his; strong, brown, and capable.

"Yes, your mother is dying," he said. "I do not know how she has held on this long: she has only been waiting for you."

He left me, and I dressed as quickly as I could, then flung my door wide open as I hurried out into the house. The blessed sunlight was everywhere, warming my homecoming for me, softening the harsh, unlovely lines that had stood out so starkly the evening before. Armand pushed his hat to a cocky angle and tilted his head to look at me, appraisingly, as an artist might. "I'm off to see if I still have a job left," he laughed. "But I will be back, fair one." He lifted my hand to his lips, barely brushing their warmth across the surface of my skin. "America must surely agree with you, *ma petite*," he murmured. "You have never looked more lovely to me."

I leaned over and kissed the brown curls that fell over his forehead. "*Merci*, Armand."

He went off through the sunlight, whistling happily. *He is trying to tell me something,* I thought suddenly, knowing Armand as I do. *No long faces.* I could almost hear him saying it. *No sadness or tears. Share everything that is joyful and good with your mother while you can.*

I walked into her room with a light step, carrying Armand's sunshine, like a rare, precious bestowal, with me.

⚭

"Tell me more of the children." My mother moved, trying to lift her head. "I feel weak as a new kitten," she admitted, sinking back in defeat. Her cracked lips were colorless, and so was her skin. There were hollows in her cheeks and temples, and purple, discolored splotches under her eyes. And her hand, when she reached out to touch me, was a claw of tightly-stretched skin and bone, with scarcely any flesh on it at all.

I smiled at her—again—and repeated the stories about Roger and Ellen. It was late afternoon of my second day home, and it seemed to me I had rehearsed every fragment of my life in Utah, repeating it two and three times for her, worn and amazed by her interest and the spark of life my stories brought into her eyes.

She could not speak much herself. She had tried to praise Armand and his excellent care of her, but speaking tired her out quickly; each word tore a terrible, wheezing effort from her. So I picked up the thread and said for her what she would say, and made her smile with my awkward but apt descriptions.

She had shown me the place in her dresser where she kept the letters I had written her, and the letters Martha had sent. Sometimes when she dozed, or slept soundly for a length of time, I would bring several out and go over them, reliving the things they told about. But this grew too painful too quickly. I had not mentioned Hans Bekker to her at all, though both Martha and I had talked of him in our letters.

But her mind was indistinct now. At times she would wake into another time and not recognize me at all when she looked into my face. Once I heard her calling out to her long-dead sister in a high, girlish voice. Once she awoke slowly and serenely and seemed to be staring off at something far in the distance. I could see the resurrection of youth glow for a moment on her wasted features as her lips parted and smiled.

"Étinne, I am coming!" Her voice trembled with emotion. "You are so handsome, my husband." I could feel her joy as she said it. "You know, all the girls envy me." Then she had laughed, and I had to reach far back to my earliest memories to reproduce such a sound, to envision the flushed womanly pride that softened and enhanced her fair features.

The morning of my third day at home she began to slip. She sunk into a sort of stupor, would not open her eyes, would not take even liquids.

"It is not long now," the nurse told me.

When Armand came at noon he sat with me, holding my hand, chafing it softly in a gentle, comforting motion.

"If she wakens again, Augustine, you must say good-bye to her and let her go."

He had said *if*, not *when*.

"Would you like me to call Jean-Paul?" he asked.

"I am not certain," I answered him honestly. "That would probably bring Sylvie as well, and noise and confusion which would not be seemly." I sighed. "I do not believe Jean-Paul wants to be here, not really, and . . ." My voice broke, but I continued tremulously, "and I wish to be alone with her, the two of us together, as it has been for so long."

His response was to nod and press my hand firmly. He remained beside me for as long as he could. When he stood to leave he stretched his long, stiff muscles briefly and replaced the hat on his head, which he had balanced on his knee as he sat.

"You must call if you need me," he said, "and then I will come to you."

He turned and bent over the sleeping form of my mother. He moved close and kissed her thin cheek, murmured words of his own under his breath to her, then left the room. For the first time since that sun-filled morning I felt alone, and a sense of bereavement began to settle upon my spirit, like a palpable hand.

⁊

The nurse came and went. The sky outside darkened. I poked at the stale food she had left on the table beside me and took a drink of the tepid water I had poured hours ago. I had grown chill and cramped with such a long time of sitting. I rose and drew the curtains, turned on a light in the kitchen, straightened up a few misplaced things, then returned to the room where my mother lay dying and walked the floor, stretching my tired and aching muscles. I remembered this room from nights of my childhood when we sat on the bed together and read all the stories we loved, one after another, until we could no longer prop our eyes open. There even were times when she would pull a blanket haphazardly over us both, and we would sleep thus all night, sweetly exhausted, arms and legs entangled with each other. And those nights there was no fear, no nightmares, no ghastly remembrances; only her love, as safe a haven as any child could wish for.

How hallowed this place! How hallowed the nights and days of her life, which I scarcely knew. How hallowed the beating of this faithful heart through the long lonely seasons of her life.

She stirred, and I bent over her. When she opened her eyes they shone more clear and rational than I had seen them since I had been home.

"When I am gone, will you go back and marry this Emory?"

Common words, spoken calmly, as though she had said, "Augustine, will you take out the cat and see that she has some fresh water and a little tidbit to eat?"

I sucked in my breath, then blew it out through my teeth. I could not lie to her now, at such a time.

"I cannot say, *Maman*. I do not think I love him enough."

Her eyes looked full at me, holding my gaze. "Marry where the soul bids, Augustine." Her words were clearly spoken and easy to follow, though the painful rasp still haunted them. "Attraction is fleeting, and so is the hot blood of passion. But the soul whispers true. Follow its promptings." Her eyes fluttered and closed. "Promise me—Augustine—"

I sank down to my knees. I drew up her withered hand and kissed it. I kissed her forehead, her cheek, her drawn, parched lips. She felt fevered, yet her skin was dry, drained of all living juices.

I turned away. I pulled open her drawer and rummaged about for the letters. I needed something, anything! Then, suddenly fearful, I froze still, and listened until I could hear the labored rise and fall of her breathing.

I tugged again. The whole drawer slid out and clattered onto the floor. I jumped at the presumptuous sound, reverberating, bruising the silence. I bent and began retrieving the scattered objects. My hand closed over a thin leather-bound volume. What was this? I held it up to the light. It looked like a journal of some kind. I left the other things where they were, sat down and opened it carefully, spreading the thin, brittle pages across my lap.

Chapter
_____

21

$\mathcal{T}$he writing was cramped and close together, and in some places quite faded with time. After a few lines, when I realized what I was reading, I let the pages fall from my hands; as though the mere touch of them scorched my fingers. Yet I had to go on. I had to *know*. All the answers were here, all the nightmares laid out for me. *The Germans are coming, that is for certain*, the journal began. *It is not enough that Gerard and Jean-Paul fight for their country. Étinne is incensed. It is as though he has a fever upon him.*

I shuddered. I could not remember my young father very well. They say he was wild-eyed that day, but steadied by a courage that was deep and unwavering. I would have named him sullen if my own memories served me. He was not altogether happy with life. A farm accident had lamed him, and it did not suit his dignity to limp through his days. Then, when the war came and he was deemed *unsuitable, inferior!* Only my mother, the pretty Idelette he had fallen in love with, could bring a smile to his face, could coax the gentleness in him back to the surface. Then there would be good times. But not often, not often. And then, of course, the war came.

The entries were sparse at first, and her fear was reflected in them; more here than in her behavior, in the attitudes she adopted. Jean-Paul always said, "Our mother is a self-contained woman. What she suffers, she suffers inside herself, and nobody sees."

But it was here when she wrote: *I cannot sleep nights. I turn in the bed and look at him, sleeping as soundly and sweetly as a child sleeps. And I think of my brother, lying dead and unburied on an un-known battlefield, only a discarded body, a statistic. Why must men fight for honor? More than often they lose all that is dear to them, and gain nothing at all.*

As I read the cramped pages I gained insight into the meticu-lous rationing of food and essential items that the war forced upon her, her ingenuity in dealing with want and deprivation and con-stant insecurity. The sketchy outline, all I possessed of those years, began to flesh out, take on form and substance.

I baked fresh bread this morning while the children picked berries, even little Augustine helping, staining her hands and mouth purple. Then we went for a picnic beside the small grotto above the church of Saint Vorles.

I glanced at the still, shrunken figure stretched out on the bed. *Where is my mother?* my heart cried. *I want to see her as she was, young and lovely, with the wind in her hair and a little girl tugging on each hand.*

Later there was a short, terse entry: *Étinne is unable to enjoy himself knowing that others are fighting and dying to save France. Per-haps only death itself will content such men as my Étinne.*

I felt myself shudder. How well she must have known him! Did that knowledge help when her premonition, her discouraged prophecy became a reality?

I read on, stopping now and again to check my mother's ragged but even breathing. Then came a horrible entry, set off by itself and rimmed in heavy black brackets: *28 May 1940. Today, after less than three weeks of resistance, King Leopold III of Belgium surrendered his army and became a prisoner of the Germans. Dear God, what is in store for us?*

I closed the thin volume and let it lie still in my lap, fighting a terrible agitation that stirred my spirit into eddies and shoals. I closed my eyes and prayed in my heart that I might have the strength to go on. After a few moments I turned the frail pages

carefully and found my place. Nothing more until: *7 June. The of-*
fensive against France has begun. Two days ago what the Germans are
calling a blitzkrieg of armored units, paratroopers and dive bombers has
been unleashed against our poor country. Chatillon is right in their path
as they push toward Paris.

I knew what happened next. I knew from the stories the boys
in the village told one another, whispering behind my back so I
would not hear. *It was Augustine's father who brought the Germans*
against Chatillon. But for his mad offensive, going in search of Germans
to slaughter . . . I knew as I grew older what I had not realized as a
young child: these boys viewed my father as a hero. When they
played war games one would vie with another as to who would be
Étinne Mousset, on the hill with his father's World War I field
gun, the French 75 mm., trained against the advancing ground
troops, or hidden in the dense forests picking off stray paratroopers. The old ones were close-mouthed and hard-faced about it. But
the young ones, too young to remember, stretched fact into legend
and romance, which is always the way of the young.

We see Germans daily now. It is a strange, eerie feeling. They say
Paris is in panic and the people are fleeing in a wild confusion. Here we
are safer in our homes than anywhere—or we would be if—

As I read I could not help thinking of the irony of it. Jean-Paul
was in the midst of the worst of the fighting in Belgium and along
our own border, but he survived. Gerard had been stationed with
our troops sent to guard against attack on the Italian border. But
Mussolini was interested in his part of the war spoils only, and de-
clared himself late in the game, and made only a brief, feeble effort, a token effort they call it, against a small section of our coast-
line. Some of our finest troops, so desperately needed elsewhere,
watched and waited in vain. But Gerard was one of the few who
met death on that border. He was killed two days after my father,
though we did not hear for some time. Both seemed such useless,
pointless dyings. The Italians did not overrun our border. And, despite my father, the Germans marched into Paris on June four-
teenth—ten days after they began their terrible blitzkrieg. What
did it matter that a seventeen-year-old boy, gentle and loved by all
who knew him, and a forty-eight-year-old man, crippled in one leg
and fiercely patriotic, were among the casualties and would be
known among the living no more?

I was there. The next entry in the journal would tell me what had happened that night. I sat clutching it to me, staring straight ahead, seeing nothing, thinking nothing, for some time before I lowered my eyes and began to read.

Yesterday what matters most in life ended for me. Étinne was in the hills much of the day, picking off German soldiers. But a small detachment must have spotted him and followed him home. They diverted themselves for a time shooting houses and businesses in the town at random. Étinne sat at the kitchen table with his leg propped on a chair, eating the cold meal I had kept for him. He did not know the soldiers were coming after him. I have heard that they bullied some of the townspeople into telling them where the crazy man lived who had been killing their men. Perhaps that is true, but I do not think about it, for what good is that now? This is my home, and I must live and get on here.

So much, so much I could understand now that had been lost to me as a child! Those few families who gave us only hard looks when we passed in the streets and would never return my mother's kind, quiet greeting—did they harbor resentment for what my father had done? Had their places of business been ruined because of my father's bold actions, and the anger and attention they engendered? And those others, who would never raise their eyes to meet ours, who walked with heads lowered when we passed by— could they have been among those questioned that fateful day? Could they have named the man Étinne Mousset and pointed out his house—happy that it stood at the far edge of Chatillon—to safeguard their own families and homes?

I drew a deep breath and lowered my head again to the paper, leaning close in order to read the words by the glow of the one dim lamp that lighted the room.

When the soldiers came it was with a wild explosion of shouting and shooting. In one minute, two minutes, it was all over and done. Étinne looked up from his sausage and cried out something—I did not hear what!—and groped for his gun, but it was not beside him. And even as he moved, several soldiers lowered their weapons against him. I saw his body twitch and then jerk violently as the bullets tore into him and spattered his blood over everything. I must have screamed. Augustine and Giselle were screaming. As I reached out to my husband, one of the soldiers shoved me against the cupboard and struck me hard with the back of his hand across my face. Giselle clung to my apron, crying and begging for mercy.

Augustine had been sitting on a low stool at her father's feet, accepting bits of food from him as he ate. As the soldiers burst in and the shooting begin, I saw one tall soldier break out from the others and grab Augustine, shielding her body with his own as he bent above her. I saw no more. But it was he who, gruff and unyielding, prodded the men into leaving once their work had been done. I know no German. But he told me later that he had frightened them into believing that the townsfolk were alerted and were even then marching against them, and they would be trapped in this house of death if they did not leave. Otherwise, what might they have done to myself and Giselle, who was fourteen-years-old?

As they scrambled out, the tall blond soldier bent close to me and whispered in French, "I will return after midnight to help you. Do not be frightened. I will come alone." "You are hurt!" I cried, for his left arm hung limp and his coat sleeve was soaked with blood. But he was out the door, running after the others, even as I spoke.

How long I stood dazed and trembling, staring wild-eyed and unseeing, I cannot say. At last I seemed dimly aware of a child's pathetic whimpering and the sound of someone calling my name. I bent over Augustine, who sat cradled in her sister's arms. A long red welt spread along the inside of her arm, a deep cut, as though someone had slashed at her with a knife. As I cleaned and tended the wound it came to me that the German soldier, rushing into the spray of fire, had pushed her aside just in time. One of the bullets had barely grazed her arm. And, in his efforts to save her, he had been wounded himself.

I closed my eyes. I was crying softly, shaking my head back and forth, as one gone a little mad. "Mother!" I called, and then again, somewhat louder. But the form on the bed did not stir. "Oh, Maman! Maman!" I reached out my hand and touched her, and sat that way, crying, for a long time. Then slowly, resignedly, I turned again to the journal and started to read.

I did not think of the German soldier again. After caring for my little one and settling her as comfortably as I could in her little bed, Giselle and I began the gruesome task of cleaning, wiping her father's life's blood from the walls and cupboards, from the chair and floor where it stood in dark pools. I wished to send Giselle from the room, but she begged to stay by my side. Work was the best thing. Keeping busy, not thinking. Étinne still lay where he had fallen as he slid from the chair and slumped grotesquely on the floor. I straightened his limbs and washed the blood from his face, then placed a small pillow beneath his head and covered his cold stiff body with my softest blanket.

While we were yet cleaning the room I heard a faint knock at the kitchen window. My heart froze within me. Giselle's eyes went wide and she covered her mouth with her hand. It was the blond German soldier! I let him inside. For the rest of the night he worked beside us, cleaning the room, setting up a plank table in the back room and laying out my husband's body in proper dignity. I could not have moved him myself. He was a singular man, not as young as I had at first thought him, but gentle and handsome to look upon. "Why do you do this?" I asked him. He looked back at me with such a sadness in his blue eyes that it startled me. "Women and children are not the begetters of war," he answered. "And no man should be faulted for fighting to defend his homeland."

His words brought tears to my eyes. He had brought food with him, and medicine for Augustine, and I noticed that his wounded arm was wrapped in a good clean bandage. "I am sorry for what you have suffered on our account," I said, glancing at his arm. He laughed a short, bitter laugh. "What I have suffered on your account!"

When all was done that could be done, he pressed me to take money from him as well, but I refused him warmly. "You have no man to care for you now," he reasoned, and dropped the money into the kettle that sat on top of my stove. "Do not forget and boil these francs into tea," he teased. And it was good for Giselle and me to let ourselves smile.

Before he left he made a strange request of me. He asked if we three might kneel down together. When we had done so he offered a prayer—such a prayer as I have never heard before in my life. His French was poor, and sometimes he lapsed into German, and then his words tumbled forth. But he spoke to God as one man speaks to another, yet with such a humble reverence that I felt its cleansing power move through me and lift up my soul out of the depths of despair from which I had thought I could never rise. He asked God to send down a blessing upon our household, and upon this poor land where the enemy, in unrighteous dominion, had set his foot. He spoke as only a priest should speak, and I did not understand him. Was he not the enemy? Why did he plead in such eloquence and sincerity for our poor sakes?

When he rose to leave I tried to thank him. But how clumsy my words were compared to his own. "You saved my daughter's life," I said. And, as though that reminded him, he tiptoed into the bedroom and kissed Augustine where she slept. "I have a daughter not much older than this one," he said, and there were tears in his eyes.

So that is the story of the coming of the German soldiers to my country and the death of the only man I have ever loved. I promised myself

I would write it. It is only right, for Étinne's sake, and for the sake of my children, that this story be told.

I paused. My mother had written this last paragraph later. The ink was a different shade, the lettering somewhat larger and bolder.

The German army brought hatred to my country and left it here. But the German soldier with the beautiful voice and the piercing blue eyes brought love and faith to my house, and they yet remain. And this has made it impossible for me to hate in the way some of my neighbors do. I believe the prayer of the German soldier helped me make it through those first dark and terrible days. I do not know his name. I do not know what happened to him. But he will always live in my heart.

I looked up. My mother's eyes were open. She was watching my face. I tried to smile. "I have been reading—"

"I know," she said.

I dropped down beside her. "It is all right, Maman, you can die in peace now. I am all right."

I was crying, but she did not seem to notice. Trembling with the effort, she reached out her thin hand and touched my face. I held it close to me and covered it with kisses and the wet of my tears. "I understand . . . so much! You need not worry about me— ever again." I bent down and kissed her lips. They parted ever so slightly and a smile lit her eyes. "I love you, Maman, more than ever! I love you! I love you!"

Her eyelids fluttered and closed. Her hand went limp in mine. I lowered it gently and placed it over her breast. *She is gone,* something told me. I closed my eyes and began to pray. Words came— from some depth I had not plumbed before. And if I can give expression to anything I was feeling, it was simply and overwhelmingly this: I was not alone.

Chapter

22

We had climbed high up on the side of the hill, above Saint Vorles. The air was fresh, with a decided nip to it. The grotto looked bare, the river beneath it appeared leaden and depthless below a colorless sky. I signed to Armand as I gazed up at the Lady, a brushstroke of white laid against the gray winter cliff.

"Look at her standing there, unchanged and unmoved all these many years."

"Unchanged," Armand agreed, "but not unmoved, *mon amie.*"

He put his arm around me and we stood in companionable silence, totally at ease, unaware of all else around us, even of that worst of all demons, time. It was I who first broke the silence.

"You will take care of the house for me, then?"

"As I promised, Augustine."

I turned in his arms. "Armand, what if I never come back?"

"You asked that before." He laughed gently and pushed my tangled black curls away from my eyes. "This is your home. No matter where else life takes you, it will remain such. Therefore, you will return, even if it is only every now and again."

I nodded, encouraged by his confidence, his common-sense wisdom. "I shall miss you," I said.

He sighed and pressed his lips to my forehead. "That is the worst thing about life—that distance parts those who truly care for one another. But . . ." His eyes took on the shine of unshed tears. "But the heart keeps them united. Will not that be so?"

My gentle lady, I thought, as I gazed up at her. *What sights you have seen. If you have a heart to break, surely it has broken ten thousand times.*

"Armand, I am frightened," I whispered. "What will happen when I go back?" I had told him, if not everything, then certainly far more than I had confided to any living soul.

"You are always frightened, little sister," he soothed. "And have you not always wished to see one step ahead, to second-guess the future?" He laughed at me again, but with a tender kindness. "You would do well to trust God, and to have faith in yourself, Augustine."

"I will," I cried. "I do now more than I ever have."

As we walked down the hill I could feel the soul of France gazing upon me through the Lady's glazed eyes. I fancied I could feel more, could feel the spirit of my people walking forward with me: common people of the earth who had lived common, everyday lives; who had stumbled, made mistakes, been less than perfect. But the dreams of their hearts and the love which life had taught them somehow lived on, became the embodiment of what all men strive for. And I was content to carry that with me into whatever the future had waiting for me.

ॐ

I had spent many long hours alone since my mother's death. Thoughts of *him* intruded into all of them. Cleaning the house, going through my mother's things, cooking my solitary meal, or walking the quiet streets of Chatillon—Hans Bekker was there. And I remembered—with searing pain I remembered—his tender insights, his gentle ways, his *care* of me. All that was bitter and frightened and unsure within me had loosened that night. Bit by bit I could feel it draining out of me. Chatillon helped; the quiet comfort of home. Armand helped. But as the days passed a sense of urgency came. I must return as soon as possible. Hans Bekker was suffering; I knew that.

Sometimes at night, with the tip of my finger, I would trace the line of the scar that ran down my flesh. I could easily imagine this man, now that I knew. His son must be very like him. Yet it still seemed so strange! Sometimes it would spook me, being alone there, to dwell upon what had transpired within these walls, to picture my mother and young sister cleaning up the gore of death while my father lay white-faced and still at their feet; to imagine them kneeling, right here in this room where I sat, and listening to a young, fair-haired stranger pray for them in another tongue. No wonder my mother had been drawn to the Mormon beliefs when she heard them. Hans Bekker had said that he had been raised a member of the Church there in Germany, that his father had been a branch president. So strange, so strange! If I had only known sooner! But my mother could never have told me, never have re-opened the horror that was locked away with those words. Besides, how could she have known what it was I was suffering, how truth and terror had twisted themselves up in my dream and created a nightmare of such tragic proportions?

Well, she was at peace now. She was with my father, and the thought of that made me glad. Gentle Gerard, who perished alone at some unknown spot, without comfort or care, and poor Giselle whose youth and beauty were snuffed out by disease before their sweet bloom could ripen, who would have been a big sister to me now; a guidance, a comfort—they were both there with her. Jean-Paul was a good man, and I loved him dearly, but his ways were not mine. He was much older, and he cared nothing for religion. Even my cherished Armand could not share this most essential, inner part of my being. To all intents and purposes, I was alone. And alone I must face Hans Bekker.

❧

It was every bit as difficult as my worst imaginings had painted it. I flew the long journey from France to America, changing planes, finally arriving tired and dazed at the Salt Lake airport. It seemed like another world. Could I fit back into it again? I was such a changed person from the girl who had been here before.

Martha, as I expected, wanted to hear everything. Rehearsing for her the dying of my mother, the bereavement, the funeral, all the things that had happened while I was in France, thoroughly exhausted me, mind and spirit. I had not been able to decide, but in the end I told her about the journal. In a way, she had a right to know. It was she who had brought the message of peace to my mother, who had given of her love and knowledge to a woman who needed them desperately. I told her many of the things that had been written, but I did not tell her who the German soldier was. I could not; not yet.

Coming "home" to the apartment was also as I had expected; a wild, noisy flurry of emotion, an expression too intense and, at the same time, too impersonal to do me much good. But, to my surprise, I did not feel as overwhelmed by the differences between us as I had thought I might. The sense of alienation my suffering had placed upon me before seemed lifted by what I had learned, by what had happened to me.

"I'll help you make up your studies," Penelope promised, squeezing my shoulder gently.

"So will I!" Clara effused. "And I'll put you on a proper diet to help you keep your strength up, and—"

"Speaking of diet," Sally interrupted with a moan. "I'll take over all your household duties for the rest of the year if you'll just cook French food for us."

There ensued an enthusiastic confusion of agreement. And, as I watched those young faces, a tenderness came over me that was cleansing and good.

Later Anja came into my room on some pretext, so I asked her how Karen was doing.

"She'll be all right," she assured me. "Now that she has a little physical strength to help her she's coming to grips with what happened. I think she'll—"

She did not know how to put it. Then stoically, almost as a form of punishment, she said bluntly, "I don't think she'll make the same mistake again."

I frowned a little. "Then she's wiser than some of us."

She smiled at my words, and seemed to relax a little.

"You look thin," she said, "and your cheeks are a bit hollow." She was choosing her words carefully. "But you look good somehow. What you've gone through—and I can imagine it must have been pretty terrible—but somehow it's made a difference in your features, even in the way you carry yourself."

After she left I thought about her words and what they could mean and realized the irony that only she had approached me on a deeper, more spiritual level and tried to express the things in her heart.

❦

I knew what I must do before I confronted Hans Bekker. I let Emory know I was back. He came blithely, happily, unaware and unknowing . . . as he always had been.

I asked him to take me someplace where we could be alone together. I had been gone just over two weeks, but the February thaw had worked itself into an early spring. He took me to the walks below the Maeser building again, and that made it so much the harder for me.

I slipped the ring off my finger and handed it to him. "I've come back," I began, "but remember what I told you before I left? *If I come back, if I remain unchanged inside.*" How could I make him understand me? "It could never work between us, Emory. I think somewhere, deep inside I knew—we both knew that."

He twisted the ring back and forth in his fingers. "Ah thought . . ." He paused, and I filled the awkward silence.

"You thought it would be easy, like things have always been for you." I tried to smile, but I could feel my mouth twist into an unhappy contortion. "Things have changed for me, Emory. I have changed." I sighed as he lifted his face and his troubled eyes met mine. "I could not make you happy, Emory. I know that, even if you do not—yet."

"You've always known better than Ah have." He was trying hard, and I felt my heart go out to him. "Ah s'pose Leroy was right all along. You're too good for the likes o'me." His smile was nearly as twisted and awkward as mine. And it did not help that he looked so boyish and vulnerable and Apollo-like standing there.

What can one do at such times? It was terrible. As the hours became more weighed down, more desultory, he gave in, as it were, by taking me home.

"Does this mean Ah won't see you again?" he asked, his voice incredulous.

"Oh, Emory," I sighed, "I care for you deeply, I think I always will. But to see each other *this way* . . . it would be fruitless—it would be as unfair to you as it would be to me."

He nodded, but I could not read his eyes. He bent over and kissed me. "Ah will surely miss that," he murmured. Then he kissed me again. Shaken and aching inside, I gently pulled away from him. Then, somehow, I was inside the apartment, leaning against the door, listening to him walk away from me, crying as shamelessly as a child.

As soon as I gained control of myself I retreated into my room. My eyes, by habit, went to Armand's painting of the Seine, dark and mysterious as I had last left it. Beneath the painting the photograph of Emory smiled rakishly at me. I walked over and lifted it from its place. Feeling not the least bit silly I kissed the full, sweet lips, then slipped it inside one of my drawers. I hoped and prayed Emory would be able to smile that way again.

Chapter

23

*W*here should I go to find him? A class-room would be too public, too hard to control. Not his home. He had posted office hours, and I determined at last that I should look for him there.

Thursday morning Penelope drove me to the humanities building. I walked inside, looking like any other student, but on an errand I believed to be most uncommon. I remembered with no trouble where his office was. It was one of several situated behind a small anteroom where a secretary sat at a desk.

"Is Dr. Bekker in?" I asked.

She looked up from her work and smiled. "He was due ten minutes ago, but that doesn't mean anything. You may wait in there if you'd like, Miss—"

"Augustine Mousset," I answered. She indicated his personal office. I walked in slowly and perched on the edge of the chair that was situated the farthest from his desk. I heard him approach. I felt the electricity of his presence, the warm surge of his personality. I heard the secretary laugh delightedly at something he said. Then she spoke, and I thought I heard my name, and there was a sudden silence which made my pulse throb in my temples.

"Are you sure?" he asked. I heard his words distinctly. Then, half afraid, he glanced in and saw me. "Hold all calls, Miss Brown," he said, "and do not disturb us, for any reason whatsoever."

He crossed the small space in a deliberate, measured tread, entered the room, pulling the door closed behind him, and continued walking until he stood behind his desk—all this before he hazarded a direct look at me. It was all I could do to force my gaze to meet his. I had rehearsed this moment a thousand times in my mind, but nothing could really prepare me.

"Augustine." He pronounced my name like a blessing, but did not seem to be able to say more, though his eyes were crowded with questions.

"I was wrong." I spoke the words slowly and carefully. "More wrong than I knew." My voice was trembling, but I could not help that. "Tell me about your father." I swallowed painfully. "Please."

He appeared poised on the edge of something, unable to take in what was happening. Then, after a moment or two of terrible silence, he answered me; graciously, withholding nothing, trusting me, as he always had.

"My father grew up in Berlin and was educated there in the twenties, and distinguished himself as a student and a gentleman. His family was not without some means and some influence. His last year of study he met and fell in love with Gudrun's mother—you know something about that."

I nodded my head and began to breathe a bit more easily. We were not to any of the difficult parts, not yet.

"He became a teacher of languages, a position of great honor in our country, and lived an ordinary life—even an honored life because of his gift as a linguist—except that he was a member of a religious party that was most unpopular, and grew to be more so and more so as politics in Germany changed. My mother was the daughter of the branch president. When he died of a stroke, my father was called to replace him. They took the practice of their religion most seriously, and spent long hours serving the people who were under their charge.

"When the war began my father wanted nothing to do with Hitler and his Nazis. When he had to enter the army he did so as a foot soldier and soon rose to the rank of captain, which is of no particular distinction."

He was becoming uneasy, but he would not spare himself. "In

June of 1940 he entered Paris when the German troops took that city. He remained stationed in Paris for some time. Meanwhile, things in Germany were growing worse. The Nazis had control of everything—industries, newspapers, the court systems, even the schools. In '41 my father was sent to Russia, as one of three million soldiers."

He sighed, and his eyes began to take on that faraway look I had seen in them one time before.

"My father had a friend or two in high places, trusted friends from his school days. After two years in Russia they had arranged for a military assignment which brought him back to Berlin as a language specialist. He at once made arrangements to remove his family to the safety and obscurity of a village in the Bavarian Alps, where my mother's sister lived—alone with small children and no one to help her now that her husband was off fighting the war. My mother was required to remain at the government job she was working in. I did not see her for nearly a year; not until, at the age of sixteen, I was instructed to return to Berlin and become an official member of the Hitler Youth. But that is not really part of my story. My father . . ." He placed the tips of his fingers against each other, pressing and releasing them, revealing an agitation I had not seen in him before. "My father delayed our leaving for month following month because he was working feverishly with the German underground to move members of the Church, of his little congregation, either out of the country, or to places of seclusion and safety. The suspense was terrible; I remember. Suspicion against him increased daily, until at last he was forced to heed it. He meant to travel with us as far as Nuremberg. But just outside Leipzig there was some bombing. The train we traveled in was badly damaged . . ."

I leaned forward. He was speaking brokenly, haltingly. He pushed his fingers through his hair, kneading the bright strands again and again in a nervous manner.

"Suffice it to say that many were killed, my seven-year-old sister, Liesl, among them."

I have a daughter not much older than this one. The line from the journal leaped out at me, but it was as though the words had been spoken, spoken in Dr. Bekker's deeply modulated voice—it was as though he and the father he talked of were one.

"I may as well tell you while I am at it that I had been in love with a certain girl since my earliest childhood, since the time when I first realized that there were differences between girls and boys. Her name was Gabrielle." His voice caught as he spoke the word. "Her family lived next door to our family, and her father served in the branch presidency with mine. She and her younger brother were on the train with us. Both were killed."

I began to shake my head back and forth, I realized I was moaning, protesting. I clamped my mouth shut, grinding my teeth together, and tried to remain still.

"She was a beautiful girl—as sweet and good a person as I have ever known." He sighed, unable to help himself. "We were both fifteen. She died in my arms." A great shudder passed through him, and he tried bravely to control his expression. As I watched his terrible struggle I remembered the class discussion we had had early in the year when some thoughtless person had asked, "What was it like to watch people you love die?" Recalling his answer I shuddered: "I cannot answer that. Perhaps a poet or an insane man could." I felt a tear spill from the corner of my eye and looked down at my hands lying like stones in my lap.

"I did not mean to earn the reputation of a fussy and loveless old bachelor," Hans Bekker was saying. "I have tried to fall in love, time after time I have tried, but the women I meet . . ." He lifted his shoulders in an expressive gesture and then dropped them. "I have special needs, you might say, and I have met no one, all these years, until now."

I moved in my chair, recrossing my legs, aware that my back hurt. He moved, too, pacing the space behind his desk for a moment. "Well, be that as it may," he continued, "my father made the necessary arrangements and we buried the three children there, before we moved on."

He was back in the past again, already; I could tell from his eyes.

"But our delay was sufficient for the SS officers who were following my father to catch up to him." A smile played at the corners of his month. "He kept the men waiting while he took us all into a small private chamber and knelt there with us in prayer, blessing each one of us, as bishop, as father—" His voice broke, and there were tears in his eyes. But he no longer cared. "He went off with the men, and we continued safely to my aunt's house. I never saw him again."

His fingers formed a pyramid once more, and he attempted to smile at me. "They would have shot him right then but for his friend's influence. He arranged to have my father sent back to Russia. But it was all the same in the end. He was part of the siege of Leningrad which was not broken until January of '44. Two months before that he was shot by a high-ranking Nazi officer—shot for insubordination."

I shuddered.

"I will never know for certain what happened. The causes given were vague: holding subversive meetings and unwillingness to follow orders. I believe it must have had something to do with the Church." He raised his eyebrows and lifted his shoulders slightly. "Holding priesthood meetings, most likely, blessing the wounded, doing missionary work—he was always a great one for teaching." He shook his head and let his hands fall into his lap. "He was on their list; it was perhaps inevitable."

The room fell silent. I was painfully aware that the next move was mine. I rose from my seat. My legs felt almost too weak to support me. I set my mother's journal, which I had been clutching tightly, on the edge of his desk.

"I could never explain to you in words what has happened," I said. "That would be impossible." I turned my eyes and lowered my face for a moment. His gaze seemed to burn through me, clear to the core of my being.

"But you are free to read this—it is my mother's journal." My voice sounded thin, little-girlish in my own ears. "In there you will find a missing link in your father's story, and the vindication you have so fiercely desired."

I turned and walked from the room. It seemed an interminable distance. He did not call me back. Although I was trembling in my desire to flee now that my formidable task was completed, I closed the door as I left—in deference. For he had buried his face in his hands, and I thought I heard the sound of his dry, suppressed sobs.

⁂

I passed the remainder of the day in a strange, faraway frame of mind. In the late afternoon I took a break from my studies and made *tarte aux fraises*—tarts with strawberries, one of the girls' favorite desserts, to go with the chicken Clara had put in the oven. I had no idea what was going to happen; I had erased everything from my life; it stood a blank, empty page with nothing yet written upon it. Yet I felt a profound sense of peace.

About seven o'clock, after the dishes were all done, and I was deep in my studies again, I heard a gentle knocking at the front door. Clara answered it and called to me to come out.

He stood framed in the doorway, his flaxen hair mussed and rumpled, as though he had forgotten to comb it. The tweed jacket he was wearing hung a little too loosely from his shoulders, and there were dark shadows under his eyes; his eyes themselves looked shadowed. But his voice, when he spoke, was still deep and beautiful, and pulsing with life.

"There is yet a little light left in the mountains," he said. "I wondered if you might come for a ride with me."

My heart beat in my throat. "I will get my jacket," I said.

As we left the apartment and he reached to close the door behind me he said, with one eyebrow lifted, "I noticed this morning, and again tonight, that you wear no ring on your finger."

"That's right." I tried to smile, though my lips were trembling. "I belong to no one now."

He lifted my unadorned hand and pressed it to his lips. "No, Augustine, my beloved." His voice was trembling. He bent and kissed the inside of my arm where the white scar of the bullet ran, though my jacket now covered it.

"You belong where you have always belonged. You belong by my side."

His eyes were such a shining, transparent blue that it stunned me to look at them. He framed my face with his fine, gentle hands, smoothing my hair back, smoothing the skin at my temples. He pressed his lips to my cheek, to the bridge of my nose, then at last covered my mouth with such anguished desire that I nearly cried out at the force of it. I had never felt this way before. Yet I knew this was right, this was what my mother had spoken of. I felt it in my mind, in my spirit, in every pore of my being. And the feeling was one of safety and goodness, of promise and light.

I took the hand he offered me. Hugging the warm, sinewy strength of it I walked with him, out into the gentle, luminous twilight, close at his side.